Born in Hertfordshire, Danielle Shaw initially studied fashion and design and worked at The Royal Opera House before moving to Geneva to work in a nursery school. Returning to England, she achieved her long-held ambition to become a full-time author and is currently researching her seventh book. She now lives in Northamptonshire with her Swedish husband.

SUNFLOWER MORNING

Catherine Wickham arrives at Whycham
Hall, delighted to help her aunt who is
housekeeper there. However, she discovers
that the new owner, property developer
Roderick Marchant, intends to alter the
Whycham Estate beyond all recognition.
Then when she learns that she is a
descendant of the original owners of
Whycham Hall, Catherine resolves to halt
Rod's plans. But she must face Rod's
determined girlfriend Francesca . . .
Forced to spend time in Rod's company,
Catherine has two choices: leave Whycham
le Cley forever, or hide her love for Rod as
she fights to save her beloved village from
property developers.

Books by Danielle Shaw
Published by The House of Ulverscroft:

MARRIED TO SINCLAIR
CRAVEN'S BRIDE
CINNABAR SUMMER

DANIELLE SHAW

SUNFLOWER MORNING

Complete and Unabridged

ULVERSCROFT
Leicester

First published in Great Britain in 2007 by
Robert Hale Limited
London

First Large Print Edition
published 2008
by arrangement with
Robert Hale Limited
London

British Library CIP Data

Shaw, Danielle
Sunflower morning.—Large print ed.—
Ulverscroft large print series: general fiction
1. Love stories
2. Large type books
I. Title
823.9'14 [F]

ISBN 978–1–84782–216–1

Published by
F. A. Thorpe (Publishing)
Anstey, Leicestershire

Set by Words & Graphics Ltd.
Anstey, Leicestershire
Printed and bound in Great Britain by
T. J. International Ltd., Padstow, Cornwall

This book is printed on acid-free paper

For Judith, with love.
Thank you for always being there.

1

Hearing the sound of a fast-approaching car, Catherine Wickham paused and dismounted her bike. Too late to reach the safety of the footpath, she considered her only options. Ahead lay the ford, recently swollen by days of relentless rain, while on either side stretched a hostile and impenetrable expanse of hedgerow and overgrown grass verge.

Alarm filled her face. What was it to be? Bare arms impaled on thorny barbs of blackthorn and her new suede loafers ruined in the muddied and rain-soaked undergrowth, or else the sun-dappled ford. Opting for the ford, Catherine knew from experience that if she pedalled carefully it should be possible to keep her feet clear of the water.

Cautiously edging the bike forward, her eyes dazzled by brilliant sunshine, she began pedalling slowly only to discover that she'd made the wrong decision. Too late she discerned a flash of shiny red bodywork ploughing a trail of murky water in its wake.

'You idiot!' she yelled, gesticulating wildly. 'This is rural Norfolk, not Brands Hatch or the M25. Can't you read the sign-post?'

Not expecting anyone to respond, Catherine was in the process of examining her clothes and soggy contents of the pannier on her handlebars, when she heard the sound of hurried footsteps.

An anxious voice called from across the ford. 'Sorry. Did you get wet? We didn't see you until . . . '

'Of course I got wet!' she cried, brushing dripping wet hair from her eyes. 'I couldn't have got any wetter if I'd swum across. Just look at the state of me.'

To Catherine's surprise, the owner of the car chose to do exactly that. Ignoring the still-swirling waters of the ford, he strode to her side where it took only seconds to gauge the true extent of her discomfort and rage. Her hair and face were streaked with mud. Her green and white striped cotton top would have gained her immediate entry to a Miss Wet T-shirt competition, and the once pale-sage fabric of her skirt was deeply mottled with slime. As for her new suede shoes . . . Catherine threw up her hands in exasperation.

'Like I said, I really am most dreadfully sorry. I didn't see you until it was too late to do anything about it. I'll pay the cleaning bill, of course.'

'That's not the point!' Catherine snapped,

blind with anger, her green eyes flashing in response to the cultured London accent. 'If you hadn't been driving quite so fast you would have seen the warning signs for the ford. You townies are all the same. Anyone would think you own the place. First bit of early spring sunshine and you decide to leave the smoke and head for the countryside. That's until you get bored with it and hurtle back at the same breakneck speed, leaving a trail of devastation in your wake.'

'Um . . . actually . . . '

'Actually what?' Catherine retorted sharply.

'I was about to say at any other time I'd welcome the chance to discuss that with you. Another day, perhaps. That's if the opportunity arises. In the meantime, allow me to introduce myself. My name's Rod Marchant. Can I offer you — '

'No, thank you. I do not want a lift. In case it had escaped your notice, I do have transport of my own. Admittedly, not quite as flashy as yours,' Catherine said, ignoring the hand held out in introduction, 'but at least I don't go round polluting the countryside and frightening the sheep.'

With a shrug of his shoulders, Rod looked back in the direction of mud-splashed, paintwork drying in the midday sun. 'Oh, I wasn't going to offer you a lift,' he said, reaching into his pocket. 'I was going to offer you my handkerchief. You're covered in duckweed. Your face and hair. If you'll allow me?'

Completely taken aback, Catherine met the gaze of the culprit she held personally responsible for her unwelcome drenching. To her surprise he wasn't at all like the Hooray Henrys who frequented the wine bar where she'd once worked to supplement her student income. Questioning eyes, the colour of melted chocolate, studied her intently. 'Shall I . . . or will you?'

Frowning, Catherine felt her mouth go quite dry, unlike her clothes, which were uncomfortably wet. 'Pardon?' she croaked.

'The duckweed. Shall I, or would you prefer to deal with it yourself? We can't have you standing here, practically soaked to the skin, looking like a . . . '

Convinced she was about to be compared to a drowned rat, Catherine was marginally distracted by the slamming of a car door.

'A frog on a lily pad,' Rod continued, smiling. Without warning, he cupped her face in his hands, brushed his thumbs gently against her cheeks and removed two stray blobs of duckweed.

Sensing he was about to reach for her hair, Catherine took a step backwards. Blushing, she pulled at her deep auburn fringe, found yet another matted clump of duckweed and flung it to one side. To her horror and Rod's subsequent amusement, it landed smack in the middle of her saddle.

'Mmm, good shot,' he said, grinning, while eyeing her neat, trim figure. 'I bet you played netball when you were at school. My sister did too. Henrietta was a brilliant wing defence.'

'For your information I played in attack.'

'Attack. Of course,' Rod said, tugging Catherine's bike free from a tangle of weeds and grass. 'I should have realized that from the way you flew at me before my knight-in-shining-armour bit, when I came to your rescue.'

Watching this self-styled knight wiping green slime from the well-worn leather saddle with his handkerchief, Catherine was suddenly reminded why she was standing ankle-deep in water. Her eyes blazed anew. 'Rescue me? Why, you pompous ass! If you hadn't been driving like a maniac my shoes wouldn't be ruined, Aunt Em's library books and shopping wouldn't be sopping wet and I wouldn't be — '

'Roddy dahling!' A sneering voice broke in, leaving Catherine's sentence unfinished. 'What on earth are you doing? I've been waiting for simply ages. If you don't hurry up we're going to be late for lunch.'

'Sorry, Francesca. Just helping a damsel in distress.'

'Is that what you call it?' snorted a thin, reedy voice. 'Then I trust there are no bones broken and we can get a move on. And, as I've already had more than enough excitement for one day, I've decided you can drive the rest of the way. First sheep and cows blocking the road and now humans. Lord knows the natives in this godforsaken place seem few and far between as it is. I suppose it's just as well I didn't drown one. Is that a hanging offence round here, do you think?'

Turning in the direction of the deeply sarcastic voice, Catherine discerned a tall, willowy blonde. Dressed in designer cashmere, she stamped her feet impatiently and glared at 'Roddy dahling', all the while taking great care to keep her fine leather ankle boots well clear of the ford. Not quite so fortunate with her own footwear, Catherine squelched noisily to the side of the verge and waited for the subsequent reply.

'Oh, well, best be on my way before I get webbed feet,' Rod said, giving Catherine a wink. 'Francesca hates having to hang about.'

Strangely unconcerned by his own ruined footwear and mud-splattered trousers, he raked a hand through his short, cropped hair and followed Catherine to drier ground. There he produced a business card from his pocket and announced, 'My office address in London. You can send me the cleaning bill. Don't worry. In case I'm called away unexpectedly, I'll leave a message for my secretary. Rest assured she'll deal with it in my absence.'

Cleaning bill! Catherine thought, incredulous. It wasn't her clothes she was bothered about. They would wash. It was the state of her shoes, Aunt Em's ruined shopping and the sodden library books that were of immediate concern.

Frowning and reminded of Francesca's haughty display, Catherine watched Rod walk back to the car, lower his six-foot frame into a comfortable position and adjust the driver's seat. Her suspicions were confirmed. It had been that stuck-up creature wearing those wonderful Italian-style boots who had been driving the car and not . . . 'Roderick Marchant,' she murmured softly to herself, reading the name printed on the business-card.

'Hmph!' she sniffed angrily, hearing the car pull away. In which case shouldn't it have been Rod Marchant's companion handing out the apologies instead of making sarcastic

7

comments about the locals? With Francesca's high-pitched, nasal-toned 'Is that a hanging offence?' still ringing annoyingly in her ears, Catherine pushed her bike to the far side of the ford, emptied her once pale green shoes of water and remounted her bike. 'Stuck up creature,' she fumed. 'I don't know about hanging, especially with that awful cackle of hers. If the history of this place is anything to go by, and she'd lived here a few hundred years ago, doubtless they would have burnt her at the stake!'

Pedalling furiously to where she knew her aunt would be waiting, myriad thoughts flashed through Catherine's head at that moment. Tales of witchcraft at Whycham le Cley soon gave way to numerous stories told by her father and grandfather and the often-repeated saga of Whycham Hall. When impressive wrought iron gates finally came into view, Catherine emitted a plaintive sigh. If only, as she'd always been led to believe by Aunt Em (her father's widowed sister and only living relation), Whycham Hall had once belonged to their own particular branch of the family she would not be using the tradesmen's entrance.

'It's not only the name we share, Catherine,' her aunt was forever reminding her, 'but also the inheritance. At least we should have if it hadn't been for that affair with your great-great grandfather and Queen Victoria.'

On hearing Aunt Em's outburst for the very first time, Catherine had raised surprised eyebrows. She'd then been hugely disappointed to discover that the affair in question had concerned not matters of the heart but money. Someone in the family, way down the line, had refused or else been unable to pay the necessary death duties. As a result, Whycham Hall had been seized by the crown and later taken over by a Victorian merchant.

Even if it is true, Catherine thought dejectedly, stepping from her bike to open the creaking side gate, the place had only ever passed to male descendants. With her father having been the last of the line and herself an only child . . . Feeling a lump rise in her throat, Catherine fought back dry tears. Hard as she'd tried, she'd never been able to imagine her father (the kindly village school teacher before his untimely death) as lord and master at Whycham Hall. Although, she acknowledged, giving a wry smile, with his wonderful sense of humour he probably would have appreciated the current irony of it all. His sister had been housekeeper at the hall for several years and now his daughter was to take up temporary residence, albeit in the old servants' quarters.

'Catherine! My dear, where have you been? Look at the state of you.'

'I'm sorry, Aunt Em. Can you believe it? There I was telling myself what a glorious spring day it was when out of nowhere — '

'There's no time for explanations,' came the agitated reply. 'Just give me the shopping and get yourself tidied up as soon as you can. The master's arrived unexpectedly and he's brought a guest.'

Catherine paused, her hand on the soggy white paper encasing the sausages. 'The master? Aunt Em, Whycham Hall doesn't have a master, not since old Mr Erskine died. No one's bothered to come near the place for ages.'

'I know. I know. But he's here now. They're here now and I doubt very much if her ladyship will be very pleased to discover it's only lentil soup and sausages for lunch. Will you please go and explain? I need to get these in the pan right away.'

Leaving her aunt to disentangle a seemingly writhing string of sausages, Catherine hurried along to the drawing-room. Master? Her ladyship? she puzzled. Pausing on the threshold, she was on the point of knocking on the door when she remembered her appearance. Deciding there was nothing for it

10

(Aunt Em had insisted she deliver her message first), Catherine tapped briskly on a solid oak panel, waited for the command to enter and began without hesitation. 'I'm very sorry, sir, madam, but Mrs Bailey said to tell you it's lentil soup and sausages for lunch. She was wondering if — '

'Lentils! Sausages!' shrieked a familiar voice, only to be interrupted by another saying, 'Good heavens! It's the girl in the ford. Jeremy Fisher's companion.'

'Who the hell is Jeremy Fisher?' Francesca sneered, still reeling from the shock of the lunchtime menu.

'Beatrix Potter. Remember?' Roderick Marchant explained. 'Didn't your nanny ever read you the story of the frog on the lily pad who . . . ?'

Furious at being compared to a frog for the second time in less than an hour and certainly not wishing to hear about Francesca's bedtime reading, Catherine turned towards the door.

'About the sausages,' Rod's cheery voice called, following her into the hallway. 'I don't suppose there's any chance of mashed potato and onion gravy to go with them?'

'I shall have to ask,' Catherine replied tartly. 'Housekeepers are usually informed when guests are expected. You obviously don't know or else have forgotten that no one's lived here on a permanent basis for quite some time. I don't suppose it even occurred to you to phone?'

'Well, no,' Rod replied, taken aback. 'We simply thought as it was a nice sunny day we'd head for the country. I assumed — '

'Exactly!'

'And what exactly is that supposed to mean?' came the curt reply.

Paying scant regard to the altered tone in Rod Marchant's voice, Catherine repeated her earlier tirade about townies leaving the city and heading for the hills. Only this time she added some equally scathing comments about them idly partying in wine bars, all the while claiming to care about the countryside and its simple inhabitants. When she'd finished, Rod fixed her with a curious glare. 'I think perhaps you too have forgotten something.'

'Forgotten something? No. I don't think so. Not unless you were expecting me to curtsey.'

'Oh, no. It's not something I was expecting you to do. It was more reminding you of our earlier conversation, particularly as you appear to have made your point most eloquently. Strangely enough, I even suggested that we might discuss it later, never realizing of course that we'd have that opportunity quite so soon.'

Puzzled by this last remark, Catherine met Rod's hostile gaze. The warm chocolate eyes had suddenly turned bitter. 'Permit me to remind you,' he continued coolly, 'you, Miss . . . er . . . ?'

'Wickham,' came the less than confident reply.

'You, Miss Wickham, as I recall, took great delight in accusing me of behaving as if I owned the place. For your information, perhaps I should explain. According to my late great uncle's will, and as far as the estate and surrounding acres are concerned, I do. Might I suggest you bear that in mind in future, particularly if you wish to remain here. I take it you are a member of staff?'

2

'Member of staff indeed!' Catherine fumed, indignant. 'Just who does he think he is?'

Returning from the gardener's cottage, Emmy placed a trug of vegetables on the draining board. 'Well, he is the late Mr Erskine's great nephew,' she replied, filling a bowl with water for the potatoes. 'Having inherited this place, I suppose he could consider himself to be the new lord of the manor.

'Then I suggest he starts by considering his own manners,' Catherine muttered through tight lips. Reaching for an onion and a sharp knife, she looked up to find her aunt was smiling at her. 'What's so funny?'

'You are, my dear. If only you could see yourself. You look just like . . . '

'Don't you dare say it, Aunt Em. I've already been compared to a frog twice today.'

Laying down her potato peeler, Emmy Bailey fixed her niece with a puzzled frown. 'A frog? No, I wasn't going to say that. Although thinking back to when you returned with the shopping, complete with traces of duckweed in your hair and those muddy splodges on your green skirt . . . '

When Catherine pulled a face, Aunt Em continued kindly, 'Actually, I was going to say how you reminded me of your paternal grandmother, the other Catherine Wickham. She had auburn hair just like yours and was also extremely feisty. Strange how the women in the Wickham family always appeared to be far stronger than their opposite sex.'

With Catherine and her aunt contemplating assorted Wickham males, the newest Whycham male opened the kitchen door and enquired tersely, 'Mrs Bailey, who was that girl you sent along with the message about lunch? I don't remember Mr Hayes, the family solicitor, saying anything about a housemaid. I thought it was just you, Mr Barnes the gardener and a couple of part-timers keeping an eye on the place.'

Housemaid! From where she was hidden away from view behind the kitchen door, Catherine chopped straight through the roots of the onion she was slicing, filling the air with pungent fumes.

Sensing her niece was about to reply in no uncertain terms to Mr Marchant's enquiry, Aunt Em shook her head in warning. 'That's Catherine, my niece, sir,' she said hurriedly. 'She's come to lend a hand, ready for the Easter holidays. Mr Hayes suggested it

15

himself, what with it being difficult to get help from the village. He assured me that he'd told you. Then again with the hall being uninhabited for a while and so much to do to the place, perhaps he forgot. As for lunch, I'm sorry it's only soup and sausages. Mr Hayes did say not to expect you until Easter at the earliest.'

'Hmm, quite,' Rod replied with a frown, doubly unsure. Had Mr Hayes informed him of the latest arrangements at Whycham Hall? And if his housekeeper was anything like her fiery relation, was she also reprimanding him for his impromptu decision to visit his recently inherited estate? Surely not, he concluded. His initial impression of Mrs Bailey had been of someone who was possessed of far more tact than her niece.

Following Emmy's anxious gaze, Rod spied Catherine, half hidden behind the kitchen door. Seated at the rustic pine table, she remained tight lipped and solemn, her once semi-transparent T-shirt now partially covered by an apron. Startled to see tears brimming in her eyes and convinced they were a result of his earlier caustic remarks, he felt strangely uncomfortable. With a murmured excuse about neglecting Francesca and fetching some wine from the cellar, he turned and left the kitchen.

'Lunch will be about half an hour, sir,' Emmy called after him. 'I'll get Catherine to bang the gong as soon as it's ready.'

'As long as you don't expect me to serve them,' Catherine sniffed, dabbing at onion-induced tears with a tissue.

'No, my dear. I'll get you to make up the beds instead. First, will you please get out of those damp clothes. You should have done that ages ago.'

Explaining that she'd much prefer to rid herself of the smell of onions, frying sausages and her morning's soaking in one fell swoop, Catherine rose from the table and untied the borrowed apron. 'Did you say beds as in plural?'

'That's right,' Aunt Em nodded. 'Master Roderick will have his uncle's old room and what did he say her name was, Francesca? I daresay she'll be happier in the blue room. Facing south as it does, it should at least be aired.'

Catherine's brows knitted into a frown. 'They're not married? Francesca's not his wife? When you referred to her as 'her ladyship' I thought . . . '

'Apparently not. I distinctly remember him asking for two bedrooms when he arrived. As for 'her ladyship', that's only because when they arrived she marched in as if she owned the place. A real Lady Muck she was, giving her orders for coffee and the like. Anyway, I'm sure I'll be able to cope with her. In the meantime, it's the other bedrooms we have to worry about. Perhaps you can help me with those this evening?'

'Other rooms? Whatever do you mean?'

'Oh, didn't I say? Before you returned from your impromptu drenching, Master Roderick asked if I could prepare a traditional Sunday lunch for tomorrow. Seems he's invited several friends and . . . '

'I suppose you said yes?'

Emmy pursed her lips. 'Of course I did. It's my job, isn't it, Catherine? It's what I get paid for, even when the hall isn't occupied. Don't forget it's also what helped keep you in college when you were studying for your librarian's exams.'

Filled with a sudden sense of remorse, Catherine turned and flung her arms about her aunt's neck. 'I'm so sorry! Please forgive me. I always get like this about the time of Dad's birthday. To think in a couple of weeks he would have been sixty-three.'

'I know,' Emmy said, patting her arm. 'How could I ever forget? He was forty when you were born and your mother had quite given up hope of ever having children. When you arrived on his birthday, the fifth of April, what a double bonus that was.'

'Even though I wasn't the long-hoped-for son and heir?'

'You know that's not true,' Emmy said, giving her niece a reassuring hug. 'You were the apple of your father's eye.'

Spying the one remaining apple in the fruit bowl, Catherine broke free from her aunt's embrace. She also caught sight of the meagre supplies on the open pantry shelves. She and her aunt ate extremely frugally. The sausages, sizzling gently in the pan, were to have been for their dinner tonight and the soup simmering on the Aga, their lunch. It didn't take long to work out there was nothing at all suitable for Sunday.

Hurrying to the door she called back, 'About Sunday lunch. Don't worry. I'll change as quickly as I can,' and found herself colliding with Rod Marchant, newly emerged from a trip to the cellar.

'Indeed!' he proclaimed, holding two bottles aloft, his brown eyes sparkling curiously. 'And what exactly will you be changing into this time, Miss Wickham? It's clear you're quite the wrong sex for the frog prince. Was there such a thing as a frog princess?'

Startled by his closeness — she could even smell his cologne mingled with the mustiness of Whycham Hall's fine wine cellar — Catherine attempted composure. Moments later she responded to his enquiring gaze with a distinctly cool, 'I meant change as in getting out of these damp clothes. As my aunt informs me you've invited friends for Sunday lunch, I shall have to go back to the village for provisions.'

'Provisions, eh? That's a word I haven't heard in a while,' Rod remarked, studying dust-covered labels on the bottles. 'Then do take care,' he continued. 'I recall Great Uncle Erskine saying the lanes around here are notoriously dangerous: blind corners, tractors and even sheep and chickens on the road.'

Stepping to one side, Catherine turned sharply in the direction of the back staircase that led to the attic bedrooms. 'Oh, I will, Mr Marchant, you can be sure of that. However, it's not sheep, chickens or even blind corners I worry about. It's blind car drivers.'

Watching her go, Rod chuckled quietly to himself. 'You certainly asked for that, Rod, old chap. She's definitely got the temperament to go with that striking auburn hair.' Then, recalling his sister's long-held obsession for horoscopes and star charts, he found himself wondering about Catherine. She could only be a fire sign, unlike the distinctly ice cool Francesca, who was waiting for him in the drawing-room.

As if on cue, Francesca appeared in the open doorway. 'Roddy dahling. Am I going to get a drink today — or have you been treading grapes down in that cellar of yours?'

'Coming, Francesca,' he called, watching her drum frosted pink fingernails against the door frame. 'I'm just going to wipe the cobwebs and dead spiders from these bottles and then ask Mrs Bailey for a corkscrew.'

Walking briskly to the kitchen (Francesca's extremely vocal aversion to spiders echoing in his head), Rod suppressed a wry smile. He doubted very much if Catherine was afraid of spiders. In fact, she probably wasn't frightened of anything at all. 'Mmm. Fire and ice, eh?' he murmured under his breath. 'Who'd have thought I'd find such a combination in sleepy old Norfolk?'

★ ★ ★

Stinging jets of ice-cold water dashed against Catherine's body, mingling with the warm, salt tears that streamed down her face. For the past five minutes she'd been trying to cool down, desperate to convince herself the reason she was crying was because of her father. It was purely renewed grief as the anniversary of his birthday approached

— wasn't it? Deep down, however, she knew otherwise. The real cause for fresh tears had been her brief but unforgettable encounters with Roderick Marchant.

'*Go on, admit it,*' an inner voice protested. '*You actually like him. Despite all your resolutions since your two-timing bastard of a boyfriend cheated on you, you've found yourself attracted to another man. Even your aunt would say Rod Marchant's got everything a woman could want: good looks, breeding, money and charm.*'

Charm? Hmm, the charm had certainly been in evidence during their first encounter at the ford, Catherine acknowledged. As for the confrontation when he'd followed her into the hallway, his manner then had been far from charming. You've only got yourself to blame for that, she told herself, shivering and turning the water to a higher temperature.

'Maybe I have,' she spluttered through a mouthful of shampoo-filled foam, reminding herself that as number one member of the FIMB (Foot In Mouth Brigade) she was very quick at speaking first and thinking later. Almost as quick, perhaps, as falling head over heels in love with the wrong man. With one broken relationship behind her, and the memory of it still too raw and painful, she'd vowed never to make the same mistake again.

'Not that you'd ever get the chance as far as Roddy dahling is concerned. He's way out of your league,' her annoying conscience sneered, breaking into her chain of thought. 'Don't forget Francesca.'

As if I could, Catherine thought glumly. Besides, she'd long since determined Whycham Hall would be the only object of her affection from now on. Other than her love for Aunt Em and her dogged persistence that Whycham le Cley should remain totally unspoiled, it was the desire to see the hall restored to its former glory that filled a special place in her heart. If only Rod Marchant would love it half as much as she did.

As heir to the entire Erskine estate, at least there would be plenty of money to lavish on the place, Catherine concluded, so perhaps he could be persuaded. If not by her, particularly taking into account her recent outbursts, then perhaps by Aunt Em and her companions from the WI. They were forever lamenting the sad demise of the hall and gardens and even Whycham le Cley itself. It was almost as if the tiny village and its inhabitants had fallen into permanent decline following the passing of the much loved Edwina Erskine. As for Cedric Erskine himself, there were those who said he had died of a broken heart.

Rinsing away all traces of citrus-scented shower gel and shampoo, Catherine tried to imagine what it must be like to share sixty blissfully happy years of marriage. Sadly, her parents hadn't been nearly so fortunate as the Erskines. The cancer that had so cruelly taken her mother's life had arrived with a vengeance and without warning, leaving them precious little time to prepare for the inevitable.

When the distant slamming of a door invaded Catherine's thoughts, she blinked back fresh tears, switched off the shower and made a grab for the towel. Rubbing hurriedly at the misted bathroom window, it was just as she suspected. Her aunt was heading in the direction of the distant compost heap carrying a bowl of potato and onion peelings.

'Dear Aunt Em,' she murmured, recalling how her father's widowed sister had stepped into the breach to care for them. Aunt Em who had seemed to be forever polishing, dusting and baking and seeing to their every need. All that wonderful home cooking, Catherine remembered fondly. All those lovingly prepared packed lunches she'd taken to school once she left Whycham le Cley Junior and headed for grammar school on the outskirts of Norwich. No wonder Mr Erskine had been so keen to approach Emmy Bailey and offer her the position of housekeeper at Whycham Hall.

Initially reluctant to accept for fear of neglecting her niece, Catherine had insisted that Aunt Em take up the position immediately. She even pointed out that thanks to her aunt not only had she been taught how to cook and sew, but also she was planning to go away to college. Emmy Bailey must therefore look to her own future. As Mr Erskine's housekeeper, that future was well and truly guaranteed and she would have a roof over her head.

Which is more than I have at the moment, Catherine sighed. With the lease on what had once been her family home recently expired, and assorted items of furniture and personal belongings distributed between Aunt Em's cottage, one of the old estate offices and a colleague at the library, her immediate future was looking extremely bleak.

Towelling herself dry, Catherine tripped against the pile of dishevelled clothing at her feet. Her poor shoes! Her one and only extravagance since starting work full-time. Now look at them. Completely ruined. Once more haunted by the sight of Francesca, she gave a derisive snort. 'I bet she's never saved for weeks on end for a single pair of shoes.'

'*Money isn't everything,*' Catherine's conscience rebuked. 'I know but at least it helps,' she whispered to her sorry-looking reflection in the mirror, all the while trying not to think of Rod's expensively attired travelling companion. As for being compared to a frog on two — or was it three — occassions? Definitely three, Catherine acknowledged grimly, recalling their brief encounter by the cellar door.

With myriad thoughts winging away to *Brief Encounter*, one of Aunt Em's favourite black and white films (not to mention the hordes of romantic novels Emmy devoured every fortnight), Catherine relived the morning's events at the ford and let her imagination run riot. In the romantic setting of a film production she would have been the beautiful, highly accomplished daughter of a wealthy land owner, astride her bay mare, with Roderick Marchant conveniently at hand when her horse reared and stumbled. Deposited safely into his arms, he would then proclaim her the most beautiful thing he'd ever seen, before carrying her off into the sunset to an elegant house full of waiting servants.

Turning away from the less than elegant reflection in the mirror, Catherine gave a wistful groan. Despite being blessed with a reasonable figure, riding a second-hand bike into Whycham Ford and getting herself covered in duckweed hardly made her heroine material.

'Forget it, Catherine,' she cautioned. 'As far as Rod Marchant is concerned, you are the waiting servant! From now on stop reading Aunt Em's library books and stick to your own.' Suddenly averse to her favourite colour, green, Catherine dressed quickly in jeans, gingham blouse and trainers, grabbed a sleeveless fleece and ran downstairs.

'That's a relief,' Emmy announced, returning from the dining-room.

'What is?' Catherine said, looking up from where she was studying her aunt's newly complied shopping list.

'At least her ladyship liked the soup, though I doubt she's ever seen a lentil before.'

'I doubt if she's ever seen the inside of a kitchen. Anyway, why the 'ladyship' bit again? That's not what she wants you to call her?'

Aunt Em smiled and began adding knobs of golden butter to a pan of creamy mashed potatoes. 'No, dear. Although I reckon Miss lah-di-dah Francesca would love it if I did. Oh, and by the way, she also asked for some more bread. Can you take some in, please?'

For a moment Catherine made as if to speak and then changed her mind. The bread had been one of the casualties at the ford. Luckily, her aunt had managed to salvage most of it. As for the remainder . . .

★ ★ ★

Once more pushing her bike in the direction of the side gate, Catherine heard a familiar voice call, 'If you're going to the village, can I give you a lift? Mr Barnes says it looks like rain. What's happened to all that lovely sunshine we had earlier?'

Catherine came to an abrupt halt. So that's where Roderick Marchant had sprung from. He'd been talking to Mr Barnes, the gardener.

'No, thank you. I'm sure I can cycle there and back before it starts raining.'

'Perhaps,' Roderick replied. 'Nevertheless, it will be a great deal quicker in my car. It's quite nippy, you know.'

Fixing him with a look that said, 'There's no need to remind me — I was there when you sped past, remember?' Catherine watched his face break into a broad grin. 'I meant nippy as in cold, not speed. North sea breezes and all that?'

Feeling decidedly foolish, Catherine forced a weak smile. Moments later she succumbed to his offer, returned her bike to the outhouse and made her way towards the bright red sports car. Halfway into the passenger seat, she remembered Francesca. 'What about your . . . um . . . friend? Wouldn't she prefer to go with you? Perhaps have a look round the village. It's steeped in history, you know.'

Rod began to laugh again. 'Francesca interested in history! You've got to be joking! Unless Whycham le Cley can boast a Harrods and a Fortnums, I'm sure she'll be far happier staying at the hall. Actually, she said she might go to bed.'

'Oh, dear. Is she ill?'

'If you mean has she got duckweed poisoning from the bread you served at lunchtime,' Rod replied, fixing Catherine with a sly grin, 'the answer is no. I think she's simply finding the Norfolk air a bit strong and has opted for an afternoon nap.' Closing the passenger door, he turned and ran round to the driver's side with a chirpy, 'That's why I'm relying on you to be my guide for the afternoon. According to Mr Barnes, you're a local history buff. I was hoping you'd give me a brief résumé on the way into Whycham le Cley. I'm afraid my local knowledge is virtually nil.'

'Even though you've inherited the hall and all the estate. You must have some idea of its history.'

Rod shook his head, spying the look of sheer disbelief flooding his passenger's face. 'Now I expect you'll be thinking I'm also a complete Philistine as well as being a rude and rotten driver.'

'It wasn't you driving the car . . . was it?' Catherine broke in, cautiously. 'Why did you let me think otherwise?'

'Let's just say I thought it best you took your wrath out on me instead. Which I hasten to add, you did most admirably.' Ignoring Catherine's blushes, Rod continued, 'Later, when we almost collided by the cellar door, it was me who wasn't terribly polite. I owe you an apology. I had no right to speak to you like that, even if you had been employed by the estate. No wonder we townies don't rate too highly with the locals.'

Not knowing how to respond, Catherine shifted uneasily within the confines of her seat. Changing gear, Roderick Marchant's left hand accidentally brushed against her jean-clad knee.

'Now, where was I?' he said at length. 'Ah, yes, Philistines. Quite simply the reason why I know so very little about the Whycham estate is because we always lived so far away. With Father in the diplomatic service, before ill health forced him to return to the UK, my parents spent so little time in England. As for myself, I never saw too much of it either, other than from within the confines of boarding school.'

'Boarding school,' Catherine repeated, keeping to herself her thoughts on boarding schools. No child of hers, if she ever had any, would be dispatched to boarding school. Which at the moment was pretty unlikely, a tiny voice reminded in her head, given that her once long-term boyfriend (the person who'd stolen her heart big-time) had himself been stolen by her so-called very best friend at college.

'Looking back, I've worked it out that the very first time I saw Great Uncle Cedric was when I was at boarding school,' Rod explained.

'I wasn't aware that he used to come and visit you. Aunt Em never said. Then again, that's quite possibly before she became housekeeper at the hall.'

'By all accounts old Uncle Erskine was always a bit of a dark horse and became even more of a recluse after the death of his good lady. Anyway, when I was at school his visits were very few and far between. If the story my father tells is anything to go by, that's when he decided to make me his heir. He'd already ruled out my mother, his niece. Can't have girls inheriting, can we?' Rod grinned.

Biting her tongue (now was not the time for a debate on female inheritance), Catherine heard Rod continue. 'One day, arriving unexpectedly at the school, he discovered me trying to protect one of the new boys from a gang of bullies. Having been the subject of similar bullying myself, I'd made a vow to stand up for those less able to fend for themselves.'

Visualizing a young Roderick Marchant fighting off a gang of bullies, Catherine frowned and bit her lip. 'I have a vague recollection of your great uncle telling my father that he loathed boarding schools.'

'Really? Do you think that's because he was sent away to one himself?'

'Quite possibly. It could also explain why he and his wife were so keen to support the village school and community. When Edwina was still alive they were always opening up the house and gardens for the local children. You know, Christmas parties, May Day festivals and the like.'

For a brief moment Rod was deeply thoughtful, almost as if hearing the sound of children's footsteps echoing down oak-panelled corridors in search of Father Christmas. And what was it Catherine had said about May Day festivals? Wouldn't the newly manicured lawns at Whycham Hall be simply perfect for that. Perhaps that was something he could organize if he ever lived there long-term. For the moment, however, there was still the family firm in London to consider and his modern Docklands flat. All in all, a far cry from Whycham and Norfolk.

Unsure as to whether or not Catherine's cough was deliberate, Rod blinked as if to clear a vision from his eyes. Slowing down to cross the ford, he checked pointedly for both cyclists and pedestrians before announcing, 'Mother's always said it was such a shame that Cedric and Edwina never had children. She's convinced things would have been so different otherwise.'

Which of course they would, Catherine thought to herself. To begin with she wouldn't be sitting within the confines of this car (conscious of her chauffeur's strong profile and expertly cropped dark chestnut hair) and her aunt wouldn't be back at Whycham Hall, worrying about a houseful of guests for lunch on Sunday and breakfast on Monday morning.

With his hand brushing accidentally against Catherine's knee for a second time, Rod negotiated the final bend into the village. Spying a trio of children, all clutching presents and presumably on their way to a birthday party, he said, 'According to my mother, that's exactly what's needed at the hall.'

'Pardon?'

'Mother believes Whycham Hall should echo to the sound of children's voices. She says it's been quiet for far too long.'

Widening her eyes in amazement (had she heard correctly?). Catherine was even more taken aback when Rod concluded, 'You know . . . in a way I'm inclined to agree with her.'

'Is that what you plan to do? Fill Whycham Hall with children?' Catherine ventured, trying to force from her mind the picture of a heavily pregnant Francesca, languishing on cushions in the conservatory or else sashaying from room to room.

Pulling in to the car park by the village green and pond, Rod fixed Catherine with a reflective smile. 'Who knows what I plan to do? For the moment, however, and family business apart, I think perhaps I quite like the idea. I'm extremely taken with what I've seen so far. So if you'd care to remind me about the local history . . . '

3

With Aunt Em's shopping duly completed, Catherine made her way to the village war memorial. Despite her protestations that she was perfectly capable of catching the bus back to Whycham Hall, Roderick had insisted he wait for her. To her surprise she found him deeply absorbed, studying the lists of casualties from the two world wars. Not sure if he'd seen her approach, she called his name softly. 'Mr Marchant.'

Turning towards her, Roderick ran a hand across his face. 'I'm sorry. I was so engrossed in reading all these names, I didn't see you coming.'

Catherine nodded in understanding. 'Even after all this time that memorial never fails to move me. I always find it hard to take in so many casualties from one small village.'

'I noticed an Edward Wickham amongst them. Was he a relation?'

'Yes. My great grandfather's only brother. He was killed in September 1916.'

'And the name, Wickham. I don't suppose there's any connection with Whycham le Cley, is there? Or is it simply a coincidence?'

35

'Oh, pure coincidence, I expect,' Catherine lied, erring on the side of caution. Now was not the time to become embroiled in a discussion on Aunt Em's pet subject, the rightful inheritance of Whycham Hall.

Spying Catherine's shopping, Rod reached out and took it from her grasp, his strong arms making light of the heavily laden basket. 'By the way, thanks for putting in my request for the onion gravy and mashed potato. And also for doing this extra shopping. I'm afraid my sudden arrival has given you and your aunt a great deal of extra work. I should have remembered this isn't London, where you can pop into the supermarket or department-store food hall. I shall have to bear that in mind next time.'

'In what way?'

'I was going to say I'll bring some provisions with me, but already I can see from the look on your face that might not meet with your approval. Am I correct, Miss Wickham? Is that something else that annoys you about us *townies*?'

'Mr Marchant, what you decide to bring with you from London is your own affair. At the same time, however, it might be worth considering what Whycham le Cley has to offer. People like yourself would be accepted far more readily if you were to patronize the village shops and local services.'

Roderick raised a bemused eyebrow. 'I see. So you don't think the locals are going to accept me as the new lord of the manor? Before you give me your answer, can I please insist that you refrain from Mr Marchant. I prefer Rod. Roderick's too much of a mouthful. If, on the other hand, you can't cope with that, perhaps you'd prefer 'your lordship' instead. I know there's no official title to go with the hall at present but in the circumstances . . . '

Catherine couldn't believe her ears. Call him *your lordship*? Why, the sheer audacity of it! He had to be joking. Turning angrily to face him, she realized all too late that he was. Suffused with embarrassment, she felt herself colour and made a hurried grab to retrieve her basket.

'Definitely not!' Rod said, chestnut eyes twinkling with amusement while transferring the basket to his other side. 'Reason number one: It's going to pour with rain at any moment, which was why in your absence I put the roof on the car. Reason number two: As you seem to think I'm in such dire need of advice on how to deal with the locals, perhaps you'd care to oblige. And . . . if I could also call you Catherine?'

On the return journey to the hall,

Catherine explained how many of the local businesses were struggling to survive. Consequently, any extra income generated from holiday-makers and day-trippers was always a welcome bonus. 'Supermarkets are all very well,' she said, recalling Rod's earlier remarks, 'but the majority of Whycham inhabitants are either middle-aged or elderly, don't have cars and would be utterly lost without the village shops and post office. As for the bus service . . .'

'You mean to say there is one? Though, come to think of it, I don't think I've seen a bus all day. Oh, dear. Is this where you're going to say that's because Francesca and I were driving far too fast to see one — '

'No. I wasn't,' Catherine broke in meekly. 'Because there are only two a day. One in the morning and one in the afternoon.'

Convinced this was her idea of a joke, Rod soon perceived that it wasn't. His passenger was deadly earnest. 'What time's the last bus in the afternoon?' he said, peering to look at the clock on his dashboard.

'Five o'clock.'

Swinging his car through the gates of the hall, Rod announced with a satisfied smile, 'Then it's just as well I insisted on bringing you back. It's only four o'clock. You would have had a very long wait in the rain.'

Thanking him for the lift and stepping from the car, Catherine paused only briefly to take in the splendour of the hall. Though not vast by country house standards, it was nonetheless an imposing family residence, completely surrounded by carefully tended gardens and wooded countryside. All in all, a tasteful composition of mellow stone, mullion windows, towering chimney pots and a seemingly endless sweep of gravel driveway.

When Rod made his way to the heavily studded, oak front door, he was surprised to see Catherine walk in the opposite direction. 'Catherine. Where are you going?'

'To the kitchen door. Aunt Em and I never use the front.'

'Why ever not?'

'Mr Erskine didn't approve of staff coming in the front door. He always insisted they use the tradesmen's entrance.'

'You're not a tradesman. Neither are you staff.'

Catherine shrugged her shoulders. 'I know but . . .'

'There's to be no buts about it,' Rod insisted. 'If I'm going in by the main door, so are you.'

'I have to go to the kitchen anyway. Aunt Em will be waiting for the shopping.'

'And I said no more buts. Now, are you

coming in by the front door or do I have to carry you and your shopping across the threshold?'

Feeling her pulse-rate quicken at the very prospect, Catherine followed Rod hurriedly inside. Once again she found him reluctant to part with the shopping. 'It's OK,' he said. 'I might as well carry it through. I need to have a word with your aunt about this evening.'

In silence and with her eyes on his athletic frame, Catherine endeavoured to keep up with Rod's lengthy strides. In no time at all, he'd made his way along the wide panelled hallway, flung open the kitchen door and deposited her basket on the kitchen table.

'Here you are, Mrs Bailey. Your niece and tomorrow's lunch all safely delivered. I hope that makes up for my unexpected arrival this morning. Goodness! What's that wonderful smell?'

Dismissing his apologies, Emmy explained she'd been baking scones for afternoon tea. She also confirmed his Saturday night dinner reservation at a nearby inn. 'I'll pop the kettle on for tea, shall I?' she said, motioning to a tea tray set with freshly baked scones, yellow slabs of butter and home-made strawberry jam. Rod nodded appreciatively and, fixing her with a beaming smile, heard her continue, 'You'll also find a nice warm fire in the drawing-room and Mr Barnes has left plenty of logs. Despite this morning's sunshine, he's convinced it's going to be a very cold night.'

Cheered by the prospect of afternoon tea by the fire (such a quaint British custom, he thought), Rod made his way to the kitchen door.

'Madam's already waiting for you,' Emmy called after him.

'Madam? Oh, you mean Francesca. Oh, well, I suppose I'd better go and tell her that we'll be eating out this evening. Though, quite frankly, Mrs Bailey, following that delicious lunch and the prospect of tea and scones by the fire, I can't help thinking it would be so much nicer to stay here instead.'

Then why don't you? Catherine thought to herself, seeing him hurry away down the hall. Five minutes later she got her answer when she held the drawing-room door open for her aunt. Watching Emmy proceed with the heavily laden tea tray and Rod spring up from his chair to assist her, she heard Francesca announce sniffily, 'Of course I want to go out this evening! Isn't that what we agreed? Besides, I've been bored stiff, stuck here alone all afternoon with nothing to do.'

'Nothing to do?' Catherine hissed, following her aunt back to the kitchen. 'How can she possibly say that about this place?

Gracious! Even if I lived here permanently I'd never get bored.'

'That's quite possibly because you've got Wickham blood in your veins, my dear. Why, I remember your grandfather saying . . . '

Not wishing to offend her aunt by saying that she didn't really want to hear (yet again) what her grandfather had said about the hall, particularly in relation to their ancestors, Catherine excused herself. She still needed to deal with her muddied clothing from this morning's drenching.

'I know most of your clothes will wash but what will you do about your shoes?' Aunt Em enquired.

Catherine emitted a desperate sigh. 'I honestly don't know. From where I'm standing it looks as if they're completely ruined. Not only that, it will take simply ages to save for another pair. It's all very well Rod Marchant saying he'll pay the cleaning bill. That doesn't solve the problem of the shoes.'

'Perhaps I can help you there, my dear, because I'm going to be in desperate need of some help tomorrow. Master Roderick's invited six of his friends to lunch, remember? I could certainly do with an extra pair of hands. Mr Hayes did insist that you were to be paid for any extra hours.'

Catherine paused by the range and picked

up her shoes. 'Indirectly, I'm already being paid for helping you. I'm living here rent free, don't forget.'

'In that dreadful attic room!' Aunt Em replied, hands on hips and her tone indignant. 'All that way up those horrid twisting stairs.'

'It's not a dreadful attic room, Aunt. In fact I love it. And the view is simply amazing. Besides, as you and I both know, Mr Hayes did suggest I use one of the bedrooms at the far end of the house and — '

'You declined,' Emmy finished for her.

'Precisely. And with extra guests arriving tomorrow that's probably just as well.'

Emmy nodded, reminded of the task ahead. Her niece certainly had a point. Although Whycham Hall possessed many bedrooms, not all of them were in an acceptable decorative state. Master Roderick's haughty companion had made that point abundantly clear when she'd insisted on a hasty tour during his absence. Making a mental note of Francesca's numerous demands, Emmy still wasn't prepared to give in as far as her niece was concerned. Yes, the attic bedroom did have a magnificent view but it was also jolly cold up there. The thought of Catherine with just two bars of an electric fire was totally unacceptable. 'I still wish you'd move into my cottage,' Aunt Em sighed, voicing her innermost thoughts.

Miles away with her own thoughts, Catherine looked up from examining her ruined shoes. Standing up, she placed a reassuring arm about her aunt's shoulders and kissed her fondly. 'Dear Aunt Em, much as I love you, even you have to admit the housekeeper's cottage is far too small for both of us.'

'But there's plenty of room.'

'No, there isn't,' Catherine said, ignoring her aunt's renewed protests. 'You're already storing loads of my belongings. In addition to which we have so many books between us, we could start our own mini-library. If I moved in with you we'd probably trip over each other's book shelves and end up fighting.'

Emmy pursed her lips in defeat. Catherine was right, of course. Nevertheless, she was still determined to have the last word. 'Are you sure you're not too cold up there?'

'Let's just say it's probably not quite so warm and inviting as the drawing-room, with its log fire and comfy armchairs.'

'That's it!' Emmy cried, triumphant. 'Your shoes. We might be able to salvage them after all.'

'How on earth can we?'

'By stuffing them with newspaper. Then,

we'll put them by the embers of the fire after Master Roderick and his girlfriend have gone to bed. With luck they'll be nicely dried out by the morning.'

'What if Rod and Francesca don't get back until late? I don't intend to stay up half the night waiting for them to come home.'

'Trust me. They won't. Master Roderick won't stay out any longer than he has to.'

'What makes you so sure?'

'Because he doesn't look the type to drink and drive. Just you wait and see. The thought of a welcoming fire and a glass of fine Napoleon brandy will soon have him heading back to the hall.'

'OK. You've convinced me.' Catherine replied, recognizing the familiar knowing glint in her aunt's eyes. 'But, before I set to with the newspaper, can I ask you something? Why do you keep referring to Rod as Master Roderick?'

'Force of habit, I suppose. Mr Hayes has always referred to him as Master Roderick.'

Watching Catherine walk towards the door carrying her shoes and a pile of newspapers, Emmy called after her, 'Anyway, if you think it strange me calling him Master Roderick, why have you suddenly started referring to him as Rod?'

'Because he told me to,' came the hurried reply.

Spying two scarlet blobs on her niece's cheeks as she made a dash for the hallway, Emmy gave a self-satisfied smile. 'Did he indeed? Well, isn't that interesting. Now I wonder . . . '

★ ★ ★

Exactly as Aunt Em had predicted, Rod and Francesca returned home at 10.30, had coffee and brandy and retired to bed (each to their own rooms) shortly after eleven o'clock. Some time later, making sure the house was quite still, Catherine crept stealthily downstairs in her pyjamas.

Until now she'd never been in the drawing-room so late at night and certainly not with the dying embers of the fire glowing warm and welcoming in the enveloping darkness. How wonderful it all was, she thought to herself. Burning embers in the soot-blackened chimney, the pungent aroma of apple and pine wood wafting from the log basket, all intermingled with the smell of lavender polish and beeswax. She even discerned the faintest aroma of brandy and coffee. In fact, it could almost be a scene from one of Aunt Em's treasured books.

Although there, hero and heroine had been sitting in a tiny Norfolk flint cottage, not Whycham Hall.

Switching on the light and bending down to put her paper-stuffed shoes by the hearth, Catherine was sorely tempted to move away the heavy brass fireguard. It wouldn't hurt for a few minutes, would it? After all, there was no one about. Wouldn't they be sleeping soundly?

'Very soundly, I should think,' she whispered, studying not only the newly opened bottle of brandy on the coffee table but also the two brandy glasses, coffee cups and empty cafetière on a silver tray. Reminded that Rod had given Emmy strict instructions not to wait up, Catherine carried the tray into the kitchen. In no time at all she had washed the glasses, cups and coffee jug and hurried back to the dying warmth of the fire.

This time feeling somewhat bolder, she switched on one of the rose-pink table lamps, turned off the main ceiling light, moved the fireguard to one side and prepared to settle herself by the fire. Barefoot, she hesitated for a moment. On either side of the fireplace was a tapestry armchair. Francesca, she knew (from the lipstick-stained coffee cup and glass she'd just removed) had been sitting to the left of the fire which meant Rod must have been sitting to the right.

Trailing her fingers across the chair to where Rod's arms had lingered, Catherine lowered herself to the floor. Then, tucking her feet beneath her, she leaned against an imaginary body and closed her eyes. 'This is exactly what one of Aunt Em's favourite authors would call a brief glimpse of heaven,' she sighed sleepily. She could even smell Rod's aftershave.

An hour later when she awoke, Catherine looked up, startled. She was not alone. Rod Marchant was sitting in the opposite chair! Quickly, trying to struggle to her feet, she found that she couldn't. It was almost as if she was rooted to the spot.

'It's all right. Don't panic. The house isn't on fire.'

Conscious of the fact that she'd not only removed the fireguard but also fallen asleep, when a single stray spark could have set light to the hall and its valuable contents, Catherine felt sick in the pit of her stomach. 'The fireguard! How utterly irresponsible of me.'

'Why? What's wrong with it?' Rod puzzled.

'I moved it. You see . . . I only intended to sit here for a little while. I'm so sorry. I had no idea I'd fall asleep. I thought the fire was safe and . . .'

Rod held out a restraining hand, insisting that she remained where she was. 'I didn't say the house isn't on fire because of that. I was more concerned about you jumping to your feet when you were still half asleep. It's OK, Catherine. Considering I've been sitting here myself for at least half an hour, I don't think these dying embers have been unattended for too long, do you?'

Catherine shook her head. Despite Rod's assurances, she remained deeply troubled. She shouldn't really be in this room uninvited. And, in addition to wearing only her pyjamas, albeit an extremely sensible pair (a Christmas gift from Aunt Em, made of cotton fleece), she'd only just realized that Rod was also in pyjamas.

At least his were silk and covered by a stylish dressing-gown, Catherine told herself. Unlike her own, which was unfortunately still hanging from a hook on the back of her bedroom door. As for the fact that he must have been watching her for ages . . .

'Tell me,' Rod began kindly. 'What brought you down here at the bewitching hour of midnight? Like me, was it the lure of the fire? Is it cold up there in that turret of yours?'

'My turret?' Catherine repeated, trying not to sound like a complete simpleton.

Rod smiled, warm chocolate eyes creasing

into tiny lines at the corners. 'Mr Barnes tells me that's where you prefer to sleep. He told me about your attic abode this afternoon, just before I offered you a lift. You don't have to sleep there, you know, Catherine. In fact, you can always sleep in my . . . '

For a brief moment Catherine was filled with inexorable panic. Was he going to say sleep in his bed? All colour drained from her face. It appeared Rod was taking this lord of the manor thing seriously after all. Frowning hard, she remembered the medieval trilogy currently gracing Aunt Em's sideboard. What was it called when the lord of the manor had his pick of the local virgins? *Droit de seigneur*.

Recalling all too vividly how she'd explained to Rod that the residents of the village were mostly middle aged and elderly, she then turned her thoughts to local virgins. Definitely few and far between, Catherine concluded, and she was one of them. The current problem being that she certainly wasn't far away and the only thing between her and Master Roderick was an Indian hearth rug!

'Catherine?' Rod urged, his voice filled with renewed concern. 'Can I get you a brandy? You're looking dreadfully pale.' Seeing her shake her head, he continued. 'I was asking about your room in the attic. If it is as cold as Mr Barnes suspects, I was going to suggest you move in to the bedroom I've allocated for my sister, Henrietta.'

His sister? How could she possibly be so stupid as to think . . . Relief flooded Catherine's face as she listened to Rod explain. 'Henrietta's working abroad at the moment for the charity ROKPA. I'm sure you'd find her room a great deal cosier. In a house this size it's totally unnecessary for you to stay in the attic. If you're now going to tell me that's another of my late uncle's antiquated rules, I want you to know I'm abolishing it here and now.'

Realizing how utterly foolish she'd been with her mind going hopelessly into overdrive, Catherine hugged her knees and explained, 'You were partly right. I did come down because of the fire . . . but it wasn't to keep warm.'

'Not to keep warm. I don't understand.'

'I wanted to see if I could salvage my shoes. Aunt Em suggested that I stuff them with old newspapers and leave them here overnight. She thought the Aga might dry them off a little too quickly and as a consequence make the toes curl up.'

Confused, Rod turned in the direction of the fire where the misshapen green suede shoes were resting by the hearth. Recognizing them as the pair Catherine was wearing when Francesca ploughed her way through the ford, he reached out to pick them up. 'Why try and salvage them when they appear totally beyond repair?' he queried, turning them over in his hands. 'Why not throw them away and buy new ones?'

'Because I can't afford to,' came the mildly indignant response. 'And also because I fell in love with those shoes the moment I saw them. Unlike you, and without wishing to be appear rude, I'm not in a position to buy exactly what I want the moment I see it.'

'Of course you can. At least you can go and buy a new pair. That's why I gave you my business card. I thought I offered to pay for — '

'You offered to pay the cleaning bill,' Catherine interrupted, plucking nervously at an embroidered bluebell on her pyjama top. 'As far as I'm aware there aren't any dry cleaners for shoes, least not here in Whycham le Cley. Of course, they might exist in London.'

Still toying with the bluebell, Catherine was vaguely aware of Rod placing her shoes back on the hearth. The next moment, however, instead of returning to his chair as expected, he was kneeling on the floor beside her, taking her in his arms. 'Oh, Catherine.

You silly goose. Of course I meant I'd pay for your shoes as well. You must get a new pair as soon as the shops open — and also send me the bill. Better still, as I intend staying on for an extra couple of days, why don't I take you into Norwich to look for a suitable replacement. That way I can pay for them myself, thus saving you further inconvenience.'

'No!' Catherine remonstrated, freeing herself from his embrace. 'I couldn't possibly agree to that. What would people think if they saw us together and you were paying for — '

'What would people think if they saw us together now?' Rod broke in huskily, drawing her back into his arms gently. 'Especially with us both in our pyjamas. And .. if I were to hold you close and kiss you . . . '

'I . . . er . . . don't know,' came the tremulous response. Failing miserably in her attempt to summon up enough willpower to free herself for a second time, Catherine heard Rod's whispered, 'Then dare I suggest we try it and see,' before he lowered his mouth to hers.

4

For a few wonderful moments, Catherine was lost in Rod's embrace, his lips searching hers and firm but gentle hands caressing her arms. Given her own brief glimpse of heaven, she was swept up in its magic, drifting back through the centuries to the earliest occupants of Whycham Hall. This was one fragment of history she didn't mind being reminded of. Back to the days when the first Lord of Whycham had brought his beloved bride to Whycham Hall for the very first time. In those days, of course, the name had been spelt Wykeham. Though whether or not there was any connection to Edward III's Lord Chancellor of England still remained a mystery. According to legend (and Aunt Em), Edmund and Eleanor Wykeham had been so very much in love. It was only when Edmund followed his king to France . . .

Catherine's brow creased into a frown. France . . . Francesca! Hurriedly, she pulled away from Rod's arms. 'I'm sorry, I shouldn't be here. I must go.'

'Please don't,' Rod begged, when she struggled free from his grasp. 'It's me who should apologize, not you. I had no right to behave like that. I suppose it was sitting here watching you as you slept. Bathed in the rosy glow of the lamp and the dying embers of the fire, you looked so lovely, almost like . . . '

Like what? Catherine longed to ask. At least this time he couldn't compare her to a frog. Wearing fleece pyjamas, she looked anything but.

'Like an angel,' Rod murmured, reaching out to stroke her hair before clasping both her hands in his. 'Like that heavenly angel I saw in Whycham church this afternoon. Living here as you do, you must be familiar with all those beautiful stained glass windows.'

'Yes. I am. But I certainly don't recall any of those angels having auburn hair and green eyes. For the most part they are blonde and blue-eyed like Francesca.'

Rod brushed his lips against Catherine's fingers. 'Ah, yes, Francesca. Unlike you, however, Francesca's no angel.'

'But she is asleep upstairs,' Catherine reminded him, convinced Rod had over-imbibed on the brandy. This time, determined to pull her hands free, she succeeded and Rod made no attempt to stop her. Instead he watched her walk away in silence. It was only when she reached the heavy oak door and her fingers gripped the handle that he called after her.

'Catherine . . . '

'Goodnight, Rod,' she whispered, turning soulful eyes in his direction.

Hearing the door close behind her, Rod replaced the fire guard. 'Goodnight, my angel. Sleep well,' he answered in reply as a sudden gust from the doorway fanned a tiny burst of flames. Knowing only too well that she hadn't heard him, his night-time wishes went spiralling up the chimney, closely followed by a plaintive sigh.

★   ★   ★

Next morning, waking from a troubled sleep, Catherine hurried downstairs to retrieve her shoes. To her surprise they had gone. Thinking that Aunt Em had already beaten her to it, she was about to return to her room when a small white card caught her eye. In exactly the same spot where she'd left her shoes was another of Rod's business cards. Picking it up and turning it over in her hand, she noticed three simple letters: IOU.

'Oh, good, you found it,' came a voice from the doorway.

Startled, Catherine turned to find Rod, freshly shaved and dressed, his short cropped hair still damp from the shower. 'That's to remind you I intend taking you into Norwich to buy a replacement pair of shoes.'

About to protest, Catherine could only gape open mouthed when Francesca appeared out of nowhere. 'Roddy dahling, there you are! I've been looking everywhere. Where have you been?'

'Just having a very quick look round the garden, which is why I'd better go and take these shoes off. They're covered in grass cuttings.'

'Oh, I see,' drawled Francesca, spying his dew-stained shoes. 'Been surveying the estate, have you? Well, I shall be expecting a proper guided tour when the others arrive but only on condition the grass has dried off a bit. I don't want my shoes ruined.'

At the mention of ruined footwear, Rod gave Catherine a sly smile, which she did her best to ignore. Pretending to rearrange the remaining logs in the basket, she announced, 'If you're both ready for breakfast, I'll go and tell my aunt.'

Watching Catherine depart, Francesca shook her head in disbelief. 'Roddy, my sweet. That girl. I mean to say, the clothes. Yesterday it was mud-spattered green garb, this morning it's jeans and trainers. Whatever next?'

'You're not exactly averse to wearing jeans

and trainers yourself, Francesca.'

'Maybe not, but at least mine are designer. Anyway, jeans apart it's not really what I expected of Whycham Hall. Shouldn't she be in uniform or something? Can't you do anything about it? Especially if she's going to be in your employ.'

Rod nodded appreciatively. Yes, it would be nice to do something about Catherine's clothes, particularly after last night. Those bluebell-decorated pyjamas were certainly something else.

'Actually, she's not really in my employ, Francesca. Catherine's merely been helping her aunt to get the house ready for summer. Mr Barnes was telling me she works in a college library.'

'A library!' Francesca snorted, her voice strangely reminiscent of Lady Bracknell and that notorious handbag. 'Lord! I couldn't think of anything more boring. Can't you persuade her to stay on for a while — or else get someone in from the village? It's obvious Mrs Bailey — or whatever her name is — won't be able to cope singlehandedly once you start having your summer house parties.'

Rod ran his finger along one of the many bookshelves. 'I'm not so sure about getting someone in from the village. I understand it's extremely difficult finding staff these days.'

'Oh dear. How frightfully tiresome. Mummy's always having similar problems in London. In that case, Roddy my dear, there's only one option. You'll simply have to exercise all your masculine charm on Mrs Bailey. Perhaps she can be persuaded to make her niece stay on.'

With his back to Francesca, Rod gave a wry smile. 'I suppose I could try — but if Catherine's happy with her job at the library . . . '

'How could anyone be happy working in a library?' Francesca said, following Rod towards the dining-room. There, casting an appreciative eye over the neatly laid breakfast table, she waited until Catherine had left the room with their order for coffee, scrambled eggs and bacon. 'About what I was saying earlier. I definitely think you should get her to stay. Can you imagine Jeremy's face if Cathy took him his early morning tea? And if you found her one of those nice little uniforms . . . ' Reaching for a glass of freshly squeezed orange juice, Francesca nodded smugly. 'You know, she could really be quite an asset when we have guests.'

'It's Catherine not Cathy,' Rod corrected, preferring to ignore the 'we' in Francesca's last remark. If the truth were told, he'd have absolutely no difficulty at all imagining

Catherine in uniform. As for leaving her alone in Jeremy's presence, that was quite another matter. No girl was safe in Jeremy's company once he'd started drinking. 'Don't worry, Francesca, I'll certainly give your suggestion plenty of thought,' he replied, reaching for a slice of toast.

★ ★ ★

When Roddy's guests and lunchtime arrived, Catherine was dressed in the pencil-slim black skirt and white short-sleeved blouse from her days spent working in the wine bar.

'Whew! She's a bit of all right!' Jeremy hissed when Catherine left the dining-room carrying the empty soup bowls. 'Where on earth did you find her?'

'On a lily pad,' Rod said, grinning.

'On a what?'

'Oh, just ignore him, Jeremy,' Francesca said. 'You know what Roddy's like when it comes to frogs and things with webbed feet. His office is littered with them.'

'You mean she's got webbed feet?'

Francesca roared with laughter, watching Jeremy drain his glass. 'No. Of course she hasn't. At least I don't think so. Then again, you never can tell with these locals. They've probably all interbred over the years.'

'Hmm . . . so she's a real local then, is she? Lucky old Rodders.'

Rod frowned, refilling Jeremy's glass. 'Why lucky?'

'*Droit de seigneur*, old chap.'

'*Droit de seigneur?*' numerous voices chorused. 'What's that?'

Jeremy winked and raised his glass, spying Catherine re-enter the room. 'That,' he began, with a lascivious grin in Catherine's direction, 'means old Roddy here can take his pick of all the local maidens. Isn't that right, my friend? Of course, if you don't want her, perhaps we could all draw lots. Come to think of it, as I noticed her first, I wouldn't mind taking her off your hands until something better comes along.'

To Catherine's consternation, Rod replied with a glib, 'I don't know about that, Jeremy. As I recall, it's me who first set eyes on Catherine. If what you're saying is true — and by all accounts they do tend to dwell on local customs hereabouts — maybe I should give some thought to asserting my lordly rights. In fact, the idea quite appeals to me. How do you suggest I go about it?'

Seething with rage and not wishing to wait for Jeremy's reply, Catherine placed a large tureen of vegetables in the middle of the dining-table before exiting as quickly as she could.

'Odious pigs!' she began, almost colliding with her aunt, who was waiting in the kitchen with the joint of meat. 'Who the hell do they think they are? To hear them talk anyone would think I was just like that leg of lamb, ready to be served up for their enjoyment. That's why I come back here. To get away from all that.' Catherine's eyes smarted with tears. 'Why, they're just like animals! On second thoughts . . . no, they're not. Animals behave in a far better fashion.'

Aunt Em pushed a silver salver to one side. 'Are you telling me Master Roderick and his friends have been — '

'Yes, I am!' Catherine broke in, fighting back a sob. 'Especially that odious creature, Jeremy. The one wearing that yellow tweed jacket. Do you know, he actually sug-gested . . . '

Not wishing to hear more (she'd already guessed what was coming next), Emmy placed a comforting arm about Catherine's shoulders. 'Dare I suggest you simply ignore it, my dear? Take it from me I've met that Jeremy's sort before, all talk and nothing in their trousers. He was at the whisky at least an hour before lunch. Why not let me take in the rest of the meal? Perhaps you can decorate the puddings instead.'

Grateful not to set foot in the dining-room again, Catherine began whipping cream for the apple pie. She was equally relieved several hours later to find herself alone in the house. Aunt Em had taken herself off to her cottage for a well-deserved rest and from the noise echoing around the garden, it was obvious Rod's guests were doing the grand tour. Only moments ago, standing at her bedroom window, Catherine had discerned the party of eight, four men and four women, laughing and joking as they made their way along the neatly trimmed lawns and gravelled walkway. At least, there had been four couples. Now she could see only three. Rod and Francesca appeared to be missing.

Contemplating their whereabouts, Catherine soon caught sight of Francesca hurrying in Jeremy's direction. Giggling and leaning heavily on his arm, she attempted to shake a stone from her shoe. As for Rod Marchant, he was still nowhere to be seen. Probably in the rose arbour and hopefully getting smothered by greenfly, Catherine thought to herself, still haunted by the snatches of conversation she'd overheard at lunch. How could Rod speak about her like that, particularly after last night?

Reminded that it was still too early for

attacks of greenfly and black spot, Catherine muttered, 'Pity!' Mr Barnes was renowned for his lethal concoction when dealing with garden pests. From the way she was feeling at the moment, Roderick Marchant and his cronies were both pests and predators. The sooner they were all out of sight and earshot the better it would be. Thank heavens for the peace and solitude of her tiny attic room. The room Rod had suggested she vacate in favour of something more stylish and comfortable. When her stomach gave a tiny lurch, Catherine tried in vain to push last night's kiss from her mind. It wasn't as if Rod had declared his love for her.

'*Why should he, when he has Francesca?*' an inner voice sneered. '*Gracious! He only suggested you swap bedrooms and only moments ago you were visualizing him covered in greenfly. Fancy letting that one brief encounter in the drawing-room go to your head. Shame on you, Catherine Wickham!*'

Angry with herself for reacting in such a way, Catherine forced her attention back to the present. Sadly, the peace and solitude she so desperately craved was shattered by the sound of footsteps hurrying along the corridor in the direction of her room. Alarm filled her face as she rose from her chair and made her way to the door. Until this instant she'd never considered locking it; now, of course, it was too late. While she'd been busy watching Rod's guests walking in the garden, one of them (she presumed Jeremy) must have been watching her!

'Catherine, quick! I need to speak to you. Open the door.'

Recognizing Rod's voice, not Jeremy's, Catherine paused with her hand on the latch. What on earth was going on?

'Thank God I've managed to find you,' Rod said, taking one step into the room.

'Oh, really.'

Rod looked cautiously over his shoulder, acutely aware of Catherine's hand fixed firmly on the door frame, barring any further progress. 'Look, I'm sorry to disturb you, but with the others still in the garden and you all alone, I thought now would be a good time to — '

'Assert your lordly rights after what happened in the drawing-room last night,' Catherine said coolly, her voice tinged with sarcasm. 'In which case, Mr Marchant, you are very much mistaken. Even though I am here on a temporary basis and living under your roof, that does not give you the right to — '

'Catherine,' Rod pleaded, taking hold of

her arm. 'Don't be so ridiculous! I haven't come here for that. I've come to apologize for Jeremy's behaviour during lunch. It was totally out of order.'

'Jeremy's behaviour! As I recall, yours wasn't any better. You even agreed to his suggestion of drawing lots for me.'

'I know. Believe it or not, I said what I did and behaved as I did deliberately. It was done to protect you.'

'Protect me! Just like you seemed to think you were coming to my rescue yesterday morning, when all along it was your fault that I got wet in the first place.'

'It wasn't me doing the driving, remember?' Rod added defensively.

'Hmph! And I suppose you're going to say it wasn't really you sitting in the dining-room at lunchtime, discussing me as if I was some kind of trophy?'

'No. Of course it was me. If you'd only give me the chance to explain. There isn't much time, Catherine. It's taken me ages to try and slip away from the others. Any minute now they'll be wondering where I am. Will you please listen to me? It will only take a moment.'

Catherine nodded begrudgingly, making no attempt to move other than to shake her arm free from Rod's grasp.

'I'd feel happier if you'd let me come in,' he pleaded, looking back in the direction of the attic staircase.

'I bet you would. Aunt Em said you were even taking bets for me when she brought in the coffee and liqueurs.'

Deeply embarrassed that Mrs Bailey should have been witness to Jeremy's inebriated post-luncheon conversation, Rod gave an exasperated sigh. 'Despite what you're thinking, I do not intend to . . . The only reason I'm asking to come in is because of the others. They've already had a detailed tour of the garden and will be expecting a tour of the house next. I'd be a great deal happier if they didn't see this part of Whycham Hall or discover that it was in use. OK?'

'OK,' Catherine repeated, taking a few steps back and motioning him inside.

Hugely relieved when the door closed behind him, Rod's gaze soon took in the room's tiny proportions and shabby furnishings: a single iron bedstead, washstand, wardrobe and loose-covered armchair, all of which had seen far better days. He was appalled. He hadn't seen anything this grim and spartan since he was at boarding school. However, one look at Catherine's tight-lipped expression reminded him that he wasn't here to discuss interior design.

'Would you mind if I sat down?' he said softly.

Nodding and pointing to the armchair, Catherine waited for him to sit before making her way to the opposite corner. Once there she positioned herself on the edge of the bed, as far away from him as she could. An action which didn't go unnoticed.

'Well,' she said, turning to look at her alarm clock, 'you said this will only take a moment. Will you please say what you've got to say and go. No doubt your friends will be expecting tea before too long and — '

'And I can't say what I have to say if you keep interrupting. I want you to know you have every right to be angry and hurt, not only with Jeremy and the others but also with me. Jeremy had had far too much to drink — not that that's any excuse, of course, but it is the reason why I went along with his suggestion. I did it to prevent a very embarrassing situation.'

Catherine glared, incredulous. 'To prevent a very embarrassing situation? Meaning that what I was subjected to *wasn't* embarrassing?'

'Of course it was, but if you'd known Jeremy for as long as I have you'd know he's capable of far worse than that. Let's just say he sometimes gets carried away. By suggesting that I . . . er . . . wanted you for myself, I knew he'd do the gentlemanly thing and back off.'

'Good grief!' Catherine gasped, flashing angry green eyes in Rod's direction. 'And for that display of gentlemanly behaviour I am supposed to be grateful?'

'No. Of course not. In your shoes I'd feel equally insulted.' Realizing only too late that his moment was well and truly up and mention of shoes did him no favours, Rod followed Catherine's gaze to the alarm clock. 'Not that I expect you to believe me,' he said, rising from the chair, 'but I was so angry with Jeremy that I think I could almost have hit him. However, taking into account the last time I hit anyone was confronting those bullies at boarding school, I suppose you could say I chose the easy option.'

'Which was?'

'By treating this *droit de seigneur* thing lightly, I hoped the whole thing would be over and forgotten. In a way I was partly right, because no one's mentioned it since and my immediate concern has been to find you, both to explain and apologize.'

To Rod's surprise and relief, Catherine said nothing. Instead she sat picking at the corner of the patchwork bedspread, all the while conscious that he was drawing ever nearer. 'I'm also sorry for what happened last night. That too was out of order. It probably sounds utterly unbelievable but . . . '

Curious to discover what he'd found so unbelievable, Catherine let her thoughts dwell on last night's encounter in the drawing-room. Moments later, waiting for him to continue his explanation, it wasn't Rod's earnest tones that jolted her back to reality. It was Francesca's thin, reedy voice, cutting through the air like a knife. 'Roddy, Roddy dahling, where are you?'

'Damn!' he hissed, looking towards the open window. 'I'd better go. Please, Catherine, say you'll try to forget this whole embarrassing business and accept my heart-felt apologies.'

Seeing her nod in reply, Rod moved towards the bedroom door, pausing only briefly for one last look at the shabby attic bedroom. Watching him go, Catherine was convinced she saw him shake his head as if in disbelief. He also muttered something that sounded very much like Poole and Rochester. What on earth had Rochester in Kent and Poole in Dorset to do with Whycham Hall?

Turning to face her haunted reflection in the oval mirror above the washstand, Catherine gave a sardonic smile. Of course. It wasn't Rochester in Kent Rod was referring to but the secretive Edward Rochester from Charlotte Brontë's *Jane Eyre*. The same Mr Rochester who'd kept his mad wife locked in an attic bedroom, in the care of his servant Grace Poole. 'How very ironic,' she said miserably, reminded of Rod's disappearing figure, 'because here you are in an attic bedroom with a secret locked in your heart. Like Rochester's wife you too are mad. Mad to be in love with Roderick Marchant.'

Blinking back tears, Catherine walked numbly to the open window. To her despair she heard footsteps on the gravel below and saw Francesca hurry to Rod's side. 'As for forgetting you,' she struggled, her voice catching in her throat, 'I don't know if I can.'

5

Moderately successful in her attempt at ignoring Rod Marchant's existence, Catherine was less fortunate when it came to his companion. At every available opportunity Francesca made it abundantly clear that she considered Rod to be her very own personal property. Today was no exception as she clung limpet-like on to his arm.

'Bye, dahlings,' Francesca called to Jeremy and his cronies as they gathered near the old stable block, preparing to leave Whycham Hall.

'Bye, Frannie, bye, Rodders,' Jeremy replied. 'See you back in civilization.'

'I'm not so sure about that,' said Rod. 'You never know, I might even stay here on a permanent basis.'

Jeremy paused, fumbling in his pocket for his car keys. Though having enjoyed his weekend at the hall, living here 24/7 was hardly his idea of heaven. For the most part he'd had to agree with Francesca: Whycham le Cley's social scene (weekly whist drives and a monthly barn dance in the village hall) was hardly riveting stuff. Hearing the clink of milk bottles, he turned and grinned lasciviously. 'Oh, well, I suppose there are some compensations, Rodders. Your little milk maid, for instance.'

Disengaging himself from Francesca's grasp, Rod turned to see Catherine placing empty milk bottles by the kitchen door, before hurrying back inside.

'Such a quaint custom, don't you think,' Francesca added, her voice laced with sarcasm. 'Mother will never believe me when I tell her the milk is not only delivered but also comes in bottles. I suppose around here they consider that's progress. At least it means Cathy doesn't have to go armed with a bucket in each hand to milk the village cow.'

'Her name's Catherine,' Rod corrected, hearing Jeremy switch on his ignition.

'Cathy, Catherine, surely it makes no difference one way or the other, as long as she knows her place.'

Rod bit his tongue, anxious not to drag Catherine's name even further into the conversation, thus avoiding a repeat of earlier embarrassment. Raising his hand in farewell, he watched Jeremy shoot off down the drive at breakneck speed.

'I do wish he wouldn't do that,' Francesca protested. 'Look at my shoes, Roddy, all covered in dust and gravel.'

'And I wish you wouldn't call me Roddy. It's almost as bad as Jeremy calling me Rodders.'

'But I've always called you Roddy — even when we were children. Roderick was always so difficult to pronounce. You've never complained before.'

'Maybe not. In case it's escaped your notice, Francesca, we're no longer in kindergarten.'

'Ooh, dear. We are in a grump today, aren't we?' Francesca said tersely. Following Rod back into the coolness of the hall, she shivered and rubbed at her bare arms.

As if reading her mind, Rod's reply was equally terse. 'Perhaps if you were to dress accordingly, you wouldn't be always complaining about the cold.'

Following his gaze to where it alighted on Catherine (wearing a mid-calf-length skirt and woollen sweater), carrying a tray of coffee and shortbread into the drawing-room, Francesca gave a derisive snort. 'I'd rather suffer the cold than go about dressed like something from a gypsy encampment. In the meantime, however, I intend to warm myself on a welcome cup of coffee and you can tell me where you're going to take me for lunch. I do hope it's somewhere less boring than here.'

'If that woman complains one more time about being bored because there's nothing to do, I shall scream,' Catherine snapped a little later, watching Rod and Francesca head towards the car. 'What did she expect to find here — a theme park?'

Aunt Em looked up from where she was polishing the silver. 'I'm with you there, dear. On the other hand, these past few days haven't been half as bad as I expected.'

'Why is that?'

'Other than breakfast, I've only had to prepare one meal a day. With her ladyship wanting to go here, there and everywhere, I've never had to do both lunch and dinner. Even today she's insisting on trying out somewhere new for lunch.'

'That's one way of looking at it, I suppose. But have you given any thought to what it's going to be like once she's moved in?'

'Moved in?' Aunt Em stopped polishing and regarded her niece. 'What makes you say that?'

'Because all weekend it's been, 'I can't wait to change this, knock that wall down, alter that and throw those ghastly drapes away.' You must have heard her too.'

'Considering they're not even engaged I

doubt she'll get very far. From what Master Roderick's been telling me, he wants everything left as it is. That's apart from some of the rooms, which appear to have been sadly neglected and untouched over the years. Added to which, Whycham Hall is a listed building.'

'Then perhaps someone should tell Francesca.'

'I thought you'd have done that already. You being the one who knows about such things.'

Catherine shook her head. 'No way! That's Rod's responsibility. As far as I can I avoid her like the plague.' Spotting a solitary fly, hovering at the open kitchen door, Catherine grinned wickedly. 'However, I wouldn't mind being a fly on the wall when Francesca does appear with her bulldozers, swatches of modern fabrics and garish colour charts.'

Mention of flies prompted Emmy's thoughts to other things that lurked on walls. 'That reminds me. Francesca says there's a spider and an enormous cobweb above her bed. I fail to see how. Only last week I gave that room a thorough spring clean. That's why I put her in there, when they arrived so unexpectedly. Would you mind, Catherine? While she and Master Roderick are out. I know spiders don't bother you.'

Some considerable time later, suddenly

remembering the unwelcome arachnid and armed with a feather duster, tumbler and an early birthday card, Catherine made her way to Francesca's bedroom. Assuming Rod and Francesca were still out, she nevertheless tapped on the bedroom door before entering. The air, she noticed, was heavy with the cloying smell of perfume and there were clothes and shoes scattered everywhere.

'If it's a lady's maid you're after, Francesca,' she murmured to herself, 'I suggest next time you bring one with you from London. I certainly don't intend to clear up after you.'

As expected, a quick glimpse of the bedroom ceiling told Catherine there was no man-eating tarantula in sight, merely a tiny spider with the misfortune to end up in the wrong room. Thank goodness she didn't go for you with one of her shoes, Catherine thought, reaching for a chair. Slipping off her own footwear, she positioned herself with the tumbler in one hand, held her birthday card in the other and climbed up. This was how Francesca and Rod discovered her, when much to Catherine's surprise the bedroom door flew open.

'What on earth are you doing?' Francesca called, hurrying into the room, leaving Rod transfixed in the open doorway.

'My aunt asked me to remove the spider that was bothering you. I shan't be long.'

For once unable to look down her nose at Catherine, Francesca was forced to look in the opposite direction. 'It's obvious what the feather duster is for,' she sneered. 'So why the glass and that . . . er . . . birthday card? Is this another quaint old custom I'm not familiar with?'

Explaining the tumbler was to place (carefully) over the spider and the card was to slip beneath the glass, Catherine proceeded to do exactly that. 'Of course I'd usually pick it up with my fingers,' she continued, 'but as the spider's so small he'd probably get squashed in my hand or else fall upon your bed. This way's so much safer for the poor little creature.'

Francesca grimaced. 'Poor little creature! I would have thought a fly swat more appropriate. If I'd had a newspaper to hand I would have used that but — '

'This way is far more humane, Francesca,' Rod offered, coming into the room. 'Poor thing's probably terrified of us. Behind the safety of that glass we must appear like three enormous giants.'

With Francesca muttering something about a rescue service for spiders, Rod crossed the floor. Shaking his head almost as if in disapproval, he sidestepped the discarded shoes and clothing and reached out to steady the chair Catherine was standing on. 'Shall I open the window, so you can let him escape?'

Nodding in reply, Catherine felt Rod's arm beneath her elbow as she lowered herself to the floor and walked with him to the window.

'Oh no you don't!' Francesca cried, spying Rod unhook the window catch. 'If you put him out there he'll probably land on all that green stuff climbing up the walls. The minute I open the window again he'll come crawling back inside and tramp all over my bed.'

'Francesca!' Rod protested. 'It's only a tiny spider. It's hardly a tarantula wearing hobnailed boots.'

Suppressing a smile, Catherine slipped her feet back into her shoes. Clasping both the glass and its occupant, she hurried to the bedroom door. 'Don't worry,' she called back. 'I'll take him out to the garden. In the meantime, perhaps you'd better keep the window closed. Just in case . . . '

'Just in case what?' Francesca enquired, deeply suspicious.

'You never know, he might have brothers and sisters out there.'

Desperate to get away, Catherine hurried along the landing. The last thing she heard was Francesca's muffled shriek and the sound of a window being secured and fastened.

Later, returning from the garden, she found Rod standing by the kitchen door. In his hand was the feather duster she'd left behind in Francesca's bedroom. 'How's Sammy?' he asked, fingering the remains of a tiny cobweb.

'Sammy?'

'Sammy, the killer spider. Our eight-legged friend.'

Catherine smiled in understanding. 'The latest report is that he's making a new home in the ivy. Which as you know is on the other side of the house. Francesca should be perfectly safe.'

'That's good. Because we can't have him upsetting the guests, can we? What about his brothers and sisters? Still lurking in the green stuff outside Francesca's window?'

'If you mean the wisteria, tell her not to worry. I'll deal with them as and when they pay her a visit.'

'Ah! So that's the wisteria. Mr Barnes was telling me all about that. He said it's incredibly old. I'm afraid I'm not much of an expert when it comes to plants. At least I knew it wasn't ivy.'

'Mmm. We can only guess that it was planted at the turn of the last century,' Catherine continued. 'I expect you've noticed how incredibly old and gnarled it is.'

'A bit like Mr Barnes and most of the other residents of Whycham le Cley, present company excepted, of course,' Rod added as an afterthought. 'Believe it or not, Catherine, I think I'm beginning to see what you mean now. Didn't you tell me the residents were mostly middle aged and elderly?'

'That's hardly surprising when there's no affordable housing for the young — '

Still clasping the feather duster, Rod held up his hand. 'No. Don't say it. Let me guess what's coming next. Something about townies looking for holiday cottages and forcing up property prices.'

When Catherine remained grim-faced and silent, Rod knew he'd been correct. Shifting his gaze from the tiny cobweb trail on the duster, he turned to look into her eyes. 'It's an issue that really concerns you, isn't it? Tell me, do you honestly believe young people would live here again — even if it were financially viable?'

'Of course they would. It's only the escalating property prices that have driven them away.'

Deeply pensive, Rod was reminded of his father's own business dealings. To afford any housing these days, be it leasehold or freehold, you had to have a fairly decent job.

'Correct me if I'm wrong,' he said, anxious not to upset her. 'Isn't there also the problem of unemployment in the locality?'

'That could soon change. There's already talk of a small business park being built on the far side of Great Whycham. They're planning to use an old brownfield site,' Catherine explained, desperate to keep Rod's attention focused on local issues. If only she could get him to use his influence to help the residents of Whycham le Cley. Maybe even convert some of the disused barns on the estate into affordable housing. It didn't need a genius to work out that where there were houses there would also be families, which in turn meant children for the village school, already under threat of closure. Yes, she reminded herself, if nothing else she owed it to her father's memory to continue her fight for the village and its inhabitants.

'I'm convinced affordable housing is the only answer to get the ball rolling,' she said, voicing her thoughts out loud. 'And if there were sufficient children to prevent the school from closing.' Conscious that she was suddenly in danger of getting carried away with all her ideas, Catherine reached out to take the feather duster from Rod's grasp. 'Sorry. I'm sure you don't want to stay here all day discussing the village. Besides, I'd better go and help Aunt Em with the tea. Next time Francesca comes it might be worth suggesting she has a different bedroom. The wisteria will soon be in full bloom. Considered by Mr Barnes to be the most aristocratic of climbers, and its growth best described as vigorous, doubtless it will be home to hundreds of insects and creepy crawlies.'

Faintly amused by such a prospect, Rod replied, 'I doubt very much if Francesca will want to come again. As time's progressed her initial euphoria with Whycham Hall appears to have worn thin. She certainly wasn't very happy when it rained, wasn't at all impressed with the nearest shops and found the smell — '

'Whycham Hall doesn't smell. Unless of course she's averse to the smell of lavender polish and beeswax.'

'I don't think it's the polish; it's more the fields and their occupants.' Rod nodded in the direction of a distant herd of cows. 'Then of course there's the chickens — or should that be rooster? Francesca says he wakes her up in the morning.'

Catherine shook her head in utter bewilderment. 'And is that it?'

'Not exactly,' Rod replied, ignoring the sarcastic edge to her voice. 'During lunch I'm afraid she also described the place as a stultifying backwater.'

As a surge of anger welled up inside, Catherine tugged forcefully at the duster, wrenched it from Rod's grasp and began beating it vigorously against the wall.

'Careful!' he teased, amused by her obvious display of abject disapproval. 'If you carry on like that it will be completely bald, then you'll be doing Francesca a favour. Mr Barnes might have to kill the rooster in order to make a replacement.'

With a mumbled apology, Catherine bent down to retrieve a cluster of moulted feathers, only to find Rod had the same idea. As their hands touched, he said softly, 'I gather you don't share in Francesca's opinion?'

'No one in their right mind could ever call this place a stultifying backwater,' she faltered, feeling her pulse rate quicken. 'If I lived here, I'd be only too happy to . . . '

'Yes? Go on,' he urged, his fingers still resting firmly but gently in place. Fully aware that Rod's searching brown eyes were now fixed intently on hers, Catherine was suddenly reminded of last Saturday night when he'd discovered her asleep by the fire. Filled with inexorable panic, she stood up, attempting to brush past him, her voice catching in her throat. 'I must go. My aunt will be waiting.'

This time it was Rod's turn to bar the way. 'All right. If you must. Before you dash off can you please explain, why is the wisteria considered to be the most aristocratic of climbers?'

Before he realized and had a chance to stop her, Catherine slipped expertly away from his grasp. 'Perhaps when it's in bloom you should come and see for yourself,' she called back.

Hearing her footsteps scurry away, Rod stared down at the solitary feather in his hand. 'Who knows?' he said, fingering its silky softness. 'Perhaps I shall.'

★ ★ ★

Two days later, having said goodbye to Master Roderick and his petulant companion, Aunt Em climbed the stairs to the bedrooms where Catherine was already waiting to help her strip the beds.

'That's funny, so it is,' she mused, her Norfolk accent sounding far stronger than usual. 'I never had Master Roderick down as a keen gardener. Yet he's suddenly become interested in the wisteria. First, he wants to know when it's going to be in bloom and then insists that I phone him the minute it's out. What do you make of that?'

Pretending to be absorbed in peeling back

a white linen pillow case, Catherine muttered something about Mr Barnes.

Rod, meanwhile, had reached Wickham Ford. There coming to a deliberate halt, he recalled the vision of Catherine ankle deep in water.

'It's OK, sweetie,' Francesca cooed from his side as she patted his knee. 'There's not a soul in sight so the sooner you put your foot down the sooner we shall be in London.'

Ignoring her subsequent comments about returning to civilization, Rod lifted a hand from the steering wheel and rubbed it across his eyes. It was almost as if he was hoping for someone to emerge from the sun-dappled shallows. Someone with green eyes to match the colour of her clothes. Someone who looked like an angel with auburn hair.

6

If Aunt Em had been surprised at Rod's sudden interest in the wisteria, Catherine was equally surprised when less than a week following his departure, she received a rectangular parcel wrapped in plain paper and with a London postmark. Frowning, she studied the address written in unfamiliar script.

'Probably an early birthday present,' Aunt Em suggested, handing her a pair of scissors.

'I wouldn't have thought so. I don't know anyone in London.'

'What about your old college friends?'

'Definitely not. Not unless one of them has won the lottery and — '

Cutting carefully through the wide parcel tape and thick brown paper, a gasp of sheer disbelief emitted from Catherine's lips.

Aunt Em waited in anticipation, deeply intrigued by the black and gold box with its heavily emblazoned designer logo. 'What is it? Aren't you going to open it? And who's it from?'

'It's a pair of shoes,' Catherine whispered, barely able to speak. 'A pair of shoes by . . . '

'I can see who they're made by, but as I've already asked, who are they from?'

Placing the green suede loafers to one side, Catherine's fingers shook as she reached into the bottom of the box for a familiar white business card. 'They're from Rod Marchant.'

'Well, now, isn't that kind of him? They must be identical to the pair you had ruined that day at the ford.'

'Hardly identical,' Catherine said, examining the exquisite footwear. 'These are the real thing, Aunt Em, not a department-store copy. I couldn't possibly wear them.'

'Don't be silly! Of course you can. They were bought for you, weren't they? They certainly look like your size. Though quite how Master Roderick would have known your size is a mystery to me. That's unless he asked you?'

Catherine shook her head. Rod had asked no such thing. She could only assume he'd examined her shoes prior to leaving his business card on the hearth in the drawing-room. And she'd never dared tell her aunt about the late-night incident by the fire. Besides, hadn't Rod begged her to forget all about it? Since his departure from Whycham Hall that task had become relatively easier. Now, however, opening the box and finding the shoes . . .

'Penny for them, Catherine?'

'Oh, I think they're worth more than that,' Catherine replied, distracted, still considering the expense of the shoes. 'Have you any idea what these must have cost?'

'Not exactly. But if they're anything like that pair you raved about in Sunday's colour supplement . . . Dare I suggest you pop them back in the box. I'm going to make a cake for the WI in a minute. We don't want them ruined by sponge mixture and butter cream icing, do we?'

With the shoes wrapped once more in pale green tissue paper, and the lid placed back on the box, Catherine noticed that her aunt was smiling. 'What's so funny?'

'Francesca,' Emmy replied, placing flour, eggs and caster sugar on the kitchen table.

Catherine frowned hard. Why should her aunt suddenly start thinking about Francesca? And why should it cause her to smile?

'Seeing you put the lid on that box made me think of Francesca's feet,' Emmy began with a chuckle. 'Don't you remember? While she was here she left her shoes lying about all over the place. Enormous, they were. Just like kipper boxes, Mrs Barnes would say, and she should know, what with her father having been a trawlerman. I reckon Francesca would have a job getting those box lids on her feet, let alone those lovely shoes inside. Talk about Cinderella and the ugly sisters.'

Beginning to follow the thread of Aunt Em's conversation, Catherine rose from the kitchen stool. 'You can't possibly call Francesca ugly.'

'Maybe not,' Emmy conceded, weighing out butter and sugar, 'but I'm still prepared to bet she's not the sort of woman Master Roderick will end up marrying. Mark my words, she'll never be mistress of Whycham Hall.'

Instinct told Catherine now was an ideal time to leave the kitchen. As far as she was concerned, Rod's name had been mentioned far too many times already. Each time it had she'd felt her pulse rate quicken and her cheeks flush with colour. If she wasn't careful, Aunt Em would soon become suspicious. 'Um . . . I think I'd better go and see the vicar about decorating the church for Easter,' she said, clutching the shoe box to her chest. 'Then I'll double check the timetable for the first train to Norwich in the morning. With heaps to do at the library before the students return from the Easter vacation, it wouldn't be fair to leave Janice to do it all on her own.'

'Right you are dear,' Emmy called, reaching for a bag of flour. 'Oh, and Catherine, I'm sure you will anyway — don't forget to thank Master Roderick for the shoes.'

Misinterpreting the look of renewed panic flooding Catherine's face, Emmy suggested helpfully, 'I'm sure he won't be expecting a letter as you'll be so busy once you return to the library. Perhaps you could ring him instead? The telephone number's on his card, isn't it?'

Telephone number! Ring Rod Marchant and actually speak to him in person? Make contact with that wonderful voice of his — a voice that was as warm and as deep as his eyes? Catherine froze in horror. Never!

★　★　★

In his London office Rod lay aside his copy of the *Financial Times*. The family business was doing well; this morning's board meeting had been a huge success and according to the FTSE index, shares were at an all-time high. Why then was he feeling so down, almost as if there was something missing from his life? Resting his head in his hands, he emitted a long, drawn-out groan.

'Good gracious, Roderick! You look as if you've lost a pound and found a sixpence. Isn't that what Uncle Cedric used to say?'

Looking up, Rod saw his father framed in

the doorway of the boardroom. 'What? Oh, yes. Or at least something like that. Although I can't think why. If Uncle Cedric's will was anything to go by, I would think in his case he more often than not lost a sixpence and found a pound.'

Charles Marchant's face broke into a broad grin. 'Hmm. You certainly have a point. Who'd have thought he would have left quite so much. So . . . is that what's bothering you? Wondering what to do with your inheritance? After this morning's board meeting it can't possibly have anything to do with Marchant Associates. The latest figures are even better than I imagined.'

While Charles Marchant poured himself a cup of coffee, Rod found himself thinking of a different set of figures. Those of Francesca and Catherine. Since returning to London — and despite her repeated messages to his office, mobile and the answer phone at his flat — Rod had avoided all contact with Francesca. As for Catherine . . .

'Coffee, Roderick?' Charles Marchant held up the coffee pot, somewhat surprised when his son shook his head. 'What's up? All that Whycham le Cley air put you off coffee? If that's the case, perhaps I'd better spend a long weekend there too. You know how your mother keeps threatening to leave me if I don't give up smoking and drinking endless cups of coffee.'

Knowing his father was only joking — his parents were extremely happily married — Rod smiled and joined his father by the office window. 'You and Mother are more than welcome to stay there,' he began, looking down on the bumper-to-bumper traffic in the heavily congested street below. 'Especially if you want to get away from all that. The last thing you'll find at Whycham le Cley is a choking traffic jam.'

'Sounds wonderful. I take it Francesca enjoyed herself too. Although, without wishing to appear rude, I don't somehow see her in green wellies and a Barbour.'

'Neither does Francesca!' Rod quipped. 'I'm afraid the minute it started raining the initial euphoria wore off. It was only her enthusiasm for what I should eventually do with Whycham Hall that kept her going.'

Charles sipped thoughtfully at his coffee. 'Really? And what does Francesca suggest you do with it?'

'Sell it. Or else turn it into a hotel or conference centre. Don't you remember? Her father's company took on a similar project in the south of England only last year. According to Francesca, they made a small fortune.'

Charles Marchant's left eyebrow shot up. 'Sell it? Surely not! You wouldn't — would you? Uncle Cedric would be horrified if you did.'

'Even though he's dead and buried in Whycham churchyard? Or do you think his ghost will come back to haunt me?'

'Most definitely,' Charles said, perturbed, draining his cup.

'It's OK. There's no need to look so worried, Father. I certainly don't intend to sell Whycham Hall or any part of the estate — yet.'

Watching his father leave the office and head back to the boardroom, Rod caught sight of a white envelope by the blotter on his desk. Marked 'personal', it must have been one he'd missed before hurrying to this morning's meeting. All the other post had been opened, sorted and filed by his PA. Who could it be from? He certainly wasn't in the habit of receiving personal letters at work. These days most of his colleagues and girlfriends used text and email facilities.

Girlfriends, Rod pondered, hunting for his letter opener. What exactly constituted a girlfriend these days? At the age of twenty-nine, of course he'd had a few but none of them had been really serious. The family business had seen to that. Not that he was complaining but the property market had been through numerous peaks and troughs in recent years. So many, in fact, that several years ago (when his father's health had again given rise to concern) he'd decided Marchant Associates would take priority over the other M word, namely matrimony.

'*Dear Mr Marchant,*' the letter began, '*I am writing to thank you* . . . ' Rod's spirits soared when he realized the letter was from Catherine. The shoes had arrived safely after all. Even though he'd taken them to the post office himself, to guarantee their prompt dispatch, he had begun to wonder. The feeling of elation, however, soon gave way to one of bewilderment. Catherine's letter was so formal. The *Dear Mr Marchant,* for a start, when he'd specifically requested that she call him Rod. And the ultra-polite tone with which she thanked him for the shoes, before closing with a simple, *Yours sincerely, Catherine Wickham.*

A frown knitted Rod's brows. What did you think she'd say? he asked himself. It was you who ruined her shoes in the first place. Correction. Francesca had ruined the shoes. He had simply replaced them — as promised — and Catherine was merely acknowledging their safe arrival. What else did he expect? 'You've hardly sent her the crown jewels,' he said, softly.

Still clutching the letter and returning to the window, Rod considered his last remark with a wry smile. From the few brief moments he'd spent in Catherine's company, even he had realized the last thing she would want to receive were the crown jewels. Jewels were the sort of thing you sent to someone like Francesca, not Catherine Wickham.

Unbeknown to Rod, his father had reappeared in the doorway where he'd been watching him for the past few minutes. 'What was that about crown jewels?' Charles queried.

'Oh, simply that they'd be ideal for Francesca.'

Pausing by the coffee pot, telling himself he'd already had more than enough caffeine for the day, Charles raised a quizzical eyebrow. Did this mean that despite earlier protestations and denials to the contrary, his son was serious about Francesca? 'You're thinking of buying Francesca some jewellery?'

Too busy studying the college emblem and letter heading on Catherine's note, before placing it back in its envelope, Rod failed to recognize the implication behind his father's question. His thoughts were elsewhere — on a certain person who already possessed jewels of her own. Hair that glinted with amber lights and eyes that sparkled like emeralds.

7

Several hours later, Catherine was dealing with a book request for an overseas student. Aware of movement from the corner of her eye, she looked up to find her fellow librarian gesticulating wildly.

'Phone,' she mouthed in Catherine's direction, pretending to hold a telephone receiver to her ear. 'You're wanted on the phone.'

Excusing herself and leaving Janice in charge, Catherine made her way to the office. 'It must be my aunt,' she said. 'I hope nothing's wrong at the hall.'

'I didn't realize your aunt had such a deep, sexy voice,' came the bemused reply.

Deep, sexy voice? Aunt Em hadn't got a deep voice, unless perhaps she'd suddenly gone down with a cold. She seemed perfectly all right when Catherine had last seen her.

'Hello. Is that Catherine? It's Rod Marchant here. I'm — '

'Rod!' Catherine gasped, looking anxiously through to the quiet of the library. Had anyone noticed how loudly she'd called his name?

'Sorry if it's not a good time to call you. I'm just ringing to thank you for your note.'

'There was no need.'

Ignoring Catherine's hurried response, Rod went on to explain how he intended to spend the following weekend at Whycham Hall. 'I was wondering if you'd care to join me for a meal on Friday evening? Maybe continue with the Whycham le Cley history lesson and that sort of thing. A little bird tells me you're coming back to decorate the church for Easter, which led me to think I ought to put in an appearance myself on Easter Sunday.'

'I'm afraid I have to work late on Friday,' Catherine replied, saying the first thing to come into her head. 'My colleague and I are planning a Wordswork event for when the students return after the Easter vacation.'

Rod hesitated, examining the handset of his phone. What on earth was a Wordswork event? More to the point, why was it so urgent, especially on Good Friday? 'Does it have to be this Friday evening? I thought the students were away on vacation for at least another week.'

'Not all of them,' Catherine said, looking in the direction of the reading-room. She blushed, making eye contact with Janice. Had Janice overheard her blatant lie about working late on Good Friday? As for the handful of overseas students who'd chosen to stay in the UK for Easter, only one seemed mildly curious as to why Catherine was looking so flustered. Usually, she was calm personified, even when dealing with the most demanding of enquiries.

'I see, and there was me thinking all students went pubbing and clubbing on a Friday.' When Catherine made no response, Rod continued, 'Even if you are working late, you'll still need to eat.'

'Yes, but Janice has already invited me to supper,' Catherine blurted out, anxious to end the conversation. This time, at the mention of her name, Janice looked up and eyed her friend suspiciously. 'I'm sorry, Rod, I really must go.'

'I'm sorry too. Another time, perhaps, when you're not so busy?'

'What? Oh, yes. Of course . . . when I'm not so busy.'

'Hmm, and who exactly is Mr Velvet?' Janice asked, returning to the office and spying Catherine's flushed appearance. 'And don't come the innocent with me. I'm talking about the guy with the gorgeous, deep, velvet voice. I trust he has the looks to match? No wonder you've been so quiet and secretive these past few days. Ever since you came back from visiting your aunt you've — '

'No, I haven't,' Catherine protested, 'because there's nothing to be secretive about.'

'Good. So you can tell me all about him. And, as it's all quiet on the western front and we're not busy' — Janice nodded in the direction of the library — 'you can begin by telling me the name of your mystery caller.'

From the emphasis Janice had placed on the words not busy, Catherine knew she would get no peace until she'd satisfied her friend's curiosity. The problem was how much of the conversation had she overheard and exactly how much was Catherine prepared to divulge?

'His name's Rod Marchant and he's recently inherited Whycham Hall.'

'Blimey! The place where your aunt is housekeeper?'

'And yes, you could say his looks match his voice. That's about it, I suppose.'

'You suppose! Catherine Wickham, you honestly don't expect me to believe that?'

Catherine looked up, dreading further interrogation.

'That's about it,' mimicked Janice, with a mischievous twinkle in her eye. 'And don't look at me like that either, because I've absolutely no intention of moving until you tell me more. Of course, I don't mean all the sordid details — just a brief résumé will do.'

'It wasn't sordid.'

'Aha! So I was right? Something did happen between you. I guessed as much. The clue was in the way he asked for you when I answered the phone.'

Longing to know exactly how Rod had asked for her but too afraid to enquire, Catherine replied brusquely. 'I'm afraid you're jumping to all the wrong conclusions. For a start Rod Marchant already has a girlfriend and secondly . . . Let's just say he kissed me in rather unusual circumstances and the very next morning apologized and asked me to forget all about it. OK?'

Janice shrugged her shoulders, sensing that was all Catherine was prepared to divulge for the present. However, what unusual circumstances, she wanted to know, and why? 'OK,' she conceded. 'I'll pass on the so-called unusual circumstances but you can at least tell me why this . . . er . . . Rod Marchant telephoned? I'm convinced he wasn't ringing just to see if you'd forgotten that he'd kissed you. That would be too much like a Whitehall farce or that old song my gran used to sing. '*I forgot to remember to forget*'.'

'No,' Catherine said, without expression. 'Actually, he rang to invite me out to dinner.'

'Why, that's fantastic! Which means he

doesn't want you to forget about him, after all. When are you going?'

'I'm not.'

'You're what?'

'I'm not going.'

For a moment Janice was speechless. 'I shall pretend I didn't hear that. How could you turn down a dinner invitation with someone like Rod Marchant? From what little you've told me he's the answer to a maiden's prayer. Gracious! If he looks as sexy as he sounds and he's owner of that wonderful Whycham Hall you're always going on about, he must have pots of money to go with it.'

'Exactly, which means he's also way out of my league.'

Janice gave an exasperated sigh. 'Lord! How daft can you get? Since when has one dinner date constituted marriage? As for being way out of his league, nothing could be further from the truth. You're pretty, you're intelligent — except like now when you're being particularly obtuse — and as your Aunt Em is forever pointing out, aren't you a direct descendant of the original owners of Why-cham Hall?'

In her enthusiasm to put across her point, Janice sent a pile of book-request cards cascading to the floor. 'If that's not the reason,' she suggested, 'it can only be something else that's bothering you. What are you so afraid of? Falling in love with him and getting hurt in the process?'

Stooping to retrieve the scattered cards, Janice noticed tears brimming in Catherine's eyes. 'Oh, shit! Me and my big mouth,' she said, suddenly reminded of Catherine's ex-boyfriend and the way she'd been so shabbily treated. 'I'm so sorry . . . '

Catherine sniffed, reached in her pocket for a tissue and blew her nose hard. 'There's no need to apologize. It's all my fault for being particularly sensitive at the moment.'

Janice bit her lip, unsure what to say next. She might have forgotten the distressing saga of Catherine's ex, but she hadn't forgotten it would soon be Catherine's birthday. The birthday she shared with her dead father, and the event Janice was hoping both to commemorate and celebrate by inviting her young colleague to supper on Friday.

Still angry with herself for opening up old wounds, Janice rearranged the request cards in silence. At the same time she tried desperately to recall what she'd overheard from the snatches of conversation between Catherine and her mystery caller. Something about working late and the Wordswork events they were planning. As far as the first

Wordswork evening was concerned, that wasn't going to be a problem. There was absolutely no need to work late on Friday evening. Romy Felden, the well-known local author, had already agreed to talk to the students about her writing career both in the UK and America. This left Catherine with only one excuse for turning down a dinner date: Janice's invitation to supper.

Anxious to make light of such a matter, Janice said with a smile, 'Black mark for you, Catherine Wickham. I'm surprised your nose is still the same length.'

'What about my nose?' Catherine queried, inadvertently touching the tip of what Aunt Em referred to as the perfect Wickham nose.

'After that whopping lie you told Mr Velvet. Of course, I didn't hear all the conversation. Nevertheless, putting two and two together I'm assuming you not only told him you had to work late on Friday but also that you'd made other arrangements.'

'OK. Perhaps I wasn't being completely honest with Rod about working late, but we are still having supper together, aren't we?'

'Of course we are. If that's what you want. I've already ordered the salmon, sole and prawns. Fish apart, I can cook supper for you any time, don't forget, whereas what's-his-name — Rod — might be feeling deeply offended that you turned him down.' Not wishing to give Catherine time to dwell on such a prospect (she was already looking decidedly sheepish), Janice fixed her with a curious expression. 'Which reminds me, taking into account what little you've divulged so far, how on earth did he know how to contact you here at the library?'

Spying a stray request card lodged by the waste-paper bin, Catherine bent down to retrieve it. 'When I wrote to thank him for the shoes, I . . . um . . . just happened to use a spare sheet of college notepaper.'

'Shoes? Good Lord, Catherine, this is becoming more intriguing by the minute.'

Realizing there was no escape from describing the whole unfortunate saga of Saturday morning at the ford and that never-to-be-forgotten kiss by the dying embers of the fire, Catherine recounted her way swiftly through each and every detail, ending with Rod's unexpected visit to her room and his gift of a new pair of shoes. Conscious of the disbelief flooding Janice's face, she added softly, 'I knew I should never have used that sheet of paper. It was simply that Aunt Em kept pestering me to ring Rod and when I found that odd sheet, left in the bin by the photocopier, I . . . '

For once completely lost for words, Janice

looked first at her watch and then at the empty reading-room. 'Time to go home, I think,' she said, switching off assorted computers and lights. 'We've had more than enough excitement for one day. If we don't get a move on, we'll be locked in for the night.'

Only too happy to get away, Catherine gathered together her belongings in silence. She was beginning to get a headache and welcomed the thought of the long walk back to her rented flat near the station. The setting might not be as salubrious as Whycham Hall but at least there she'd find other things to occupy her mind. Decorating the church for Easter Sunday was one such project and hadn't the new vicar also asked for her advice on local history and ancient traditions? Thankfully, she didn't feel quite so ill at ease in the company of Reverend Cooper.

Spying Catherine's pensive expression, Janice grabbed her gently by the arm. 'Come along,' she said, anxious to make amends for her earlier faux pas. 'Let's make a deal. You buy me a glass of plonk from round the corner, and I'll promise not to report you for snaffling college writing paper.'

'Done,' Catherine said, forcing a weak smile. 'Only anywhere other than Dino's, if you don't mind.' The last place she wanted to go this evening was the wine bar with its Hooray Henry clientele. It would be too painful a reminder of Sunday lunchtime at Whycham Hall, notably Jeremy and his fellow cronies.

8

Back in the sanctuary of her flat, Catherine made herself a coffee and picked up a notebook and pen. With this being Reverend Cooper's first Easter since arriving in the village, Aunt Em and the church wardens wanted St Andrew's to look extra special. As usual Aunt Em would be doing the main altar flowers and pedestal by the lectern. This year she'd also sought the advice of someone younger.

'I'm getting far too old to clamber on pews and decorate window ledges,' she'd remarked to her niece. 'I also think those huge old jugs, that I always fill with daffodils and goat willow, are beginning to look a bit decrepit — just like me.'

Ignoring her aunt's comments regarding the passage of time (she had more energy than most women half her age), Catherine had to admit the description of the jugs was spot on. Those same chipped and stained terracotta pitchers had been hauled out of the ancient wooden cupboard, near the bell tower, for as long as she could remember. Totally unsure as to what she could use in their place, she had accepted the challenge.

Trying to rack her brains for a suitable alternative, Catherine was adamant. This year not a single daffodil would grace the windows at St Andrew's. Nevertheless, she reminded herself, the window ledges themselves were rather high and on the deep side. In turn they'd be requiring something fairly substantial to make an impact. In her mind's eye, Catherine paid a whistle-stop tour of Whycham le Cley, pausing only briefly in the garden of every dwelling (be it cottage, almshouse or bungalow and even Whycham Hall itself) before her face brightened with a glimmer of inspiration. Yes, she would still use the goat willow. There was plenty of that in the hedgerow near Kazer's Farm. As for her other idea . . .

Smiling to herself, she scribbled down her plan for gathering what was needed. If her idea did work she would also be doing the village a favour. With everyone already planning ahead for the annual summer show, there'd be no need to detract from any horticultural handiwork. Happy with what she was proposing (which meant not having to forage in people's gardens), Catherine was forced to acknowledge the one overriding problem. How to gather everything together *and* get it into St Andrew's. 'No wonder Aunt

Em always sticks to daffodils,' she said glumly, making her way to her galley kitchen. Carrying a bucket of daffodils through the lych-gate was never a problem. What she had in mind was quite another matter!

Washing her coffee cup and saucer, Catherine faced up to reality. What she really needed to see her project through was a strong pair of arms and someone with a Land Rover or estate car. To her dismay the only strong pair of arms she could think of belonged to Rod Marchant. Hardly the best person to be reminded of at present. Wasn't she trying to forget all about him? And failing miserably in the process. Not only that, Rod was still in London.

'Aha! But he won't be on Saturday,' a tiny voice echoed in her head. 'Didn't he say he was planning to attend the Easter Sunday service?'

Deciding that although Rod was paying another visit to the hall, she'd do her utmost to keep out of his way, Catherine gave a self-satisfied smile. To begin with, he wasn't bringing any guests this time, she would have plenty to keep herself occupied at St Andrew's and Aunt Em wouldn't be needing an extra pair of hands. Then, of course, there was the issue of Rod's cramped two-seater sports car. Absolutely no use to her whatsoever. Whereas the Revd Cooper did possess an ancient Volvo estate.

* * *

'I think what you're planning sounds absolutely super,' Janice called from her kitchen. 'If it wasn't for the fact we've been summoned to lunch with Dave's parents, I'd come along on Sunday to admire it in person.'

'I only wish you could,' Catherine said, watching Janice appear with her renowned luxury fish pie. 'I've a feeling I'm going to need all the support I can get. Regrettably, some of the congregation are totally opposed to change.'

'I thought you were too, at least as far as Whycham le Cley is concerned.'

'I am,' Catherine insisted, 'only this has nothing to do with the future of the village. It's all to do with the usual jugs of daffodils.'

Scooting back to the kitchen and reappearing with a bowl of mixed salad, Janice nudged aside her own jug of flowers. 'Actually, I think daffodils are rather pretty. Look at all those lovely golden trumpets, for example. As for those little frilly edges . . . '

Catherine's face filled with renewed concern. 'Janice! You're supposed to be making me feel better, not worse.'

'Don't worry. I'm only teasing. Come on now, let's eat, drink and be merry, as they say, especially as we're celebrating your birthday.'

'My birthday isn't until Sunday.'

'I know, but as I've already mentioned I shan't be around. Furthermore, having commandeered this rather special bottle from Dave's vintage collection, I for one intend to enjoy it. My husband's having a night out with the boys and subjecting me to Easter Sunday with the in-laws, don't forget. At the very least we're entitled to a decent drop of wine before he comes home full of bonhomie and smelling of drink.'

'That's a drop?' Catherine said, her eyes widening, watching Janice fill their glasses.

An hour and a half later she clasped her palm across the top of her glass, declining another refill. It was all right for her friend. She only had to climb the stairs at the end of the evening. Catherine, on the other hand, had to make her way to the station and the last train to Whycham Halt.

'Thanks for a lovely evening, I really enjoyed it,' Catherine said, following Janice to the front door. 'As usual the fish pie was delicious. You must let me have the recipe and I'll make it for Aunt Em on her day off. What's the main ingredient — wine or fish?'

Janice nodded and smiled, secretly pleased by this request. She'd heard Emmy Bailey made a mean fish pie herself. 'Thank you for joining me,' she replied, passing Catherine her coat. 'It was certainly a vast improvement on last Friday's supper when I was all alone.'

'What did you have then?'

'Three vodkas and a doughnut. That's only because I was feeling so damned lonely and fed up,' Janice said, in quick response to Catherine's horrified expression.

'All I can add to that is thank heavens Dave's finished his project.'

'Amen to that,' Janice sighed. 'Now, are you sure you don't want me to walk with you to the station?'

'Positive. I've already told you, it's not far. And I'll do exactly as you suggested: I'll keep to the main road, walk on the opposite side — facing the on-coming traffic — and scream like mad if anyone suspicious-looking comes anywhere near me. OK?'

Janice remained unconvinced. 'I still think — '

'And I think you've been watching too much *Crimewatch*. You should be here when Dave comes home. Furthermore, you never know where the last of that wine and a little bonhomie might lead. Weren't you saying only the other day that the pair of you haven't exactly . . . er . . . been getting it together for quite some time? Now he's completed that major systems project at work the pressure should be off for a while. Hopefully, he'll come home suitably relaxed, all ready to whisper sweet nothings in your ear and . . . '

'Hopefully not too relaxed,' Janice reflected, a sly grin playing on her lips. Perhaps Catherine was right. Dave had been under so much pressure at work in recent months. With everything resolved in time for the end of the financial year, the next crisis shouldn't loom its ugly head until the onset of November or December.

Standing at the front door waving Catherine goodbye, Janice struggled to remember exactly where she'd put last year's surprise Christmas present from her husband. Peering into the toe of her stocking on Christmas morning, she'd been slightly shocked and not best pleased with her husband's unexpected gift. What a thing to give her, particularly as they were spending Christmas with the in-laws in their tiny bungalow. If her mother-in-law had even chanced to come across it . . .

'Don't have nightmares, sleep well,' Catherine called back, breaking into Janice's chain of thought.

'Oh, I'm not planning to sleep,' Janice murmured, closing the door and checking her watch. 'Neither will Dave, if I have anything to do with it.' First, preparing a cafetière of very strong coffee, she dashed upstairs and headed for the spare bedroom. Ten minutes later, rummaging through the bottom of a wardrobe, she nudged aside her sewing box and found what she was looking for. A jar of chocolate body paint and a black lace thong, decorated with a sprig of mistletoe.

Pausing for a moment with a pair of scissors in her hand, Janice contemplated attacking the satin embroidered motif. Hardly appropriate for this time of year, she told herself, reminded of daffodils and Catherine's plans for Easter. Moments later, with the mistletoe still in place (those tiny embroidered berries were rather pretty), Janice heard her husband's key in the lock. That in itself was a good sign, she thought, placing the scissors to one side. As promised, Dave had kept to his word and not stayed out too late. This meant all she had to do was tell him the Easter bunny wouldn't be putting in an appearance this year. Instead, Christmas was coming early!

★ ★ ★

Highly relieved when the station came into view, Catherine allowed her hurried footsteps to slow down to a more relaxed pace. For the past five minutes she'd had the distinct feeling she was being followed. Yet, every time she turned round, there was no one there. Telling herself it was her own stupid fault for making fun of Janice's concern for her safety (aided and abetted by that wonderful drop of vintage white), she gave silent thanks for the small group of middle-aged men and women making their way across the station forecourt.

In this instance, her thanks were twofold: firstly, continued use of the last train to Whycham Halt guaranteed the service for a little while longer (though quite how Dr Beeching had ignored this particular branch line was anybody's guess) and secondly, because it meant company on the journey home. With luck, at least one or two of the passengers would remain on the train until she arrived at her destination.

Lulled by the gentle rocking motion and still savouring the delicious bouquet of the Tre Venezie pinot grigio, Catherine's thoughts chugged back to early evening. With no hint of a serenading gondolier from the finger-smudged train window (merely a car slowing down for the level crossing), she hoped with all her heart that Janice and Dave were sharing a little Venetian magic together. Chuckling quietly to herself at her friend's delightful sense of humour, Catherine looked up to see if anyone had noticed her grinning like the proverbial Cheshire cat. To her astonishment, she discovered she was all alone in the compartment. Even now the train was slowing to a stop at Whycham Halt. Deeply perturbed that at some time or other she must have inadvertently dropped off to sleep, she hurried from the train.

Once more on terra firma, Catherine pulled her coat collar up to her ears and breathed in the chill of the early April night. Looking around as she did so, she checked both directions of the platform. At one end was old George Baldry, the crossing keeper, and at the other young George, who at forty-three was already the spitting image of his father. Stepping down from his cab, young George reached into his uniform pocket, located his keys, locked the driver's door and ambled towards his father.

'G'night, Miss Catherine,' father and son called in unison.

'Goodnight,' Catherine replied, pausing briefly. It was just as she thought. She'd been the only passenger left on the train.

Initially preparing to walk the relatively short distance (at least as far as she was concerned) to Whycham Hall, Catherine hesitated and looked about her. With the clear night sky studded with stars and a full moon overhead, why didn't she check out her idea for St Andrew's? Wasn't that better than waiting until morning? This way I'll know whether or not it's feasible, she thought, walking briskly in the opposite direction. And, if what I have in mind isn't suitable for the windows, no matter. There'll be plenty of time to think of something else while making my way back to the hall.

9

Comforted by the lingering smell of old George's pipe tobacco, Catherine walked the entire length of what the locals referred to as the main road, before heading in the direction of the village green, pond and church institute. Only then did she remember her aunt. She'd told Aunt Em she'd be back by eleven o'clock. What time was it now?

In answer to her unspoken question, St Andrew's clock chimed the half hour. Half past eleven. Impossible! Why hadn't she rung her aunt the minute she'd stepped from the train? Knowing only too well that was quite possibly because she was still half asleep (or should that be half hungover?) Catherine came to an abrupt halt. It didn't take much to visualize Aunt Em pacing the floor anxiously, or else peering every now and then from her cottage window.

Prompted by a vision of her aunt in purple candlewick dressing gown, and hair rolled tightly in curlers, Catherine reached into her pocket for her mobile. Five minutes later, having explained the reason for her late-night mission, she told her aunt not to wait up, picked up her overnight bag and continued on her way.

Somehow or other, though, this time she didn't feel quite so confident as she approached her goal: three huge willows that bordered the village pond and car park. With their ancient, sweeping branches casting huge shadows in all directions, Catherine felt a shiver creep up and down her spine. How strange that one's senses became so much more acute in the dark and familiar sights and sounds so disparate. Trying not to be such an alarmist, she forced herself to stop and listen. By identifying each sound and reassuring herself that none of them meant danger, she could at least suppress the mounting anxiety in her breast.

Beginning with the distant slamming of a car door, followed by the barking of a dog, the clink of newly rinsed milk bottles put out for Mr Jipson the milkman, and the gentle plop of something in the village pond (she presumed a frog), Catherine took a few deep breaths and made her way to the largest willow tree. There, resting her bag against a tree trunk, and grateful for both the recent spell of rain and sunshine, she ran her hands along the trailing branches, cascading majestically to the ground.

'Oh, yes. If this works it could look

absolutely perfect,' she whispered, likening this year's growth to a giant crinoline while her fingers caressed feathery fronds of newly unfurled willow leaves and catkins. 'If it doesn't, I'll still be doing the village a favour.' Only last week (according to Aunt Em), the parish council had received several complaints about the willows encroaching both the pond and car park. By pruning back some of the more vigorous growth, and using it to decorate the church, wouldn't she be doing what her aunt called killing two birds with one stone?

With a satisfied glow, Catherine smiled and walked even deeper into the fresh green foliage. Then, closing her eyes as if to picture the finished result at St Andrew's, she stretched out her arms to feel the branches swaying gently in a sudden gust of breeze. 'Mmm, sorted. All I want now is someone with . . . ' The words 'suitable transport' froze on Catherine's lips while her earlier thought of killing two birds with one stone sprang uncomfortably to mind. Unless she was very much mistaken, someone had thrown (or kicked) a stone into the village pond, causing a pair of roosting moorhens to startle and flee their nest.

All at once wide-eyed and conscious of her heart pounding uncomfortably in her breast,

Catherine was glad of the enveloping greenery. If whoever it was was merely passing by in all innocence — perhaps even walking their dog — she would have nothing to fear. On the other hand, however ... Willing herself not to think of her unattended bag and the possible dire consequences, she decided to stay put. Perhaps it wasn't only Janice who'd been watching too much *Crimewatch*.

Keeping her body pressed up against the ancient tree trunk, desperate to remain undetected in the shadows until any semblance of danger had passed, Catherine listened and waited. When, after several minutes she heard nothing more, other than St Andrew's strike a quarter to midnight, she began to breathe more easily. Maybe the weird sound she'd heard hadn't been made by a human after all. Maybe it was just another frog or even a water vole. In an effort to keep calm, she took great pains to remind herself she hadn't seen a soul on her way into the village. And she had been the only passenger to get off the train.

'*As far as you know,*' an inner voice cautioned as the hairs on the back of her neck stood up once more and another gust of wind rustled the branches. '*Don't forget you fell asleep. Isn't it possible that someone could* have jumped off the train before it even stopped at Whycham Halt? That same someone whom you sensed was following you once you left Janice's?'

Reproaching herself for all these foolish notions, Catherine looked about her in abject panic. This time she not only heard the sound of footsteps, she also discerned a cadaverous shape looming ever nearer through moon-bathed swathes of willow. Definitely not a ghost, she concluded, wiping away tiny beads of perspiration forming on her brow. All Whycham le Cley ghosts were supposed to be female, who floated through walls and doors. These footsteps, however, were most certainly human and very much man-sized.

'D-don't you dare come any nearer!' she cried, her voice starting out as a tiny squeak before becoming stronger. 'If you do, I swear I'll scream. I'll scream so loud that — '

'Really? I certainly don't advise you to do that, Catherine,' came a voice, as one strong arm held her in a firm embrace, while the other was clasped gently across her mouth. 'I think we'd both be the talk of the village if you did. What on earth would people say finding the two of us grappling together in the moonlight, beneath this magnificent willow?'

'Rod! What the . . . ?' Catherine gasped, her voice muffled, struggling to free herself from Rod Marchant's vice-like grip.

'Making sure you get home safely,' he replied, refusing to slacken his hold on her. 'And, unless you stop kicking me in the shins and promise that you won't scream the place down, we shan't even make it across the village green, let alone back to Whycham Hall.'

Yielding to Rod's request, Catherine shrugged her arms free, stepped back and hissed angrily, 'Just what the hell do you think you're playing at? If I'd been old Mrs Bannister from the almshouses, I would probably have had a heart attack.'

'Luckily for me you're not, though I doubt she's as accurate with her feet as you are. Did you play football as well as netball?' Rod said, rubbing his shins. 'Anyway, I thought I'd heard she was as deaf as a post.'

'That's not the point!'

'Tut tut. Remember what I said about making a noise.' Rod cast a knowing look in the direction of the row of almshouses. Convinced that most of the residents had been in bed for at least two hours, complete with teeth soaking in Steradent and zimmers at rest, he still didn't want Catherine making a scene. 'If you'd care to tell me what you were doing dancing about the willows at midnight, as I'm still familiarizing myself with

Whycham le Cley customs . . . '

'I wasn't dancing and it isn't mid — '

'Oh, really.' Rod gave a wry smile, listening to St Andrew's strike twelve as he retrieved her bag and they walked away from the shelter of the trees. 'You could have fooled me.'

Still bristling with anger and indignation, Catherine snorted. 'Hmph! And what about you! What about you sneaking up on me, scaring me half to death.'

'Yes, well . . . I'm sorry if I frightened you. I had hoped, by throwing that stone into the pond, I might have alerted you of my presence. In answer to your query, I came to find you because your aunt asked me to.'

'I was alerted, all right,' Catherine snapped, before registering all of Rod's explanation. 'My aunt? Why should Aunt Em . . . ?'

'Quite simply because she was concerned for your safety when you rang and told her you were heading in this direction. At the time I confess to being slightly confused, especially when she mentioned something about the church. For all I knew you might have had a secret assignation with the vicar. It was only when I remembered old Catchpole wasn't exactly up to a midnight saunter through the willows — '

'For your information, Reverend Catchpole

has recently retired. We now have a new vicar, who's extremely young and . . . '

'Yes?' Rod urged, spying Catherine's blushes as they walked beneath a lamppost.

'Um . . . very good looking.'

'And also very unmarried?'

'Yes, he is,' Catherine announced softly.

Rod sucked in his cheeks, contemplating this snippet of information, and for several minutes they walked along in silence until they reached the main road. 'Not that way,' he said, when she started to turn right. 'My car's back there behind the school house. I parked it out of the way because I didn't want to disturb the locals when I came looking for you.'

Once more reminded that Rod still hadn't fully explained his mission for finding her, Catherine waited for him to continue. 'Your aunt was extremely anxious, you know. When I arrived back at the hall, having missed you at Whycham Halt, she seemed deeply agitated. I don't mind admitting it came as quite a shock, seeing her running out of her cottage wearing her dressing gown and slippers. At first I thought there was a fire. In time of course I discovered you'd told her you were heading off to the village alone.'

Catherine's brow creased into a frown. 'I also told her not to wait up. What's so wrong with that? Didn't Aunt Em explain why I was going in to the village?'

'No, and neither have you.'

'It's because I'm decorating the church windows for Easter.'

'At this time of night? Good God! Oops, sorry. This new vicar must be something special if he has you decorating the church at — '

'I've already said I wasn't meeting the vicar. I went to look at the willows.'

Taking Catherine by the arm, Rod led her gently in the direction of his car. 'OK. Point taken, although I'm still none the wiser. While we're driving back to the hall, perhaps you'd better explain why those trees are of such particular interest.'

Secretly glad of the warmth and comfort of the car, Catherine clarified her ideas for decorating the church in readiness for Easter Sunday. 'Of course, it might not work at all, but I really don't want to use daffodils again,' she concluded.

'Sounds like a great idea to me, and by all accounts quite a contrast to the usual Easter themes. Not wishing to throw a spanner in the works and bearing in mind your usual form of transport, how do you plan to collect all this greenery?'

Knowing full well Rod was referring to her

bike, Catherine toyed with the buttons on her coat. 'Um . . . I'm not sure, exactly. I thought I might ask Eric, the herdsman at Kazer's Farm. Mr Kazer sometimes lets him borrow their Land Rover. Or else there's the vicar. He's got an old Volvo estate.'

With a sideways glance in her direction, Rod guessed from the look on Catherine's face that she was referring to the new vicar and not the old. He also sensed, from the twitching curtains at his housekeeper's cottage, he was in for a second viewing of Mrs Bailey in dressing gown and slippers. This time, complete with baby-blue hairnet and pink curlers, she came scurrying out on to the cobbled forecourt.

'Catherine, my dear! At last! Where have you been?'

'You know where I've been. I rang and told you.'

'But you've been gone so long and when Master Roderick said you weren't at the station . . .'

Fixing both Rod and her aunt with a curious stare, Catherine tried to put two and two together. From what she was hearing now (in addition to something Rod had said a short while ago), was she correct in thinking that he'd been waiting for her at Whycham Halt? Other than the two Georges, she'd seen no one at all.

'I'm afraid I was held up at the level crossing,' Rod began, as if reading her mind. 'It was only when I came back to the hall, your aunt explained that I must have missed you.'

And I've obviously missed out on something too, Catherine refrained from adding, watching him unlock Whycham Hall's back door and motion both aunt and niece inside. Earlier on in the week, when Rod had telephoned to invite her to dinner, hadn't he remarked how a little bird had informed him she was coming home for the weekend? Therefore, had that same little bird, now following him into the kitchen (wearing hairnet, dressing gown and slippers) also told him of her niece's whereabouts on Friday evening?

Casting her mind back to less than an hour ago, Catherine recalled the distinct feeling of terror before discovering her stalker's identity. Curiously enough, that had soon metamorphosed into the peculiar lurching in her stomach whenever Rod was near. That apart, something was still troubling her. What about even earlier in the evening? Had Rod also been following her, watching her, ever since she'd left the library with Janice? Unsure quite how to deal with the current situation and the mixed emotions bubbling inside,

Catherine said flatly, 'Well, Aunt, as you can see, thanks to Mr Marchant, I'm home now. With us both having to make an early start in the morning, I suggest you go to bed.'

Breathing a deep sigh of relief as if waking from a very bad dream, Emmy was soon transported back to another one. Her niece might be home safely but she suddenly remembered she was standing in her employer's kitchen, wearing only her night-dress and dressing gown. Worse than that, she had rollers in her hair!

'And I'll have to clean the lectern and fetch the flowers for the altar,' Emmy replied, acutely embarrassed and keen to make her exit. 'If you'll just make Master Roderick a nightcap, Catherine.'

'I'm sure that won't be necessary,' Rod said, trying to suppress a smile. He'd never seen Mrs Bailey looking quite so flustered. As for Catherine's horrified expression of complete incredulity . . . It hadn't gone unnoticed that she'd earlier referred to him as Mr Marchant.

Anxiously patting at her head, in a desperate but futile attempt to conceal her hairnet and rollers, Emmy made a dash for the door. 'Oh, Catherine won't mind, will you, dear?' she called, and in a swirl of purple candlewick and blue net, disappeared into the darkness.

Calling goodnight and closing the door behind her, Rod turned to face Catherine, already filling the kettle. 'I thought you said you needed to get to bed,' he remarked, watching her gather together a jar of coffee, the sugar bowl and biscuit tin. 'I'm really quite capable of — '

'And I'm afraid it will have to be instant,' Catherine said tersely, spooning coffee into a mug. Tonight Rod Marchant would have to make do with earthenware. If he wanted the usual Royal Doulton, then tough!

Bemused, yet at the same time bewildered, Rod pulled out a chair and studied her intently.

'Catherine, I don't honestly know what this is all about, but do you think we could call a truce? I said I was sorry for frightening you. I thought you were happy with your aunt's explanation.'

'I'm happy with my aunt all right,' Catherine snapped, tearing open a packet of Rich Tea biscuits and throwing them on to a plate. 'Delirious, in fact, knowing that she must have told you exactly what I was doing this evening and where I was going.'

'That's not fair. She was deeply concerned for you. Do you usually take yourself off to

Whycham Common at midnight?'

'I'm not talking about Whycham Common, I'm talking about earlier in the evening. And don't try to deny it. Were you or were you not stalking me when I left my friend's house?'

Rod looked up, mildly affronted, from where he was joining together two halves of broken biscuit. 'I think the word stalking is a bit strong. I simply happened to be in the neighbourhood and thought I'd just make sure you got to the station unharmed.'

'Oh, really! Well, yes, having left your London office I suppose you would have to pass directly outside Janice's door, at the exact same time I was leaving to catch my train. How silly of me not to realize. It must have been all those thugs at her front gate, waiting to pounce on me, that prevented me from seeing you. Considering how proficient you are at coming to my rescue, I'm surprised you didn't send them all packing and offer me a lift home there and then.'

'I was going to, but I didn't want to embarrass you in front of your friend,' Rod said, ignoring the distinctly acerbic tone in her voice. 'You also set off up the road at a vast rate of knots.'

'That's only because I sensed someone was following me.'

'There was. For your information, it wasn't me.'

'Wasn't you?' Catherine repeated, aghast. 'After what my aunt said, I thought . . . '

'Then you thought wrong. You were being followed by an unsavoury-looking fellow in black jeans and a hooded top. Your handbag might have been secure slung across your shoulder. Not so the overnight bag you were carrying, which he seemed to be taking a keen interest in. In case you're wondering, I was sitting in my car, so he wasn't aware of me at first. It was only when I pulled away from the kerb and headed in your direction that he took off and disappeared down a side street. By that time, of course, you'd reached the station and the company of other people, leaving me with the only available option. Doing a U-turn and trying to beat the train back to Whycham Halt.'

'Where you got held up at the level crossing,' Catherine finished for him, her face ashen.

'Precisely,' Rod said, reaching for another mug. 'Might I suggest you join me for a coffee — even if it is instant. You look as if you could do with one.'

'I — I'll make you a cafetière, if you'd prefer.'

'Instant will be fine,' Rod said, fixing her

with a lazy smile, watching her fill two mugs with hot water. 'Now, are we going to drink it in here — or shall we head for the drawing-room?'

Already ill at ease, Catherine mumbled something about there probably not being a fire made up and promptly sat down at the kitchen table.

Declining the sugar bowl herself, Catherine passed it back in Rod's direction. He meanwhile hesitated for a moment before stirring two spoonfuls of sugar into his coffee. 'Like my father trying to cut down on both coffee and cigarettes, I suppose I should really try and cut down on the sugar. As for you,' he ventured, 'at any other time I'd probably say you were sweet enough without it. In your current frame of mind, you'd probably go and kick me again. My shins are still smarting from that earlier attack.'

Catherine froze, pausing with her mug to her lips. If she'd kicked Rod that hard he'd probably be needing the bottle of witch hazel Aunt Em kept in the cupboard above the sink. 'Rod, I'm so sorry . . . not only for kicking you as I did, but also for what I said earlier. I honestly had no idea. Like that day at the ford, I simply jumped to all the wrong conclusions.'

'Then dare I suggest you stop jumping. Sit

down, finish your coffee and have a biscuit.'

Unintentionally both reaching for the same Rich Tea, Rod and Catherine faced one another across the table, each with half a biscuit in their hand. Rod laughed, reminded of the one he'd tried to piece together and the others flung unceremoniously on to the plate. Knowing that he'd already made reference to Catherine's prowess with a netball and football, he decided against further mention of other likely sporting abilities, namely the discus.

'What's so funny?'

'Nothing,' he lied.

'Yes, there is. You were going to say something. What was it?'

'Truce,' Rod said, watching Catherine examine her share of the biscuit.

'Truce,' she replied shyly, as Rod held out his own half across the table, joining the two pieces together as one.

10

'Come along, sleepy head, time to wake up. Master Roderick's waiting downstairs with the Range Rover.'

Crawling out from beneath the duvet, Catherine peered first at her aunt and then at her alarm clock. 'Why? What time is it?'

'Time for you to get up. You're going willow gathering, remember.'

Catherine groaned and rolled over on her side. 'It's only half past six.'

'That's right,' Aunt Em said, placing a cup of tea on the washstand before walking to the window to draw back the curtains. 'And you know what they say. It's the early bird that catches the worm.'

Failing desperately in her attempt to keep her eyes open, Catherine also lost her struggle to sit up. Why was Aunt Em talking about cars and worms? It was all extremely confusing and she was so very, very tired. 'Why are you going worm gathering in a Range Rover?'

Emmy shook her head and laughed. 'Not me, you. At least, it's you going in the Range Rover. And it's willow you're collecting, not worms. What on earth did Janice give you to drink last night? Now, are you getting up or not, or shall I tell Master Roderick you've changed your mind about decorating the church?'

The church! Catherine sat bolt upright. The willow for the church windows. Last night . . . It was all starting to come back to her. The only thing that didn't fit was Rod and the Range Rover.

'Rod doesn't have a Range Rover,' she yawned.

'He does now,' Aunt Em explained, watching her tumble out of bed and head for the shower. 'That's another reason he came back this weekend. He realized he'd be needing something other than that sports car of his if he's going to oversee the estate. You can't go driving across the fields in that little thing. Had it delivered yesterday, he did.'

Muttering through a mouthful of shower gel and shampoo, Catherine heard her aunt call out, 'I'll interpret that as you'll be down in ten minutes, shall I? Don't forget your tea and I'll make a fresh pot for Master Roderick while he's waiting.'

* * *

'Sorry to have kept you,' Catherine called, out of breath, running into the kitchen. 'I must have forgotten to set my alarm.'

'That's OK,' Rod replied, eyeing her towel-dried hair, where it framed her face like an amber halo. 'For a minute I thought it was my mistake. You did say you intended to make an early start when I offered my services.'

Yes I did, Catherine wanted to reply, but that was when she was still relatively alert and racking her brains as to whom she could call upon to assist her with her task. Suppressing yet another yawn, she peered through the window at the shiny new vehicle parked outside the stable block. Funny how Rod had never mentioned it last night — or should that be this morning? It had been almost one o'clock before they'd said goodnight, Rod going to Uncle Cedric's old room and she to her turret.

Reluctantly, taking the slice of toast Aunt Em thrust into her hand, Catherine looked anxiously in Rod's direction. 'Better eat it,' he told her, smiling. 'I don't really want crumbs in my new car.'

'I'm sure you don't want half a forest, either,' she replied.

'Probably not. So perhaps we'd better get a move on before I change my mind.'

For one truly awful moment, Catherine thought that he was being serious. Then she saw the faintest glimmer of a smile playing on his lips.

'Right, Mrs B.,' Rod called, heading for the door. 'Let's do a recap. Number one on the list: I help Catherine collect the willow and take her to St Andrew's. Number two: I come back for you, take you to the florist's and on to the church with your flowers. Number three: once you clever ladies have finished your handiwork we all head off to the pub for an early lunch.'

While Catherine looked on in amazement, puzzling over when all these arrangements had been made, Emmy Bailey shook her head and exclaimed, 'Oh, no, Master Roderick. Like I said before, I couldn't possibly do that. It wouldn't be right.'

'You mean you're teetotal?'

'No, she means she's staff,' Catherine corrected, joining him at the kitchen door.

Hesitating on the threshold, Rod was about to remonstrate with his housekeeper. To his surprise, she was looking almost as flustered as when he'd caught sight of her in her dressing gown. There'd also been that hint of warning in Catherine's voice, when she'd replied on her aunt's behalf. Erring on the side of caution, he opted for silence and reached for his car keys.

'Sorry if I put my foot in it back then,' he

said ten minutes later as they passed the village pub. 'I know your aunt is officially my housekeeper, but was suggesting us all having lunch together such a dreadful *faux pas* on my part?'

'Not dreadful, merely a bit tactless — at least as far as Aunt Em is concerned. Don't forget she's spent most of her life in service. I expect she was simply embarrassed by your generosity,' Catherine added, trying to make Rod feel less uncomfortable.

'Not half as embarrassed as me, each and every time she calls me sir or Master Roderick.'

'She can't call you Rod, can she?'

Pulling into the car park near the willow trees, Rod sighed and switched off the ignition. 'Oh, well, I suppose I'll have to be content with one out of two. At least you call me Rod . . . that's when I'm not upsetting you.'

'I'm also not staff,' Catherine reminded, stepping down from the 4×4.

Busying herself with a pair of secateurs, Catherine spied Rod, opening the hatch of the Range Rover, adjusting the seats and making room for all her willow branches. Though a good idea in principle, she told herself, she remained deeply anxious about all this greenery going in the back of his new car. Perhaps she should have asked the vicar after all? The only problem being that although she found Revd Cooper extremely obliging, he also had five parishes to run. It was hardly fair to expect him to hang around for her by the village pond at 7.15 in the morning. 'And it is his busiest time of year after Christmas,' Catherine said, voicing her thoughts out loud, unaware that Rod was behind her.

'Why are you talking about Christmas? I thought this little lot is for Easter.'

'It is,' Catherine replied, without thinking. 'I was talking about the vicar.'

Rod frowned, rubbing a hand across his chin. Why this feeling of immense disquiet whenever the new vicar was mentioned?

'Ahem, I think I should warn you we have an audience,' Catherine said, giving a sideways glance at the almshouses. 'It looks as if we're the current topic of conversation. Old Mrs Bannister and some of her neighbours appear to be gathering in their front gardens.'

'Why are they up and about so early? They're not decorating the church too, are they?'

'No, but the majority of them are in bed by ten o'clock. Unlike us,' Catherine added as an afterthought.

Leaving Rod to reminisce about last night,

particularly the incident with the broken biscuit, Catherine made her way towards the trio of elderly ladies.

'What are they doin'?' Mrs Bannister asked her neighbour.

'I don't know,' came the reply 'No doubt Miss Catherine will tell us.'

'What?'

'I said, I expect Miss Catherine will tell us!'

Taking into account the old lady's less than perfect hearing, Catherine explained to Mrs Bannister and her companions she was collecting greenery for the church. 'I'm also helping my aunt to decorate the windows.'

'You'll never get all that in those earthenware jugs,' a voice cried. 'Won't be any room left for daffodils.'

'There aren't going to be . . . ' Catherine began and quickly changed her mind. Not a good idea to tell these kindly souls that this year there were to be no daffodils in the window displays at St Andrew's. Plucking a stray willow catkin from the sleeve of her sweatshirt, Catherine was grateful for a diversion. Rod was already carrying an armful of willow branches towards the 4×4.

Leaning heavily on her zimmer frame, Mrs Bannister called out, 'Surely he's not goin' to put those in that lovely car o'his? Miss Catherine? You tell that young man to come over here an' get my curtains.'

Curtains? Rod stopped in his tracks. Why on earth should he need this old lady's curtains?

'I think she means you to put them in the car to protect the upholstery,' Catherine explained. 'It's a bit of a tradition in Whycham le Cley — especially amongst the older generation. No one throws anything away, least of all curtains. They have umpteen different uses.'

Rod stood and scratched his head. Umpteen different uses?

'Protecting the car seats from muddy feet, children and dogs,' Catherine began. 'Picnic cloths and picnic blankets, not forgetting how handy they are when taking produce to and from market. The list is endless. In fact, if you were to look into the back seats or boots of cars round here, nine times out of ten you'd find some discarded furnishings. I'm surprised you haven't noticed already.'

'Oh, I see. Come to think of it, I have seen someone driving around with what looks like a rose garden in their car.'

Catherine smiled, 'That will be Hayley, Mr Barnes's daughter-in-law. She's married to Eric, the herdsman at Kazer's Farm. Those curtains are an absolute must as far as Hayley's concerned.'

'Really, why is that?'

'Because if Hayley has to go and fetch Eric from work, he doesn't exactly come home smelling of roses.'

Catherine's wry sense of humour was lost on Rod at that moment. He was far too busy watching Mrs Bannister's neighbours totter towards him, each carrying an armful of curtains.

'They'll be just the job, young master. You'll see.' The old lady beamed from her front gate, overseeing proceedings (the Steradent having worked wonders overnight). 'An' don't you go worryin' about bringin' 'em back in a hurry. They'll make that car o' yours look nice 'n' bright an' sunny.'

* * *

'If only you could have seen your face,' Catherine giggled, once they'd waved good-bye and set off for the church.

'Hmm, well, bright and sunny wasn't exactly what I had in mind when I picked out this black leather interior.'

'An' you know you don't have to worry 'bout bringin' 'em back in a hurry,' Catherine mimicked.

Looking in his rear-view mirror, Rod's gaze registered the pile of willow branches nestling amongst what looked like a field of golden sunflowers. 'I'd be very careful if I were you, Miss Wickham. Remember what you were saying earlier . . . about the umpteen different uses for old curtains.'

'Yes.'

'It might interest you to know I've just thought of another one. Wrapping up a certain annoying person and throwing her in the village pond!'

On arriving at St Andrew's, Catherine was relieved to see the church door already open. True to his word, Barry Martindale, the church warden, was already checking through the hymn books while Maureen, his wife, was busying herself amongst the pews. Explaining that Aunt Em would be along shortly, once she'd made her early morning visit to the florist, Catherine announced that as long as it was all right with them (and she wouldn't be in their way), she'd make a start on the windows.

'You go right ahead, my dear,' Maureen replied. 'I've already washed the jugs, not that it's made any difference. They still look grubby.'

Catherine gulped and took a deep breath; not another member of the congregation expecting a profusion of King Alfred's. 'Um . . . I hadn't intended to use the jugs. I've already suggested to Aunt Em that I might try something different this year.'

'Thank the Lord for that.' Maureen beamed. 'My prayers have been answered at last. Horrid old things they are. If it wasn't for the fact that I thought He'd be watching me, I would have *accidentally* dropped those years ago. What did you have in mind instead?'

'Weeping willow.'

Catherine could see from the look on Maureen's face that she was already beginning to wonder how and where they were going to locate weeping willow at this time in the morning. They'd only got the church for a couple of hours. The choir were due for choir practice and the vicar had a wedding on the other side of the benefice, immediately after lunch.

'It's OK,' she assured. 'I've already collected the willow and Rod — I mean, Mr Marchant — has kindly offered to bring it in his car.' As if on cue, Rod appeared in the open doorway carrying several branches of willow. Much to his surprise, Maureen practically fell to her knees and curtseyed.

'I'm afraid I can't shake your hand,' he said, when Catherine introduced them. 'As you can see I'm doing an impersonation of a willow tree at the moment.'

'And probably not a good idea to bring it in branch by branch. It will take simply ages,' Catherine declared, once she'd freed Rod of his burden and Maureen had scurried away with her cans of Mr Sheen and Brasso.

Rod pursed his lips. 'I'm afraid I can't get the Range Rover any closer. It certainly won't fit though the lych-gate.'

'Obviously not,' Catherine said, fixing him with a knowing smile, 'but I know something that will. The curtains. If we each take a couple of corners, a bit like a hammock, we'll probably only need to make two trips to the car.'

'Don't tell me, you've done this before,' Rod said, as they manoeuvred the first pair of heavily laden curtains through the gate, into the churchyard, and up to the heavy oak doors of St Andrew's.

'Maybe I have and maybe I haven't,' Catherine teased.

'Or maybe it's simply another example of Whycham le Cley resourcefulness.'

'I see. You think we're resourceful, do you? We're not just a bunch of backward-thinking yokels.'

Rod's eyes glinted mischievously. 'Don't even go there, Catherine. Remember what I said about the village pond.'

'Truce,' she whispered, holding out her

hand, conscious of both Maureen and Barry watching them suspiciously from the shadows.

With all the willow laid out resplendently on its bed of sunflowers in the Lady Chapel, Rod pulled back the sleeve of his sweater to check his watch. 'Right. This is where I love you and leave you. Your aunt will be wondering where I am. Is there anything else you need before I go?'

Just a strong pair of arms in case I fall, Catherine wanted to say, eyeing the height of the windows. Strange how they appeared much higher than she remembered. No wonder Aunt Em was pleased to step down in more ways than one, this year. 'No, I'll be fine, thank you. The worst bit will be getting the first branches in to place. As for the corners, I'm intending to fill those in with goat willow. Don't worry, that's already taken care of too. Eric was going to drop it in to Aunt Em after early morning milking. If you could remind her to bring it when she comes.'

'Will do,' Rod called back, starting to walk away. All these names and all these people, he pondered. Would he ever remember each and every one? He'd only been here once before since he'd inherited the estate, and already he was both deeply touched and amazed at the willingness within the community to help one another out. When a rustle of leaves, followed by a thump and an 'Oh, drat!' prompted Rod to halt by the bell tower, he turned to find Catherine wedged awkwardly against a pew, covered in willow catkins and rubbing her right hip.

'It's all right,' she called, when he came running to her aid. 'I think Maureen overdid it with the polish on this pew. I shall have to be more careful when I climb up on the others.'

'For goodness' sake, take care,' he urged, suddenly aware of the difference in height between the pews, Catherine, and the church window ledges. Wanting to stay, yet at the same time knowing Mrs Bailey would be waiting for him at Whycham Hall, he hesitated for only a moment longer. Nodding in Barry and Maureen's direction, Catherine fixed him with one of her looks and mouthed the word, 'Go.'

11

Almost an hour later when he returned, Rod didn't know what to expect. Following Mrs Bailey into the church, his initial view was somewhat marred by the enormous bunch of Arum lilies she was carrying in her arms.

'My goodness! You have been busy,' Emmy called to her niece. 'And doesn't that look wonderful?'

Although the comment wasn't aimed directly at himself, Rod still nodded in approval. Not only had Catherine finished the first window, she was starting on the second.

'You really think it's OK?' Catherine queried.

Emmy placed the Arum lilies carefully on the red carpet by the lectern. 'I'd say it looks more than OK. I think it looks stunning . . . just like a green waterfall and extremely restful. Don't you think so, vicar?'

Vicar? Rod did a double take. He certainly hadn't noticed anyone else in the church (other than Catherine) when he'd arrived. Then again that was quite possibly because he only had eyes for the young woman, wearing jeans and sweatshirt, perched somewhat precariously on a distant pew.

'Very much so, Mrs Bailey. And a perfect vision to behold,' echoed a voice, prompting Rod to look towards the altar. There to his surprise he saw a young man, presumably in his mid to late twenties, looking nothing at all like the vicars he remembered from his youth. At about five feet ten inches in height with light blond, short spiky hair and wearing rimless glasses, he was a far cry from the recently retired Revd Catchpole. Unlike Revd Catchpole, however, this man of cloth had a distinct spring in his step as he strode towards the lectern, where his gaze alighted once more on Catherine and her handiwork. Hmm. Exactly what or whom did the vicar have in mind when talking of a perfect vision to behold?

'Do be careful,' Revd Cooper warned, watching Catherine (who as yet hadn't acknowledged Rod's presence) struggling with a particularly stubborn and twisted branch of willow.

'Don't worry. I will. But why is it that one side always goes better than the other? Never mind. Hopefully, I can cover that bit up with goat willow. That's if Rod remembered to bring it.'

Still standing just inside the church door, Rod felt three pairs of eyes turn in his direction.

'Ah, Mr Marchant, I presume,' the vicar said, walking towards him, his hand extended in friendly greeting. 'We meet at last. I'm so pleased you're going to be here for our Easter Sunday service. Mrs Bailey's told me so much about you. You must come and have lunch with me at the vicarage one day. With us both being new boys at Whycham le Cley, I'm sure we have a great deal in common.'

Intrigued as to what exactly Mrs Bailey had been telling the Revd Cooper, Rod saw her cast a suspicious look in his direction before murmuring something about getting on with her lilies and altar display.

'I'm sure we have, Reverend,' Rod replied, eyeing the attractive figure of at least one thing they both had in common. 'And you must come over to the hall. In the meantime, I think I'd better fetch that goat willow. We can't have Catherine balancing on the pew like that, can we?'

Leaving the vicar to watch over his charge (secretly acknowledging that he'd rather be the one left in church), Rod raced back to the Range Rover. On his return he was relieved to see everything was just as before.

'Still all in one piece,' the vicar confirmed, offering Catherine his hand as she stepped down to examine both the quality and quantity from the hedgerow at Kazer's Farm.

Then, as an after-thought, he said to Rod. 'By the way, do call me Damian. I'm well aware that hasn't gone down too well with some of the older members of the congregation — they probably expect to see the three sixes branded on my forehead — but I've always thought the reverend tag a bit impersonal when getting to know my flock.'

'Only if you call me Rod,' came the good-natured reply.

With Catherine and her aunt finishing their tasks, Rod followed the vicar out into the churchyard, where they continued their conversation. Ten minutes later, saying goodbye, Damian disappeared in the direction of the ancient Volvo estate, while Rod reorganized the seats of the Range Rover and then set off for Uncle Cedric's grave.

'I know, I know,' Rod said quietly, as if the kindly old gentleman had been there in person, and not in spirit. 'He's a really nice guy and probably just what Whycham le Cley needs to bring it into the twenty-first century, without treading on too many toes. Shame about the Damian, though,' he chuckled. 'I can't see Mrs Bannister and the curtain bearers consenting to first-name terms, can you?'

Once more reminded of the sunflower-patterned curtains and their assorted uses,

Rod remembered his earlier invitation to his housekeeper and her niece. From the sound of footsteps echoing in the stone-flagged porch of St Andrew's, he could only assume that Barry Martindale had returned to lock up the church and those left inside were now ready to leave.

'See you tomorrow morning, Mr Marchant,' Barry called, placing the heavy iron key back in his pocket. 'And thank you again for your help. Much appreciated.'

'Don't mention it,' Rod replied, waiting for Catherine and Mrs Bailey to catch him up.

'Well, I certainly will,' Aunt Em puffed, out of breath, anxious not to keep him waiting. 'We don't know what we'd have done this morning without your help, do we, Catherine? Getting up so early as you did and I still haven't thanked you properly for last night.'

'Last night?'

'Going out to hunt for Catherine and bringing her home.'

'Aunt Em,' Catherine protested, 'you make it sound as if I was in darkest Africa, not Whycham le Cley.'

'That's as maybe, my dear, but you can't be too careful these days. People get attacked in all sorts of places.'

'Don't I know it,' Rod said, with a wink, once he'd helped Mrs Bailey up into the rear passenger seat of the 4×4. Making a deliberate point of rubbing at his shins, he returned to open the front passenger door for Catherine. 'However,' he continued in hushed tone, 'I might be prepared to forget all about it if you'll join me for lunch.'

'You know what my aunt said about that,' Catherine reminded, struggling to fasten her seat belt.

'Yes, she said she couldn't because she's staff. However . . . as you've already pointed out on more than one occasion, you are not.'

Conscious that Rod was now so close he was able to whisper in her ear (while at the same time helping her with the seat belt), Catherine looked behind for moral support. To her surprise, it looked as if Aunt Em was dozing.

Rod held a finger to his lips. 'Ssh. Isn't it better to let her sleep? Goodness knows what time she got up this morning. She was already pegging out washing when I came down at six o'clock. Just think,' Rod said kindly, switching on the ignition and selecting first gear, 'if you join me for lunch, she can even have a rest this afternoon as well. Besides, I need to pick your brains for when I have Sunday lunch with the vicar. He was suggesting that you might be able to help me.'

Catherine fixed him with a bewildered

frown. Why on earth did Rod need to pick her brains when both men had seemingly got on so well? More to the point, why had they been discussing her when they went outside to the churchyard?

Rod regarded Catherine with a reassuring smile. 'There's no need to look so alarmed. We new boys merely want to ask your advice about doing something for the younger people of the village. Perhaps reinstating some of the old Whycham le Cley traditions. For instance, do they still dance around the maypole and that sort of thing?'

★　★　★

With Aunt Em putting her feet up and contemplating a lazy afternoon, Rod and Catherine sat in a quiet corner of the Whycham Arms. Watching her finish the remains of her sausage casserole, Rod sighed appreciatively. 'Hmm, that was almost as tasty as the first meal your aunt cooked for me. Now, shall we get down to business?'

For the briefest of moments, Catherine's mind went into overdrive thinking of all the possible connotations of the word. One of the problems of being a librarian, she supposed, watching Rod reach into his jacket pocket for a notepad and pen.

Pleased to have covered several pages with numerous ideas, Rod closed his notebook and looked about him. Apart from two old chaps finishing a game of dominoes, he and Catherine were the last in the bar. 'Time to go, before we get thrown out,' he said, nodding towards the clock on the wall.

'I don't think Reg would dare do that.'

'Why ever not?'

'Aren't you forgetting you're the lord of the manor?'

Rod groaned. 'Oh, no, not that again. Shall I ever be allowed to forget that and have a normal life if I live here?'

'Of course,' Catherine assured. 'A little bird tells me you've made quite an impression already.'

'That wouldn't be the same little bird who told me to go searching for you by the village pond last night?'

'Quite possibly. She also said the PCC are very appreciative of the fact you're going to attend the Easter Sunday service and even do a reading.'

Looking distinctly uncomfortable, Rod held back Catherine's chair while she stood up. 'Yes, well . . . to be honest I'm not so sure about a reading. I haven't exactly agreed to it.'

'They'll be terribly disappointed if you

don't. And, providing you carry on as you've done so already, you'll find it won't be long before they all welcome you with open arms.'

Tempted to say there was only one pair of arms he'd care to be welcomed into, Rod decided against it and followed Catherine to the door. 'Oh dear, now it looks as if I'm going to be in need of yet another favour.'

'What's that?'

'You'll have to instruct me in the ways of the church as well. I confess it's been several years since I last took communion.'

Marginally comforted by Catherine's repeated assurances that he had nothing to fear, Rod swung the 4×4 through the gates of Whycham Hall. Five minutes later, thanking him for lunch and also his help, she paused with her hand on the banister rail before heading up to her room.

'And we'll still see you in church tomorrow?'

'Yes. But unlike this morning I shall be relying on you to give me an alarm call. I don't suppose you'd care to bring me up a cup of tea?'

'I might,' Catherine replied, spying the twinkle in his eye. 'But only on one condition.'

'What's that?'

'You do the gospel reading at the Easter service.'

'OK. Slave driver!'

Unable to believe her ears, Catherine turned to fix him with a grateful smile. Knowing the older members of the congregation as she did, she knew only too well how much it would mean having Mr Marchant in church. And if he were to read the lesson . . . Why, it would be just like old times. When her father and Mr Erskine had been alive, they'd both taken it in turns to do the readings at St Andrew's.

'Catherine,' Rod's deep, warm voice broke into her trail of thought. 'What you were saying earlier about Africa. When you told your aunt you'd only gone to Whycham le Cley and not darkest Africa. I was wondering . . . have you ever been?'

'Of course not. I've barely been out of Norfolk. Why do you ask?'

'Because I'd like to tell you about it sometime. And show you the family photos.'

Catherine's eyes widened in interest. 'You lived in Africa?'

'Only briefly. It was when my father was in the diplomatic service, before he took early retirement and set up the business in London. Of course, my sister knows more about Africa than I do. She stayed on to work for a local charity.'

'Is she still there?'

Rod shook his head. 'No, she's now working for another charity in Nepal.'

Surprised to hear about the sister that even Aunt Em didn't know too much about, Catherine was even more surprised when Rod announced, 'I'd really like you to meet Henrietta one day. Perhaps when she comes home on leave. I'm sure the two of you would get on really well.'

'Yes, I'd like that too. She might also be interested in meeting Damian,' Catherine reflected. 'I'm sure I heard him mention something about supporting a family in Africa.'

'What a good idea,' Rod heard himself reply, knowing full well he didn't think that at all. He had his own plans for wanting his sister to meet Catherine and they didn't include the Revd Cooper!

Feeling decidedly churlish, Rod made his way to the library in search of Uncle Cedric's family Bible and a book of common prayer. 'Hmm. Love thy neighbour,' he murmured, running his forefinger down the list of commandments.

Once more reminded of his neighbour at the vicarage, Rod snapped the Bible shut and reached into his pocket for the familiar notepad and pen. Hurriedly jotting down a message to ring his sister, he also found himself writing down the name Damian. Until today he'd only ever associated it with that disturbing film The Omen and an unfortunate sheep in a tank of formaldehyde. Feeling a bit like a lost sheep himself, Rod replaced the Bible on the bookshelf and reached for a well-thumbed dictionary. What did constitute an omen these days?

Mulling over the words — portent, sign, warning, premonition, prediction, forecast, etc. — Rod slumped down in an armchair and raked his fingers through his hair. After last night and early this morning (and even during lunch), the signs were looking extremely promising as far as Catherine was concerned. Now, however, he wasn't quite so sure. Every time that wretched vicar's name was mentioned, he'd been filled with a deep sense of foreboding. As for making a forecast, that was the last thing he wanted to consider.

Heading upstairs, persuaded that exactly like Mrs Bailey he was also suffering from the effects of a late night and very early morning, Rod contemplated having forty winks himself. That was until he spied his scowling face in the bathroom mirror. 'Definitely not,' he chastized. 'Don't forget you've more important issues to deal with.'

Five minutes later, splashing his face with cold water, Rod returned to his bedroom, reached into his briefcase and took out the heavy folder he'd collected from the estate agents on Friday afternoon. Containing an extensive range of properties and possible sites earmarked for future development, within a fifty-mile radius, he'd have plenty to take his mind off portents and omens.

12

'Go on,' Emmy urged, watching her niece tap on Master Roderick's bedroom door. 'You don't want him to be late for church, do you?'

'No, but it doesn't seem right somehow.'

'Rubbish. I thought you said he asked you to wake him up. It's not as if you've never been in that room before. You often took Mr Erskine his breakfast or medication.'

Longing to say there was a great deal of difference in ages between the previous owner of Whycham Hall and the current one, Catherine thought better of it. Instead, concentrating more on steadying the bone china cup in her trembling fingers, she turned the handle and made her way through the gloom towards the large tester bed. To her immense relief, Rod was still sleeping.

Now what do I do? she asked herself, placing the cup on the nearby chest of drawers and looking about her. Do I wake him up by whispering in his ear, shaking him by the shoulder or simply making a noise? Certainly tempted to sit on the bed and reach out to touch the slumbering form, Catherine decided it was probably safer to draw back the bulky velvet drapes. With the subsequent noise of solid brass rings sliding along the curtain pole, followed by shafts of sunlight flooding the richly patterned Indian carpet, she knew she'd made the right decision. Rod stretched and stirred.

'Now, there's a surprise,' he murmured, his voice heavy with sleep. 'Who'd have thought it?'

'You did ask me to,' Catherine said quickly, silently cursing her aunt while fixing the curtains into place with huge tasselled tie-backs. If it hadn't been for Aunt Em she'd be elsewhere by now.

'Yes, I know. But I never dreamt you would.'

'I thought we made a bargain.'

Intrigued, Rod propped himself up on one elbow. 'You said you'd do the reading if I brought you an early morning cup of tea,' Catherine reminded.

'Ah, yes. Church. Easter Sunday. So . . . you're my Easter bunny, are you? Lucky me. I don't suppose you fancy hopping over this way for a bit.'

'Certainly not.'

'Not even to pass me my cup of tea? I can't reach it from here.'

'You've got arms, haven't you?'

'Oh, yes, I've got arms. And just like the

wolf in *Little Red Riding Hood*, all the better to hold you with,' Rod teased. 'The only problem being they're completely bare, just like the torso they're attached to. No matter. As long as you don't mind, and as you're not going to pass me my tea, I suppose I'll have to get out of bed and fetch it myself.'

Blushing as deep as the rich crimson drapes, Catherine rushed towards the bedside table and pushed a cup and saucer within his reach. She then turned hurriedly in the direction of the door and called back, 'Don't be late for church, Mr Marchant.'

'Don't worry, Miss Wickham,' he chuckled, watching her go and throwing back the bedclothes, shuck off silk pyjama bottoms and made his way towards the bathroom.

Showered, dressed and following a solitary breakfast, Rod paused by the grandfather clock in the hall. It was only 8.45, which meant he still had plenty of time to make his way to St Andrew's for the 9.15 service. Deliberating between his two sets of car keys, he opted for the Range Rover. Declining his offer of a lift to church, Catherine and her aunt had decided to walk as it was such a fine morning. They needed to get there early, Mrs Bailey had explained, taking his order for breakfast. Catherine had volunteered to help Maureen Martindale prepare an Easter egg hunt for the children.

Smiling fondly at the memory of waking up to find Catherine standing by the bedroom window, Rod recalled yesterday's decision about wanting her to meet his sister. Unfortunately, with Henrietta working in Nepal and not due home on leave for quite some time, that meeting was totally out of the question. Even so, he decided, doing a quick calculation, there was still time to make a phone call before leaving for church. Mindful of the four and three-quarter hours' time difference, and providing his mental arithmetic was up to scratch, it should be about 1.30 in the afternoon in Kathmandu. All in all, a good time to ring the children's home. Lunch would be over and the children preparing for their afternoon nap.

Surprised by the lack of cars in the vicinity of St Andrew's, Rod was equally surprised to find the church practically filled to overflowing. Presuming that most people had walked, he was also relieved to find a familiar face waiting just inside the door.

'Seems news of your anticipated arrival has brought everyone out to meet you, Mr Marchant,' Barry Martindale said proudly, holding out a hymn book and a pamphlet containing the order of morning service. 'Now, if you'd let me escort you to your pew.'

'My pew? Can't I just sit anywhere? Over there, for instance?'

With 'over there' being the pew Catherine was sharing with her aunt, Barry shook his head and placed a hand on Rod's elbow. 'Oh, no. That wouldn't be right at all. Aren't you forgetting? The owner of Whycham Hall has his own pew. Your uncle, and his father before him, insisted on it. If you'd like to come this way, Mr Marchant. Solely for the use of Whycham Hall residents and their guests, it is,' Barry continued in hushed tone. 'I take it you don't have any guests staying with you?'

Rod shook his head, strangely ill at ease. When he'd attended Great Uncle Cedric's funeral, he'd not paid too much heed to the layout of the church. It had been too emotional an occasion. Wondering why he hadn't thought of inviting several friends to join him this weekend, he answered his own question. Jeremy, Francesca and the others hadn't exactly endeared themselves to the residents of Whycham le Cley. As a consequence he was now facing the prospect of following Barry down the aisle accompanied by murmured voices, furtive nudges and numerous pairs of eyes following his every step. Feeling more like a gladiator thrown into the lion's den (than someone attending Sunday service for the first time in ages), he took some comfort in knowing he was at least wearing appropriate body armour: exquisitely tailored Savile Row suit, Jermyn Street shirt, classic silk tie and he'd remembered to polish his shoes.

Pausing for several moments by the ornately carved Whycham family pew, Barry beamed with delight when Rod mentioned that he was perfectly happy to do the reading as requested.

'Wonderful!' he mouthed. 'Vicar will be so pleased.'

Infinitely less pleased was old Mrs Bannister. For the past few minutes she'd been admiring Rod's sartorial elegance, while at the same time registering that he was utterly alone.

'Don't the young master look 'andsome today? Tho' it ain't right Barry leavin' him on his own like that. Why don't Catherine go an' sit next to him?'

'Shh, Mother,' came a voice. 'You know that pew's only for people who live at the hall.'

Suffused with embarrassment, her face blushing as pink as her rose-petal hat, Mrs Bannister's daughter placed a restraining hand on the nearby wheelchair. To no avail, however, the old lady announced to all and sundry, 'But Catherine do live at the hall,

168

don't she? An' I saw the two of 'em together yesterday mornin'. Collectin' willow for them there windows, I reckon. Gave 'em my curtains for that new car o' his too. You know the ones with those lovely sunflowers that I got on Norwich market — '

'Mother, *please!*'

While half the congregation turned to look at Catherine, the remainder were watching Barry and Rod in earnest conversation. 'Of course,' Barry replied in response to Rod's last remark. And sensing that vicar and choir were about to begin their procession from the bell tower towards the nave, he hurried back to confront Catherine.

Dreading what was coming next, Catherine offered up a silent prayer. It was no use. All eyes were on her now and her aunt was prodding her annoyingly in the ribs. 'Go on,' Aunt Em entreated for the second time that morning, her voice thankfully several decibels lower than Mrs Bannister's. 'Poor chap looks so lost and alone up there.'

Glancing quickly to her right, Catherine saw the Revd Cooper fix her with a benevolent smile and gesture for her to make her way forward. Further down on her left, however, and looking back with pleading eyes, was Rod. How could she resist?

'Alleluia! Christ is risen,' the vicar proclaimed, his jubilant voice drowning out the hum of approval as Catherine took her place by Rod's side.

'He is risen indeed, Allelulia!' The congregation replied, with those nearer the front (including the two George Baldrys) nudging each other. Unless they were very much mistaken, *the young master* had just taken hold of Miss Catherine's hand and given it an affectionate squeeze.

Comforted by her presence and with Catherine guiding him through the beginning of the service, Rod began to relax. Even the prospect of the reading became less daunting. That duly completed he returned to his seat, preparing himself for the Liturgy of the Sacrament. Just like the Sunday service, it had been some considerable time since he'd last taken communion.

'We are the body of Christ . . . ' the vicar intoned. 'The peace of the Lord be always with you.'

'And also with you,' echoed the members of St Andrew's, eager to see how Rod would react.

'Let us offer one another a sign of the peace,' Damian said, smiling in his direction.

Sensing a pregnant pause, wondering what on earth came next, Rod felt Catherine fumble for his right hand. 'Peace be with you,' she faltered, turning to face him.

'Oh, right. Peace be with you,' he replied, and, looking over her shoulder, watched various members of the congregation striking a similar pose with their neighbours.

'Now follow Damian,' Catherine said softly, knowing from experience that at this stage in the proceedings Revd Cooper usually set off down the aisle to offer his own sign of the peace.

'What, to all of them?' Rod asked, horrified, squeezing past her. It would take simply ages to shake hands with every parishioner present.

'No. Just a few on either side. Then come back here for the sacrament.'

Stirred by all the friendly faces, the subsequent taking of bread and wine and the final rousing hymn, Rod was almost sorry when the service came to an end. Eventually, fastening his hassock back into position, he emitted a deeply satisfied smile.

'That wasn't too bad — was it?' Catherine said, making ready to leave the pew.

'No. But I'm jolly thankful for Mrs Bannister's vocal contribution. At least it brought you to my rescue. Sorry if it caused you any embarrassment, Catherine. If there's anything I can ever do for you . . . ?'

'Right now there is. You can take yourself to the end of the church and join everyone for a coffee. Perhaps get to know a few more of the locals.'

'Coffee! You have coffee?'

'Yes, and biscuits. Plus of course the Easter egg hunt for the children. Though I think I'd better go and remind Damian all about that. He forgot to mention it before the service began.'

Hardly surprising, Rod thought to himself, suddenly finding himself alone. The vicar's attention had been undoubtedly elsewhere. On an angel with copper-coloured hair, perhaps?

'Ladies and gentlemen, how very remiss of me,' a voice called out. 'I do apologize. Catherine has just reminded me there's an Easter egg hunt for the younger members of the congregation. This will take place both inside St Andrew's and outside in the churchyard. Once you've partaken of your coffee, if you'd care to give the little ones a hand.' Amid the excited squeals of children, Damian held up his own hands. 'And, before I bid you all a Happy Easter, could I just offer my personal thanks for the wonderful floral decorations this morning, courtesy of Catherine and Mrs Bailey, not forgetting Maureen's sterling efforts with dustpan and brush,

Brasso and Mr Sheen.'

To a mixed chorus of, 'Hear, hear, well done, ladies, a magnificent effort,' Damian was seen to take Catherine to one side. 'A little bird tells me birthday greetings are also in order. I did suggest mentioning it before the service, and getting Mrs Basford to play 'Happy Birthday' on the organ. To my surprise your aunt advised against it. She didn't think you'd want to draw attention to yourself.'

Pausing with her cup of coffee to her lips, Catherine almost choked. That well-meaning little bird again. Watching an array of brightly coloured feathers bobbing about on Aunt Em's hat (behind the tea urn), she knew she couldn't be angry for long. Anyway, it wasn't only her aunt who'd been responsible for all the attention-drawing. Even now, Mrs Bannister's voice was distinctly audible above the milling throng.

With the old lady hidden from view in her wheelchair (and her daughter anxious to take her home), Catherine flinched every time she heard mention of the early morning willow gathering and the sunflower curtains. She still needed to explain to Rod the importance of such a donation. To begin with he'd never be able to get rid of them. Mrs Bannister was now adamant that he should keep them. This meant it was far safer to keep them in the Range Rover. If, for any reason they ever made it into Whycham Hall . . . Heaven forbid! Catherine thought to herself with a wicked glint in her eye. She could just imagine Francesca's reaction.

Still pondering Rod and Francesca's relationship, and why exactly he'd chosen to spend Easter Sunday alone at the hall, Catherine was reminded how her heart had gone out to him, big time. Mrs Bannister had been quite correct in one respect. It hadn't been terribly polite expecting Rod to sit all by himself — no doubt there would be words at next month's PCC meeting. In addition to which, and despite her initial embarrassment, it had been rather enjoyable sitting in the Whycham family pew. Rod had indeed looked 'andsome in his suit.

From the positive looks on people's faces, it also appeared as if he'd made a lasting impression on the community. I only hope it remains that way, Catherine thought to herself, a tiny cloud hovering in her mind. She couldn't tell for certain, of course, but that pretty hefty folder on the table by the window in Rod's bedroom, had it really been from Tyrrell and Robinson the estate agents? If so, what was Rod interested in — buying or selling?

Meeting his gaze from where he was standing by a willow-draped window, Catherine saw a young child clutch at one of his knees. 'Lift me up, please, mister, cos there's an egg up there and I can't reach it.'

His attention drawn to the freckle-faced child with carrot-coloured hair, Rod stooped down and held out his arms. Then, with the egg gathered safely in a pair of tiny hands, Rod said brightly, 'Right, then, shall we go outside and look for some more?'

Watching them go, Catherine made her own way into the churchyard, where her mission was not to hunt for Easter eggs. Instead, she planned a quiet visit to her parents' grave. With her solemn thoughts interrupted only now and then by further delighted laughter from Rod's new-found friend, she allowed her mind to drift back to her own childhood. Unlike Rod, she hadn't been sent hundreds of miles away to the strict regime of a boarding school. Her formative education had been here at Whycham le Cley under the gentle guidance of Miss Archer and of course her father, the village school's head teacher.

'Ah, here you are,' said a voice by her elbow. 'I was wondering where you'd disappeared to.'

Blinking through her tears, Catherine saw

Rod's eyes scan the writing on the marble tombstone. 'Oh, I'm sorry. Am I interrupting? If you'd like to be left alone?'

'No. It's all right and you're not interrupting. I was preparing to leave anyway.'

'Leave for where?'

'Initially to go and help with the general tidying up after the service, and then back to the hall. I need to pack my bag.'

'You're going home tonight?'

'No, I'm going before lunch.'

Rod's face filled with renewed confusion. Just as he was leaving for this morning's service, the vicar had rung and invited him to lunch. 'All very last minute,' Damian had said, himself on the verge of leaving. The only difference being that the Revd Cooper had only to cut through his garden and cross the churchyard to reach St Andrew's.

'I thought you'd be having lunch at the vicarage.'

'No. Why should I be?'

'After the service when Damian took you to one side, I assumed he'd — '

'No, he didn't,' Catherine interrupted. 'He simply wanted to say Hap — '

Stopping almost as quickly as she'd begun, Catherine soon changed her mind about mentioning her birthday. Not that she'd expect Rod to do anything about it. It was probably best left unmentioned, that's all. Fortunately for her, the young child, still holding tightly on to his hand, was now jumping up and down, prompting further attention.

'Please, mister, I need a wee.'

'A what?'

'Don't worry,' Catherine said, watching Rod's face fill with alarm. 'You can leave Daisy with me and I'll deal with the necessary. Believe it or not, St Andrew's also has a loo.'

'Daisy. So that's her name. I've been trying to work out what it is. Munching her way through all that chocolate, I could only fathom out something that sounded like Maisie.'

'Daisy Barnes,' Catherine called back, as she hurried away. 'She's Mr Barnes's youngest granddaughter.'

Rod gave a wry smile, reminded of a character in an old children's annual his mother had had as a little girl. 'Oh, well, I suppose it's far better to be named after a flower than a mouse.'

Minutes later, still hoping that Catherine would return, he took a sideways step to look at the nearby tombstone. Registering the names of both Catherine's parents, he recalled the sadness in her eyes when he'd come across her, completely unawares. If it hadn't been for young Daisy hanging on to his every word — and his hand — he would in all probability have taken Catherine into his arms and brushed away her tears. Though definitely not with this, he thought, regarding the chocolate-stained handkerchief clutched in his palm. Thank goodness that just like his father, he always carried a freshly laundered handkerchief.

Hearing a commotion at the church door, Rod turned to see young Daisy trying to free herself from someone's grasp. Catherine, meanwhile, was trying to act as a go-between.

'But I wanna go an' see mister,' Daisy wailed.

'Definitely not! You mustn't go bothering Mr Marchant again,' a young woman cried, trying desperately to keep hold of Daisy's hand. 'Have you any idea who he is?'

'Yeah, he's Catherine's friend. Anyway, I wasn't botherin'. We was lookin' for eggs.'

'And by the look of your face and hands, young lady, you found them all.'

'No, we didn't cos mister said he saw anuvver one under the seat and anuvver one by the *lynch-gate*.'

Not in the least bit interested in Easter eggs, Hayley Barnes was more concerned about her father-in-law's job as head gardener up at Whycham Hall. What on earth was Daisy thinking of? Mr Marchant hunting high and low all over the churchyard for chocolate eggs — whatever next? Worse still, one look at her daughter was more than enough to remind her of old Mrs Bannister's comments. Oh, Lord! The *young master* might have looked handsome when he'd first arrived in church; now wherever he was (and if the state of Daisy's face and hands was anything to go by) he'd probably be trying to clean melted chocolate from that wonderful navy blue suit of his.

Unsure as to what all the fuss was about, and assuming Catherine had done the necessary with young Daisy, Rod scooped up the two remaining Easter eggs and headed in their direction.

'Oh, Mr Marchant, I'm so sorry,' Hayley began. 'Your lovely suit. I hope it's not ruined. Daisy's a naughty girl running off like that and — '

'I didn't run. We walked, didn't we, mister?'

'Yes, Daisy. We did,' Rod said kindly, anxious to quell the mounting tension. 'And a lovely walk we had too, looking at all the pretty spring flowers and . . . '

'Huntin' for Easter eggs,' Daisy finished for him, her face eager with anticipation. It hadn't escaped her notice that 'mister' was holding two more eggs behind his back.

Desperate for support, Rod made eye contact with Catherine. To his relief she came to his aid almost immediately. 'Oh, look, Daisy. Mr Marchant's found the other eggs. How about if we give them to Mummy and she takes them home for you? If you eat any more chocolate now you'll probably spoil your appetite for lunch.'

'And it will be something for you to look forward to,' Rod added, slipping his grubby handkerchief into his pocket.

Deeply pensive, Daisy studied the trio of adults standing before her. Although Mister and Catherine were smiling at her, Mum still didn't look very happy. In fact, she had what her older brothers and sisters called 'that funny look on her face'. The only problem being Mum never laughed when she had it. In Daisy's case, it usually meant she had to sit on the naughty stair and go without her pudding. Remembering that today they were all due to have lunch with Grandad and Nana Barnes, which meant lots of lovely puddings, Daisy gave a begrudging nod.

'All right. I s'pose so,' she said, watching her mother place the eggs carefully into her handbag. 'But Brett and Carl mustn't have them. They've got loads of eggs at home.'

Mention of her three-year-old twins, left at home with their older brother and sister, was enough to prompt Hayley on her way. Unbeknown to their mother, Brett and Carl had found their clutch of Easter eggs within minutes of their father leaving for early morning milking at Kazer's Farm. 'And what do you say to Mr Marchant?' Hayley enquired.

'See you later, mister.'

Too embarrassed to hang around, Hayley grabbed Daisy firmly by the hand with loud mutterings of how about remembering to say please and thank you, leaving Catherine and Rod convulsed with laughter when Daisy piped back, 'I did say please when I wanted a wee.'

'Oh, I really like her. Isn't she great?' Rod chuckled. 'Tell me, do you think they'll go through the *lynch-gate* on their way home?'

'I hope not,' Catherine replied. 'I certainly don't fancy Daisy's chances if they do. Speaking of going, I really had better be on my way. As Aunt Em looks as if she's ready to leave too I can only assume I missed out on all the washing up.'

Rod sucked in his cheeks and looked hurriedly at his watch. 'OK. Just give me a couple of minutes to say my goodbyes and I'll be right back.'

Leaving Catherine to ponder back for what, Rod turned and gave her a knowing wink. 'I've already arranged it with your aunt. I'm giving you both a lift back to Whycham Hall.'

'Have you really?' Catherine murmured under her breath. At least this time the little bird had been given a name.

13

Catherine faced her aunt squarely across the kitchen table. 'All I'm saying is that I still wish you hadn't.'

'As if I could have done anything to stop him,' Emmy protested. 'We were both glad of a ride home from church, weren't we?'

'That's not what I'm talking about, Aunt Em, and well you know it.'

'And I don't know why you're making such a fuss. He's only offered to give you a lift back to your flat. Which is no distance at all in that sports car of his. I thought you'd be pleased. It means you won't have to mess about with trains — or have that walk at the other end.'

'I don't have to mess about with trains, nor do I mind the walk at the other end. In fact, I quite enjoy it.'

Not used to seeing her niece quite so put out, Emmy added feebly, 'It's like I said to Mr Marchant when he first suggested it, that Sunday service from Whycham Halt is far from reliable. There's only one or two trains in the afternoon.'

'Yes. And I only need one of them. As for you saying 'when he first suggested it', I don't know how you've got the nerve to sit there and say that. As I recall, it was you who mentioned it first, five minutes before Rod left to have lunch at the vicarage.'

'That's where you're wrong, Catherine. Master Roderick did suggest it first. He approached me about it when I took him his breakfast. And, before you go jumping down my throat again, I not only told him I thought it was a very kind gesture on his part, I also warned him that you'd be too proud to accept a lift all that way and would no doubt make a scene. Which you have.'

Feeling deeply ashamed, Catherine made to leave the table. In a way her aunt was right. She had made a scene. Though, thankfully not in front of Rod. Was that why he'd not mentioned the offer of a lift until the very last minute? Fixing his housekeeper with that secretive smile . . . What was it he'd called back? 'Catch up with you later, Mrs B. Mustn't keep the vicar waiting.'

As for waiting, Catherine concluded, right now her aunt was probably waiting for an apology. If she wasn't, she certainly deserved one. 'I'm sorry, Aunt Em. I don't know what's got in to me just lately. It was very wrong of me to snap at you like that. I ..'

'Tut tut. No apologies and no tears,' Emmy said kindly, 'and certainly no reason to leave the table before you've finished your lunch. You've simply been going through a very emotional time just lately, that's all.'

Catherine forced a weak smile. 'That's all?'

Leaving the table herself, Emmy pushed her chair back into place. Seconds later, she was cradling Catherine in her arms. 'There, there, my love. Maybe I was wrong about the tears after all. If you want to cry, you go ahead. These past few weeks haven't been exactly easy for you. Things can only get better, you know.'

'Really? I'm not so sure about that.'

Emmy demurred, not exactly sure herself where she should go from here — at least with regard to this conversation. On the positive side, Catherine seemed at long last to be getting over that very unsavoury business of her two-timing ex-boyfriend (some twenty-first birthday present that had been!) and she was extremely happy with her job at the library. Thank heavens Janice had proved to be a proper friend, not like that scheming hussy her niece had befriended at college.

Waiting for Catherine to wipe away her tears, Emmy continued to look on the bright side. Thanks to Mr Hayes (or should that now be Mr Marchant?) there was a distinct possibility Catherine would be spending even more time here at Whycham Hall. A place she'd loved ever since she was a little girl. All those endless carefree days walking in the bluebell woods with her father or else looking for frogs and tadpoles and other assorted wildlife down by the stream.

Reaching in the pocket of her apron for a tissue, Emmy blew her nose hard and dabbed at the corner of her eyes. She too was missing Catherine's father. When she'd been widowed during the Falklands War, he'd been a truly caring and supportive brother. Oh, so many mixed emotions, Emmy surmised: laughter, tears and heartache. Laughter and celebrations when Catherine had been born on her father's birthday; tears shed for those three special people buried in Whycham churchyard (her niece's parents and her own dear husband) and now the heartache that had prompted Catherine's lunchtime outburst. Convinced she knew the root cause, the next hurdle to overcome was bringing it out in the open.

Busying herself with clearing away the dishes, Emmy decided to risk it. 'Catherine about Master Roderick. You do like him — don't you?'

'Yes. Of course I do. Believe it or not I also appreciate his offer of a lift. At least it meant you and I could have lunch together today. And I'm extremely grateful to him for taking me to collect the willow so early yesterday morning.'

'Hmm, that's as maybe, only that wasn't quite what I had in mind when I asked *do you like him*? It's obvious he thinks a great deal of you.'

'What makes you say that?'

'Gracious me, child! I might have spent the best part of my life in sleepy old Whycham le Cley. That doesn't mean I can't tell when a young man's fallen head over heels for my niece. First the new vicar and now Master Roderick.'

'What! Y-you mean . . . '

'Are you saying you haven't noticed?'

'Apart from that initial meeting at the ford, I suppose Rod and I have been getting on rather well lately. We certainly share a similar sense of humour. As for Damian . . . I had no idea. Are you sure?'

'As sure as the twenty-three candles on your birthday cake.'

'You've made me a — '

''Course I have,' Emmy interrupted, 'You're never too old for a birthday cake. I thought you could take it back with you — perhaps share it with your friends at the library. In the meantime, why don't we have a piece with a nice cup of tea before Master Roderick takes you home?'

'I see,' Catherine said, fixing her aunt with a sly smile. 'And is the vicar coming too?'

'Lord! I hope not,' Aunt Em cried, completely taken aback. 'Not that he wouldn't be welcome, of course,' she added as an afterthought. 'We don't want to complicate things, do we?'

'Taking into consideration what you said only a few moments ago, aren't they complicated enough already? I confess I had no idea about Damian. Lovely as he is, I thought he was simply doing his job and being friendly. Less friendly, however, is Francesca.'

'What's Francesca got to do with it?'

'Everything. To begin with she's got her heart set on Whycham Hall.'

Emmy beamed, triumphant. 'At least you didn't say she's got her heart set on Master Roderick. It's as plain as the nose on my face she doesn't love him.'

'I'm not so sure about that. She certainly treats him as if he's her own personal property.'

'That's only because she's merely in love with the sort of life she'd live if they were married. You mark my words, Catherine. Master Roderick wouldn't marry someone he didn't love. He's not the type.'

Nevertheless, Catherine refrained from

adding for fear of offending her aunt a second time, there was still a hell of a difference between liking someone and marrying them. From the way things were looking at present (and even though she'd admitted they got on very well together), the thought of Roderick Marchant marrying a college librarian and making her mistress of Whycham Hall was extremely unlikely.

Leaving Catherine to pack her overnight bag, Emmy looked at her watch and set the kitchen timer. In an hour she hoped to finish her preparations for Master Roderick's supper and also make a start on Monday's lunch. This time tomorrow, she reflected, she would be alone again. Catherine would be safely installed at her flat and Mr Marchant heading back to London. Which didn't leave much time this afternoon. If only Catherine would stop looking for obstacles instead of letting things happen naturally, as they had this morning in St Andrew's.

Chuckling quietly to herself, Emmy offered up silent thanks for old Mrs Bannister's intervention in proceedings. Even she couldn't have arranged that better if she'd tried. As for seeing Master Roderick and Catherine sitting side by side in the Whycham family pew, that had really brought a lump to her throat. And if in five or ten years time there were junior versions of her employer and her niece, what could be more perfect?

Telling herself not to let her imagination run away with her just yet, Emmy turned her attention to the rest of the afternoon. How could she best deal with that? What if Revd Cooper kept Rod talking too long at the vicarage? What if Catherine suddenly changed her mind and took the train after all? Determined that nothing should go wrong, Emmy made a mental list preparing for all eventualities. Number one on the list: making sure she kept the young people talking long enough to miss all the trains at Whycham Halt.

Guessing that when Master Roderick caught sight of Catherine's birthday cake, he'd insist they had tea in the drawing-room, Emmy was already one jump ahead. That simply wouldn't do at all. Instead, she hurried back to her cottage and returned with a prettily embroidered tablecloth and matching napkins. Her only concession as she prepared the kitchen table was regarding the china. Mr Marchant, like his uncle before him, pre-ferred drinking tea from bone china cups.

'Goodness, that looks very tempting. Is it someone's birthday?' Rod called, popping his head round the kitchen door.

'That's right, sir. It's Catherine's. I always

make her a chocolate cake for her birthday. It being her favourite.'

'Lucky Catherine,' Rod replied. 'It must be years since someone baked me a cake for my birthday. By the way, where is she?'

'She's just this minute finished packing her bag and gone outside. Going hunting for flowers for the table, she said.'

Relieved to discover that Catherine was still in the vicinity (and presumably agreeable to his offer of a lift), Rod was nevertheless surprised to hear she'd gone *hunting* for flowers. The gardens at Whycham Hall were a profusion of spring flowers. Even he, with his limited knowledge of flora and fauna, had recognized daffodils and tulips. Half expecting Catherine to return laden with blooms, he was equally surprised to see she carried nothing other than a simple posy. At the same time, Mrs Bailey was hastily removing the pink and white candles from the birthday cake.

Rod scratched his head. 'Correct me if I'm wrong — aren't you supposed to light the candles and sing 'Happy Birthday' before you take them off?'

'Unless of course it's Catherine Wickham celebrating her birthday,' Emmy explained through pursed lips. 'Just before you arrived,

Master Roderick, I was given strict instructions to remove every single candle.'

'I see. So you don't want us to sing 'Happy Birthday'?'

'Definitely not,' Catherine replied. Meeting Rod's gaze, she reached for a tiny posy vase into which she placed some ivy, violets and primroses.

'Oh, well, considering I can only croak like a frog, that's probably all for the best. As I told the vicar over lunch, I'd be absolutely no use in the choir. I can't sing for toffee.'

Knowing that wasn't completely true — she had stood beside him in church — Catherine said without thinking, 'How was lunch at the vicarage?'

'Very nice, thank you. In fact, your name came up on more than one occasion.'

Trying to suppress her blushes and ignore her aunt's look of 'I told you so', Catherine hurried to the sink to fill the posy vase with water.

Sensing they could be treading on dangerous ground, Emmy resolved to draw attention away from the vicarage. No doubt they'd find out soon enough why her niece had been the topic of conversation. 'That's a pretty posy, dear,' she said, watching Catherine place the vase in the middle of the table. 'Like I always say, the simplest arrangements are often the best. Take that willow for a start. Everyone thought those windows at St Andrew's were absolutely beautiful, not to mention the fact you also gave those willow trees a jolly good pruning.'

'And it will be easier to park near the village hall,' Catherine said. 'You also know my thoughts on picking garden flowers.'

Rod looked up from where he was admiring the newly picked posy, sweet-pea-embroidered tablecloth and napkins, and dainty blue and white china. It was all so quintessentially English. 'Is that why you never picked any tulips or daffodils?'

Catherine looked at him in surprise. 'Oh, I'd never pick anything from the gardens at Whycham Hall.'

'Another of my great uncle's rules?'

'No. One of my own, in fact. As far as possible I prefer to use wild flowers. And only then if they're in plentiful supply. Those violets and primroses, for instance. There's a carpet of them in the woods beyond the tennis court.'

'Speaking of tennis,' Rod continued, 'I don't suppose you play, do you? Damian was suggesting we might get together for a mixed doubles later on in the year.'

Alarmed by such a prospect and spying the dark clouds from the kitchen window,

Catherine muttered something about it being too early in the year to think of tennis.

'Ah, but not too early to think of May. That's why you were the main topic of conversation during lunch. Damian and I thought it would be a jolly good idea to hold a May Day celebration here at the hall. Naturally, we both decided you were the ideal person to help organize it. That's of course if you don't mind? You did say how much you wanted to keep the old traditions going.'

Knowing only too well how much she wanted to preserve the way of life at Whycham le Cley, Catherine was less sure about what it would involve, especially if it meant dealing with the vicar of St Andrew's and the owner of Whycham Hall.

14

Kissing her aunt goodbye, Catherine made her way to where Rod was loading her travel bag into the car.

'I hope you've got everything,' he said, opening the passenger door. 'Birthday cake, home-made scones and biscuits, clean laundry . . . '

'If I haven't,' Catherine replied, knowing he was only teasing about the laundry, 'don't be surprised to see Aunt Em come running after us before we've even reached the bottom of the drive. She usually thinks of something. It's almost as if she doesn't want me to go.'

'That makes two of us,' Rod said, fixing her with a disarming smile before making his way to the driving seat.

About to remind him that he was also going — going back to London, immediately after lunch tomorrow — Catherine got no further. Just as she'd predicted, Aunt Em came hurrying towards the car. To her surprise it was Rod she was heading for.

'Oh, Master Roderick,' she said, out of breath, 'I'm so sorry. I forgot to ask, what time would you like supper? I know you said you'd only be wanting something cold, as you had lunch with the vicar, but — '

'Don't worry, Mrs Bailey. For the moment I'm not sure what time I'll be back. You never know, I might get held up. It depends what the traffic is like and . . . '

Emmy's brow creased into a frown. The chance of getting caught in traffic was extremely remote, particularly on this side of the county. With it being Easter Sunday, most folk who'd gone away for the weekend wouldn't be returning until tomorrow. On the other hand, she pondered, meeting Rod's gaze, he could perhaps get held up if Catherine were to invite him in for a drink or something . . .

Pleased to see her niece's attention was elsewhere, Emmy nodded as if in understanding, highly delighted when Rod suggested, 'Why not leave supper on a tray and then take the rest of the evening off. What with Damian's hospitality and that wonderful chocolate birthday cake, I daren't even think of food. I've eaten far too much already this weekend.'

'Right you are, sir. I'll leave supper on a tray in the kitchen. You can decide whether or not you take it into the dining-room or have it on your lap elsewhere. I'll see you in the morning, shall I?'

'She's a real treasure, isn't she?' Rod said, watching Emmy disappearing in the direction of the kitchen, just as it began to rain. 'Has she always been that conscientious?'

'Always,' Catherine affirmed, and proceeded to tell Rod about the years she and her father had spent in Aunt Em's tender care.

Leaving Whycham le Cley behind and heading through the rain towards the outskirts of Norwich, Catherine began to wonder what she should do once they arrived at her flat. Should she invite Rod in for a coffee, or merely say thank you for bringing her home and wish him a safe trip back to London? Reminded only too well of Aunt Em's standards when it came to hospitality, Catherine thought in this instance it could only be tea or coffee. Definitely not wine. Her usual standby bottle of supermarket plonk was hardly comparable to those in the cellar at Whycham Hall.

'So . . . what do you think about holding a May Day festival?' Rod said, breaking into her train of thought.

'I think it's a wonderful idea. We always had May Day celebrations when my father was head teacher. I'm sure the current head, Mr Lowther, would be keen to get involved.'

'Great. And you'd be happy to help out?'

'Very much so. My only concern is that there isn't much time to arrange things. I take it you do mean May of this year?'

Rod pursed his lips and drummed his fingers against the steering wheel, 'Mmm. You're right there. With barely four weeks to go we're going to be somewhat limited. Damian was spot on when he described us as new boys. I'm afraid we did get rather carried away with all our plans. By the time we'd got round to the cheese board we'd not only dealt with May Day but also midsummer, harvest festival, bonfire night and Christmas.'

'Gracious! You have been busy,' Catherine replied, hardly daring to think ahead to Christmas. Did that mean Rod was planning to spend Christmas at the hall?

With Catherine's thoughts winging away to December, Rod's immediate concern was remembering her directions to the flat. Ten minutes later he pulled up outside what had once been an elegant, three-storey, late Victorian townhouse.

Reminded of the remains of birthday cake, tin of scones and biscuits, plus her travel bag, Catherine soon realized she'd need help getting everything up the stairs to her front door. In a way this was the moment she'd been dreading. Part of her wanted very much to invite Rod inside, especially as he'd taken the trouble to bring her home. At the same time, however, she'd vowed never to invite anyone she didn't really know into what she regarded as her own private space.

But it isn't as if I *don't* know him, she told herself, watching Rod switch off the ignition and windscreen wipers before hurrying to the rear of the car.

'*Ah, but once bitten twice shy,*' an annoying inner voice cautioned. '*Besides, do you really know him? Can you trust him? Look what happened before with Jason and your so-called best friend. What about Rod's friend . . . Francesca?*'

'Shut up! I'll deal with that later,' Catherine muttered, hunting in her handbag for her keys.

'Pardon? What was that?'

'Oh, I was just saying what a problem it is to shut this handbag,' Catherine lied, pretending to struggle with the clasp. 'I'll have a proper look at it later.'

Seemingly convinced by her reply, Rod held out an assortment of tartan-decorated cake tins. 'Right, lead on, Macduff,' he said. 'You take the tins and I'll take your travel bag. That's if you're OK about me accompanying you to your front door?'

'Y-yes. That would be a great help. I'll go and unlock it. Be careful of the steps, though.

They can get a bit a bit slippery in the rain.'

'I see what you mean,' Rod called, hurrying up behind her.

Conscious of the rain dripping from the overhead porch, Catherine pushed open the communal front door and motioned him inside. 'Thank goodness it wasn't like this for the Easter egg hunt,' she said, saying the first thing to come into her head, while trying to gauge what she should do next.

Rod came inadvertently to her rescue. 'Where do you want your bag? Shall I leave it here in the hall or else . . . ?'

Seeing him nod in the direction of the nearest door, Catherine shook her head and smiled. 'No. Not there. That doorway leads into Mrs Minns' sitting-room. She's my landlady. I'm two flights up, on the top floor. If you're not averse to climbing a few more stairs and would like a cup of coffee?'

Delighted to have the opportunity of spending a little while longer in her company, Rod followed Catherine up two very steep flights of stairs. 'Call that a few,' he said, grinning, when he paused for breath outside her door. 'Now I know how you keep in shape. What with these stairs leading to your flat and those at Whycham Hall, leading to your turret. Most of my friends in London would positively balk at climbing one flight, let alone two. Tell me, do you have a thing about staircases? What's the attraction or is your middle name Rapunzel?'

'No. Actually it's Edwina. And, as you can see from the state of my hair, I'm certainly no Rapunzel. In truth, the reason I live here is largely due to cost and proximity to the station, whereas at Whycham Hall it has to be privacy and the view. On a clear day I can see for miles, almost as far as the marshes.'

Hesitating as she juggled the cake tins, unlocked the door to her flat and switched on the light, Catherine turned to face him. 'Rod . . . what I said just now about cost. Are you aware that I don't pay any rent when I stay at the hall?'

'To be honest, I wasn't at first. However, one quick call to Mr Hayes soon put me in the picture, particularly in relation to your invaluable help and support. Rest assured, Catherine, I have absolutely no intention of charging you rent. In fact, I think it's me who should be paying you for your services.'

Momentarily taken aback when Catherine fixed him with an old-fashioned look, Rod was instantly reminded of Jeremy and that awful *droit de seigneur* debacle. 'Um . . . when I said services, I meant . . . '

'It's OK. I know what you meant,' she replied, placing the tins on a nearby table, 'and do please sit down. I'm afraid the choice is pretty limited. As you can see space is at a premium up here. I should imagine this was the domestic's quarters at one time. According to Thelma — Mrs Minns — when these houses were first built everyone had live-in help.'

'Goodness! How old is Mrs Minns?'

'About eighty-five. She inherited this place from her parents.'

Still reeling from the shock of Catherine having such an elderly landlady, Rod was also reminded of post Victorian values. 'How does Mrs Minns feel about you having gentlemen callers?' he said, reminded of an old black and white film where gentlemen callers were an absolute no-no.

'As I've only been here since Christmas and you're the first, I suppose I shall have to wait and see.'

Unable to believe his ears, Rod looked about the cramped yet cosy lounge/diner and opted for one of the two fireside chairs. Presumably it would have been an impossible feat trying to get even the smallest two-seater settee up the narrow staircase and into this unusual-shaped room.

'I won't be a moment,' Catherine said, unbuttoning her coat. 'I'll just go and hang this up and wash my hands. Will you be OK with coffee or would you prefer tea?'

'Coffee would be fine,' Rod called after her, still puzzling the layout of the flat. Somewhere in the dim and distant past he was sure his mother had possessed a novel about an L-shaped room.

Assuming that this particular L-shape was a result of partitioning off a section for a bedroom and possible bathroom, Rod's gaze quickly took in the remains of Catherine's so-called flat. A dark-oak, gate-leg table and two dining chairs at this end (in addition to the two fireside chairs and a small coffee table) and at the shorter end of the L what looked like a reasonably well-stocked galley kitchen. All in all a far cry from his extremely spacious and minimalist flat in London's Docklands. Feeling strangely uncomfortable at his own good fortune, and reminded once more of a certain attic room at Whycham Hall, Rod looked up when Catherine reappeared, moved aside a bottle of wine and reached for the kettle.

'I . . . um . . . didn't offer you the wine,' she began. 'I'm afraid it's only supermarket plonk. Hardly what you're used to.'

'If that's a reference to Uncle Cedric's amazing wine cellar, how about us having a wine tasting as well when we get together to discuss the proposed May Day festivities?'

'Not a good idea. My nose starts tingling after two glasses of wine or sherry. Any more and I'll probably be dancing on the table.'

Rod smiled, intrigued, regarding the barley-twist legs of the nearby table. 'What a delightful thought. Maybe we should open that bottle of plonk after all.'

'Definitely not! I need to be in control of all my faculties tomorrow. I've a great deal of work to do.'

'Spoilsport. Wait a minute! Isn't tomorrow Easter Monday? You're not going in to the library?'

'No. But you did say Damian wants the list for May Day ASAP. In addition to which I still have to put the finishing touches to the Wordswork events at college.'

'Ah! That reminds me,' Rod said, moving forward to help Catherine with the tray of coffee. 'I knew there was something I wanted to ask you. What exactly is a Wordswork event?'

Always happy to talk of books and anything connected with writing, Catherine explained how thrilled they were to have the author Romy Felden as their first guest of honour. 'It's quite a coup,' she said, her eyes sparkling. 'Romy usually steers well clear of the limelight but as she's fairly local and often features East Anglia in her books . . . She's also extremely supportive of literary events for young people.'

'Romy Felden,' Rod repeated. 'My mother and sister are huge fans of her writing. Isn't she married to that actor fellow?'

'Mmm. Yes. That very dishy actor fellow — Stephen Walker.'

'Oh dear,' Rod announced glumly, recalling Stephen Walker in the recent TV mini-series *To Love the Hero*. 'And there was me hoping to be your hero. Come to think of it, Mother and Henrietta are huge fans of his, too. I don't know, some chaps have all the luck.'

'Stephen might be very dishy but he's also very happily married. That's one of the reasons they like to escape to Romy's cottage. At least there they're away from the prying eyes of the tabloids.'

Rod nodded in understanding and reached across for his coffee. 'I can't think of anything worse than stepping out of the front door in the morning to be confronted by hordes of photographers. Can you?'

'I think I can safely say that's one thing I won't ever have to worry about,' Catherine said, smiling, and passed him the sugar.

An hour later and, not wishing to outstay his welcome, Rod glanced at his watch before reaching into his jacket pocket. 'How very disappointing. There was me hoping that two cups of coffee might have the same effect on you as two glasses of wine. As it looks as if there isn't going to be any dancing on the table this evening, I suppose I ought to be making a move. Before I do, I'd like you to have this. Happy Birthday, Catherine.'

Catherine stared, intrigued, at the tiny package Rod was holding in the palm of his hand. If he hadn't known until this afternoon that it was her birthday, when had he been able to go shopping? The village stores only opened for a couple of hours on Sunday morning to deal with the delivery and sale of newspapers and he'd had lunch at the vicarage.

'It's all right. It won't bite,' Rod said, mysteriously, watching her unwrap the single layer of tissue paper. 'But you never know . . . it might croak.'

'If that's supposed to be a hint, I can only assume it's something froggy.' Voicing her thoughts out loud, Catherine carefully unwrapped a walnut-shaped green leather box, containing a tiny glass frog. Then, before she realized what was happening, Rod was standing by her side.

'As you've probably gathered it's not new. In fact, it belonged to Great Aunt Edwina. Cedric bought it for her years ago during one of their many trips to Venice. I understand it's made of Murano glass and if you look very closely you'll see the heart is set with a piece of *millefiori*.'

Discovering the delicate *millefiori* heart for herself, Catherine fixed Rod with a confused smile. He, meanwhile, continued. 'Mother says that Great Uncle Cedric was quite a romantic in a reserved sort of way and was always adding to Edwina's collection. Apparently, she never went anywhere without that little chap. It's strange, really, Edwina's frog collection is one of the few things I can remember from my earliest visits to Whycham Hall. Perhaps that's why I share a similar passion. I already have her letter opener and paperweight on my desk in London.'

'Doesn't this belong there too? It doesn't seem right that I should have it,' Catherine added, looking deeply flustered.

'Why ever not?'

'Because as you've already mentioned it belonged to Edwina, which means it's also very special.'

'Exactly,' Rod whispered, closing her fingers gently around the frog. 'And you're very special too, Catherine. Didn't you say only moments ago that you also share Edwina's name? That can't be purely coincidence. To me that makes this gift even more significant. Just look at the lid of the box.'

Prising her fingers free from Rod's grasp, Catherine examined the faded gilt lettering. Yes, she supposed in a way he could be right. Though not sure what had been there originally, two letters still remained. An intertwined C and E.

'Cedric had everything he ever bought Edwina engraved with their two initials, such was his devotion,' Rod explained. 'As far as I'm concerned that's fate, Catherine. Those initials C and E could easily stand for Catherine Edwina. Which means this little frog can only ever belong to you. In fact, in the short space of time that I've known you, it's almost as if you're exactly like that piece of *millefiori*. You too have a special place and it's here in *my* heart.'

'Rod . . . I don't know what to say.'

'Then dare I suggest you say nothing at all,' came the murmured response as Rod's mouth closed lingeringly on hers.

15

Bleary eyed, Catherine padded from the bed and made her way to the window. The same window where she'd stood less than six hours ago waving Rod goodbye. Following the unexpected turn of events last night it was hardly surprising that she'd been unable to sleep. Now after several hours of tossing and turning, she decided she might as well get up and face the dawn.

Shivering, and grateful for the warmth of her bluebell pyjamas, Catherine trailed her fingers against the sun-bleached curtains. How strange to think that yesterday morning she'd drawn back heavy velvet drapes and fixed them in place with ornate silk tassels, whereas here it was faded chintz and matching tie-backs. Resolving to do something about all the curtains in the flat, that's if she decided to stay here long term, Catherine gave a wry smile. Even Mrs Bannister's discarded sunflowers would look a great deal more welcoming. Thank goodness she hadn't brought Rod into the bedroom. Although, and blushing at the very thought of it, if she was to be perfectly honest with herself, the temptation to do so had been palpable. A temptation that she now acknowledged had never existed in quite the same way with Jason. How glad she was she'd never succumbed completely to her ex-boyfriend's charm and persistent cajoling.

Briefly reminded of Jason and Coral's duplicity, Catherine felt a brief wave of anger flood over her. Moments later, however, and feeling less enraged, she attempted a more benevolent frame of mind. Though Jason had purported to have loved her, he obviously hadn't loved her enough to wait for what Catherine had often referred to as 'the right moment'. How ironic, therefore, that her chosen *right moment* was to have been on her twenty-first birthday, the very day she found Jason and Coral together. Catherine bit her lip and closed her eyes, almost as if hoping to shut out the painful and cruel discovery: her boyfriend and her supposed best friend (whom as it turned out was acquiring quite a reputation as what fellow students called a 'bed-hopper') naked and in her bed!

Giving silent thanks for her tutor's bout of flu on that fateful day (resulting in the cancellation of the afternoon's lecture), Catherine opened her eyes once more and gazed out of the window. How wonderful it would have been to see Rod's car parked in the street below. Instead, he no doubt was sleeping soundly in his heavily carved tester bed (furnished with monogrammed bed linen and finest merino wool blankets) whilst Catherine's single divan resembled the aftermath of a pillow fight. Retrieving one nocturnally discarded pillow from the floor, she plumped up the other, straightened the crumpled bottom sheet and folded back her duvet. No wonder she'd slept so badly. What on earth had she been thinking about — or more to the point, dreaming about — to have left her bed in such disarray? The answer to her first question was immediate. There was only one thing she could have been thinking about and that was Rod's declaration of love. As for what she'd been dreaming about, she hadn't a clue. She supposed she could have been dancing on the table.

Heading from the bedroom to the bath-room, she faced her reflection in the mirror. She might not have had two glasses of wine or sherry but she'd certainly had far too many cups of coffee. To the extent she'd probably gone to bed with eight pints of caffeine in her veins. No wonder she'd had such a troubled sleep.

Equally restless was Rod. Pacing the corridors at Whycham Hall, half of him was still with Catherine at her flat, while the other half was telling himself to pack his belongings and head back to London before the Easter Monday snarl-up on the roads. The only problem being he didn't want to go back to London. He wanted to stay here.

Hearing the grandfather clock in the hall strike six, Rod raced down to the kitchen with his briefcase. If he wasn't careful, Mrs Bailey would be putting in an appearance before too long. And if she saw the untouched supper tray, she might start jumping to all the wrong conclusions. Certainly, he had arrived back at the hall far later than anticipated, but two less-than-comfortable fireside chairs were hardly conducive for a romantic *soirée à deux*. Nevertheless, Rod thought, pondering the problem of what to do with a ham salad, a slice of fruit cake, an apple and a banana, it had still turned out to be a very pleasant evening. To his immense relief, once she'd recovered from his shock proclamation, Catherine hadn't laughed in his face when he'd expressed his feelings of love for her. Quite the contrary, in fact, she'd even responded to his kisses.

Deeply pensive, Rod rubbed a hand across his chin and shook his head. At any other time a situation like that could quite easily have ended up in the bedroom. Thank goodness it hadn't and that he'd also had the self-control to recognize the warning signals. Catherine deserved better than that. She was, without doubt, completely different from any girl he'd ever met before.

Busily wrapping the apple, banana and fruit cake in clingfilm and secreting them in his briefcase, Rod looked up to see his housekeeper stepping from her cottage door. What on earth should he do now? In a matter of moments she would arrive to find him confronting a plate of ham salad.

'Good morning, Mrs Bailey. Er . . . as you can see I wasn't very hungry,' he faltered.

'Not to worry, sir. At least you had the fruit. You know what they say about having your five portions a day.'

'Oh, I think I had far more than that yesterday.'

Only too aware that his choice of words could have been completely misconstrued, Rod continued, hurriedly. 'I always do when I'm in Norfolk. It's when I'm in London I let things slip as far as fruit and veg are concerned.'

'Then I'd better make sure you have a decent lunch before you leave. I take it you are still going back to town today? And don't worry about this,' Emmy said, removing the uneaten salad. 'Nothing gets wasted around here. What the chickens and birds don't eat always gets put on the compost heap.'

Rod breathed a huge sigh of relief when Mrs Bailey turned to leave the kitchen. For one truly awful moment he'd been expecting a Henrietta-type lecture. His sister was forever reminding him of the thousands of starving people in the world. Only yesterday, Damian had broached a similar topic of conversation. At the time, Rod had considered it slightly hypocritical. Ten minutes later, however (just as they were tucking into roast beef and Yorkshire pudding), Damian had confessed an ulterior motive for serving the proverbial fatted calf. He'd asked Rod if he'd care to offer his support in any way for the village he was sponsoring in Africa.

Checking to see that his briefcase was shut, Rod waited for Mrs Bailey's return. Now then,' she said, beaming. 'What can I get you for breakfast? Or is it too early to think of bacon and eggs?'

Rod nodded; for the moment he'd rather have a stroll round the estate. There were certain buildings he needed to make note of before returning to London. Reminded of the details from the Norwich estate agents, the proposed business lunch with Henry Davenport (Francesca's father) and also his own father later in the week, he opted to delay breakfast.

'Shall I just make you your usual pot of coffee before you set off, or even do you a flask?' Emmy queried, seeing Rod had placed his Barbour and wellingtons by the back door. 'You might be glad of something warm inside you. It's still very damp out there after all that rain last night.'

Coffee! Rod couldn't think of anything worse. Following last night's coffee consumption, he was now on a par with his father. 'No thanks, Mrs Bailey. I think I'll pass on the coffee for the moment. Tell you what, bearing in mind what you were saying earlier about five portions a day, why don't I take a couple of apples with me instead? When I get back, if you could see your way to making me a pot of Assam and some scrambled eggs and bacon, that would be wonderful.'

'Right you are, sir,' came the reply as Rod emerged into the misty morning.

Happy to be alone with his thoughts, Rod surveyed the nearby cottages, estate office, stable block and outhouses within the immediate vicinity. That completed and numerous photos taken, he then ventured further afield in the Range Rover, surprised to find so many buildings with connections to Whycham Hall. Having been taken on a detailed tour by Mr Hayes when he'd first inherited the estate, it was only now that the immense size of it was beginning to sink in. All those empty barns on the periphery and why had this row of four cottages that he was approaching been left to fall into such a state of disrepair? Anxious to explore further, Rod turned off the road in the direction of the abandoned dwellings.

Having spent nine years working for his father at Marchant Holdings, in addition to innumerable conversations and site visits with Henry Davenport, Rod knew only too well the dangers of venturing into derelict buildings alone. Nevertheless, his curiosity was still getting the better of him.

'Damn!' he hissed, stepping down from the Range Rover, when a splash of gold and green caught his eye. Mrs Bannister's sunflowers had only served to remind him there was no safety helmet in the car. His own safety helmet — sunflower yellow and complete with *Marchant Holdings* in leaf-green lettering — was sitting on a shelf in his office. Making a mental note to bring it the next time he came (no, better still, bring three — he wanted his father and Henry to see this particular plot), Rod pushed aside a rotting front gate and stepped warily through the overgrown garden towards the nearest cottage door.

Instantly reminded of the ubiquitous

Marjorie Allingham cottage illustrations that appeared on birthday cards and calendars (a great favourite with his mother), Rod tried the first of the four front doors. To his dismay it wouldn't budge.

'Probably just as well,' he told himself, trying the remaining three tarnished door handles. 'If this was London, the place would probably be overrun with squatters or, even worse, drug addicts. Either that or every pane of glass would have been smashed to smithereens.'

Taking a couple of steps back in order to take yet more photos and examine each and every window, Rod nodded approval. Not a single one showed any sign of vandalism. A bit of weather damage, perhaps, but with some new putty, a couple of coats of weather-proof paint, replacement period window catches and . . . With his imagination running into overdrive, Rod was even more desperate than before to see inside these cottages. OK, so it wouldn't take more than a swift tap at one of the downstairs windows with something solid but that would have been sacrilege. What was it their old family doctor used to say? 'If it ain't broke don't fix it.'

Hmm. Maybe not a good idea, he thought, kicking aside the broken fence post he'd had in mind as *something solid*. At the same time, however, he still might be able to find a way inside if he went round to the rear.

Having no luck with each of the back doors, Rod contented himself with rubbing at all but one of the ground-floor windows with his handkerchief. As a result, it wasn't long before today's handkerchief was even more grubby than the one he'd used for Daisy's chocolate-covered fingers. He also noticed that his Barbour and moleskin trousers were now covered in an assortment of dead insects, spiders' webs and ivy. Rod chuckled quietly to himself; Francesca would positively hate it here. In addition to the safety helmets, he thought, coming face to face with a huge house spider, maybe some J-cloths and the odd empty jam jar wouldn't go amiss either.

Surprised when the spider disappeared completely from view, Rod felt his heart soar. The very same creature suddenly appeared on the inside windowsill. To his delight, a quick examination of the final window, not to have received the attention of his handkerchief, yielded at the slightest touch of his fingers. In a matter of moments he dashed back to the 4×4, grabbed one of the infamous curtains and, placing it across the assorted debris and broken window catch (the last thing he wanted was torn trousers), heaved himself inside.

'Oh, if only Catherine were here,' he sighed, directing his comment to the eight-legged squatter. 'To begin with she'd make sure you were taken somewhere safe, while fixing me with one of her mischievous smiles and declare that I'm learning fast. Curtains aren't just for hanging at windows!' Warmed by the reminder of yesterday evening and wishing once more that Catherine was here to share the hidden treasures of these isolated cottages, Rod stared about him in the semi-gloom. On a clear day, of course, the sun would come streaming through the windows. Today, that was not the case. The heavy skies outside were as dreary as the soot-blackened, cream-tiled hearth.

Still conscious of the safety aspect of examining the rest of the cottage alone, Rod erred on the side of caution. The exterior walls of these four dwellings (presumably once estate workers' cottages) might have been constructed from sturdy Norfolk flint, and their overhead beams hewn from old English oak, but even at Whycham Hall a recent survey had shown isolated traces of woodworm. Why should here be any different? As if to prove a point, Rod opened a nearby cupboard and dislodged the bottom shelf. One look at the tell-tale dust, settling on rose-patterned lining paper below, was all the evidence he needed. Today he would not be risking the stairs.

Whether or not it was from the sudden pangs of hunger gnawing away at his stomach, Rod found himself thinking of another set of stairs. The stairs leading to Catherine's flat and the welcoming aroma of coffee. Now despite having declined Mrs Bailey's earlier offer, anything, even a cup of coffee, would be acceptable. You're certainly not going to find it here, Rod old chap, he told himself. Exactly like that children's nursery rhyme, the cupboards are bare. Old Mother Hubbard would be wringing her hands in despair and her dog whining pitifully, a bit like little Daisy Barnes, desperate to reach those Easter eggs. Easter eggs! Rod's face brightened as he squeezed his way back through the open window and retrieved the curtain. He might not have any Easter eggs in his pocket but he did have a couple of apples.

Consuming his al fresco two out of five, Rod secured the window back in place as best he could and set off down the garden path. It was only when he neared the Range Rover that he turned for one last lingering look. Yes, his earlier gut instincts had been right. There was no end to the list of possibilities for the empty buildings he'd come across this morning. As for Henry Davenport's reaction, that could be echoed by his favourite saying as he scoured the countryside looking for suitable sites to develop. *'Get in there quick, make a killing, tart it up, hear the cash registers ringing.'*

Far from happy with the Davenport approach to property development (Marchant Holdings would never operate like that), Rod nevertheless found Henry's ditty ringing annoyingly in his ears. So much so that he narrowly avoided making a killing of his own when a frog leapt out from the grass beneath his feet. Unsure as to whom had been the most startled, man or frog, Rod fixed the tiny amphibian with an inquisitive smile. 'It's OK. I know what you're thinking, especially as Catherine's probably sent you to keep an eye on me. Rest assured, I shan't be building any tower blocks here.'

★   ★   ★

Much to Mrs Bailey's surprise, Rod opted for breakfast in the kitchen. As he explained, pulling off his wellingtons and hanging up his Barbour, he was far too hungry to wait any longer. He also had no intention of spoiling Cedric and Edwina's magnificent set of dining chairs with his muddied trousers.

'Of course that's only if you don't mind. I promise not to get in your way,' he told Emmy, still reeling from the shock of seeing him wash his hands at the kitchen sink before sitting down at the kitchen table. Her previous employer would never have sat down to eat here. On reflection, Mr Erskine hardly ever came into the kitchen at all.

'N-no. I'll see to it right away, sir. As for getting in my way, that's not a problem. I prepared the chicken casserole yesterday and I've only the vegetables to finish off.'

Newly breakfasted, Rod emitted a deep sigh of satisfaction and patted his stomach. 'If only I could take you back to London with me, Mrs B. I don't suppose you'd fancy it, would you?'

Emmy shook her head, knowing he was only half serious. 'I'm afraid not, Master Roderick. Apart from the time I was living in married quarters, I've never lived anywhere other than Whycham le Cley. Like a lot of folks round here, and my parents before me, I was born here and expect to die here. London's not for the likes of us.'

'By 'us' do you also mean Catherine?' Rod ventured. If only he could get Mrs Bailey to divulge a bit more of her niece's past. He was convinced there was something he still didn't know.

Emmy, however, would not be drawn. It hadn't escaped her notice that Mr Marchant had arrived home far later than expected last night. A light sleeper, the sound of his car and the accompanied sweep of headlights across her bedroom ceiling were more than enough to arouse her suspicions. If she was to be perfectly honest, nothing would make her happier than to see Catherine and Rod together as a couple, perhaps even living here full-time at Whycham Hall. That was only if Master Roderick's intentions were honourable. As for her niece living in London, of that she wasn't sure. Besides, Emmy thought through clenched teeth as she reached for the vegetable peeler, by rights Catherine belonged here anyhow. Wasn't she the rightful heir to the Whycham estate?

Sensing her non-cooperation and spying her unusually determined set of jaw, Rod rose from the table. 'Oh, well, best get on, I suppose. I've heaps of paperwork to do before leaving this afternoon. If anybody calls I shall be in the study.'

Reminded that Rod still hadn't had his usual pot of coffee, and that perhaps she'd been less than polite, Emmy called after him. 'What about coffee, sir? Shall I bring you a pot later?'

'No, thank you, Mrs B. As I mentioned

earlier, I'm giving coffee a miss today. However, if you could take the sherry decanter and a couple of glasses into the drawing-room at twelve o'clock.'

'You're expecting a visitor?' Emmy asked, dropping the potato she was peeling. She'd not been told about an extra guest for lunch.

'No,' Rod replied, flashing her a winning smile. 'But I'd like you to join me for a glass of sherry beforehand.'

★ ★ ★

As instructed, Emmy took the sherry and two glasses into the drawing-room dead on the dot of twelve noon, where Rod was already waiting. Dressed in navy blue slacks, pale blue shirt and a navy blue guernsey, he looked a great deal cleaner than when she'd last seen him. One look at his still-damp hair and the underlying smell of his aftershave was enough to tell her that as well as dealing with his paperwork he'd also dealt with the removal of Whycham le Cley flora and fauna *collected* on his early morning walk. If only she was forty years younger!

Conscious of Mrs Bailey's eyes on his sweater, Rod poured out two glasses of sherry. 'My sister says I always look as if I'm going sailing whenever I wear this guernsey.

224

She even joked about me buying a boat on The Broads. My excuse is that it's the ideal thing to wear when it's cold and damp. Personally, I think Henrietta would quite like it for herself. I gather it gets a bit nippy in Nepal. Perhaps I should give it to her the next time she comes over. In the meantime, I suppose you could say I'll be sailing back to London after lunch.'

Almost wishing that he wasn't, particularly from her niece's point of view, Emmy accepted her glass of sherry, unsure whether or not to sit or remain standing. As if reading her mind, Rod motioned her to an armchair. What was it Catherine had said? Two glasses of wine or sherry and she'd be dancing on the table. If only the same applied to her aunt. Not that he was expecting Mrs Bailey to do any dancing, he acknowledged, momentarily consumed with guilt for his ulterior motives.

Ever since he'd first arrived at Whycham Hall, he really had been full of good intentions to invite the few members of staff in for drinks. Today it was only one particular member of staff (if you could call her staff?) that he was interested in. His housekeeper's niece — Catherine Wickham.

Exchanging general chit-chat about Cedric and Edwina and the day-to-day running of the estate, Rod soon stepped forward to refill

Emmy's glass. 'I won't have another, because I'm driving,' he explained, when she put up her hand to protest. 'And if that delicious smell wafting from the direction of the kitchen is anything to go by, I shall assume lunch is well and truly under control. In my book that means you're entitled to another glass, Mrs Bailey. Don't forget, with me out of the way this afternoon you'll soon have the place to yourself again and . . . '

'That doesn't mean I'd take liberties,' Emmy began, mildly affronted.

'No. No, of course not,' Rod said, cursing his clumsiness. 'I was thinking more in the direction of you and Catherine getting together to discuss the May Day celebrations. Damian and I would be most grateful for any input on your behalf. Incidentally, have your . . . er . . . spoken to Catherine today?'

Emmy nodded and took another sip of sherry. Yes, she had spoken with her but other than telling her aunt that Rod had kindly carried her bag all the way upstairs to the flat and that she'd invited him in for coffee, Catherine had sounded distinctly cagey. Perhaps if Emmy herself were to steer the conversation away from the May Day festivities and back to her niece, she might become somewhat the wiser.

Twenty minutes later, Rod and Emmy

faced one another across the room, each one deeply satisfied with how the conversation was developing. Rod had told Mrs Bailey about the gift of the Murano glass frog, for the simple reason he hadn't wanted her to think it had gone missing from the dressing table in Edwina's bedroom. She in turn had begun to tell him all about Catherine's ex-boyfriend.

'The trouble with Catherine is that she's far too trusting,' Emmy declared, placing her half-empty glass upon the coffee table. 'Of course, I never liked that Coral from the moment I first set eyes on her. A skinny little thing and as hard and as prickly as that horrid lump of white coral gracing Mrs Bannister's mantelpiece. A present from Cornwall, I think she said. Yes, that's right, cos her niece also sent her a Cornish pixie. Anyway . . . where was I?'

'Telling me about your niece, Catherine and her friend, Coral.'

'Friend!' Emmy snorted. 'That wretched creature was never a friend. All that pretending to be nice when behind her back she was just using Catherine. Do you know what really makes me angry, Mr Marchant?'

Rod shook his head, willing her to continue. Pausing for a moment, Emmy took another sip of sherry and looked behind her as if making sure no one else was in the room. 'Well, just after Catherine had helped that so-called friend of hers out of a very sticky situation — I won't go into details because it's far too sordid, let's just say it involved a married man — Catherine received a card from her professing undying gratitude that ended with the line, 'I hope I never take your friendship for granted'.'

'And?' Rod said, slightly puzzled, trying to work out the significance of such a statement.

Draining her glass, Emmy stood up, her face flushed from a combination of anger and sherry. 'Isn't that obvious? If you had a good friend who you claimed to love and care for, would it even cross your mind to write something like that? '*I hope I never take your friendship for granted.*' Deep down, I reckon that little trollop knew herself to be a liar and a cheat and utterly untrustworthy. All I can say is thank God Catherine found out about her and Jason before it was too late. No wonder it's taken the poor girl so long to get over it.'

'Thank God, indeed,' Rod murmured to himself, watching Emmy totter somewhat unsteadily towards the kitchen. Hmm, as well as their devotion to the hall and Whycham le Cley itself, that was something else niece and aunt both shared. A desire for social justice and an uncommon reaction to two glasses of sherry.

'Mrs Bailey,' Rod called out. 'I knew there was something I've been meaning to ask you. What you were saying earlier about your family being born here. As Catherine's already told me about the young man commemorated on the village war memorial, I was wondering . . . have you ever thought of tracing your ancestors? It seems to be all the rage at the moment.'

With one hand on the kitchen door, Emmy turned back to face him. Fortunately, her earlier rage had dissipated, and her expression altered to one of serene calm. 'Trace our ancestors, Master Roderick? Why, there's no need for that. Anyone round here will tell you my father's side of the family is related to the earliest occupants of Whycham Hall. In fact, if it hadn't been for Queen Victoria and some stupid rules concerning male inheritance and death duties, Catherine would be mistress of Whycham Hall. I'm surprised she's never told you.'

★   ★   ★

Clearing away the remains of lunch, Emmy still couldn't believe her boldness. Not only had she drunk two glasses of rather potent

229

amontillado sherry (her nose was still tingling) but also she'd been far too outspoken when talking about her niece. Thank heavens Catherine hadn't been here to witness her aunt's outpourings of anger and indignation. Though if she had, no doubt none of it would have happened. What would Catherine say if she knew? Worse still, what must Mr Marchant be thinking of her? Telling herself that she must now remain completely teetotal — at least until Christmas, Emmy reached for the kettle and a jar of Nescafé. Master Roderick might have declined coffee today but she most definitely needed one. And it had better be black!

16

Four months later, Rod picked up a bulky envelope containing photographs and made his way to a Chelsea wine bar. In the past few months he'd seen less and less of his London friends and more and more of Whycham le Cley and above all, Catherine. Further proof (as if it was needed) that he'd be far happier living in Norfolk with the woman he loved. The only problem now was how to go about it. So far his father had been extremely understanding in relation to the amount of time he was spending away from the London office. How long would he be allowed to take liberties?

Usually, one to leave the latest in information technology to his son, it was Charles Marchant himself who eventually recommended taking the twenty-first century to Whycham Hall. As a result, the latest state-of-the-art PCs, flat screens, USB flash drives and multi-functional compact units had been installed in Great Uncle Cedric's old study without detracting too much from the original decor.

Passing an extremely swish five-star hotel

(famous for its penthouse suite and spa), Rod thought how good it would be to bring Catherine here for an entire weekend of unadulterated luxury. As yet they hadn't consummated their love, not through lack of desire but more from lack of the appropriate setting. At Whycham Hall, Catherine was always conscious of Aunt Em's presence and, as they'd recently discovered to their embarrassment, her bed and the L-shaped room at her flat was hardly suited to a night of romance. In an attempt at sparing her blushes, Rod even joked Queen Victoria had probably slept there too. It was thinking of Queen Victoria that prompted Rod to recall Mrs Bailey's startling revelation: her niece's rightful claim to the Whycham Estate. How very appropriate and satisfying, therefore, that he would be installing his future bride-to-be as mistress of Whycham Hall.

At least you will once you've officially proposed, bought her an engagement ring and set the wedding date, his other self reminded, when a sudden flash of diamonds from a nearby jeweller's caught his attention. Regrettably, also to catch his attention was the sight of Jeremy and Francesca, stepping from a taxi, up ahead. Highly relieved they hadn't seen him, Rod paused to look at several trays of eye-catching diamond solitaires, clusters and huge sapphires. The first favoured by footballers' wives and the latter by royals. Convinced Catherine wouldn't want anything quite so ostentatious, Rod recalled to mind Great Aunt Edwina's engagement ring: an exquisitely fine, square-cut emerald, set on either side by a tasteful solitaire.

'Of course! What could be more perfect,' Rod murmured to himself. With Catherine's eyes and colouring, it could only be emeralds for his precious jewel. As for the showy and extremely ugly diamond rings (at least in his opinion) glinting before him, there was only one person he knew who'd delight in flaunting something of that size on her engagement finger. She was waiting with the rest of the gang in the wine bar.

'Roddy dahling! Where have you been? We've been waiting here for simply ages.'

Knowing that wasn't entirely true, Rod subjected himself to a kiss on both cheeks from Francesca before reaching across the table to shake Jeremy's hand.

'Rodders, old chap! We'd almost given up and thought you weren't coming. Someone even suggested you might have got run over by a tractor or else buried beneath a pile of slurry.'

Francesca sniffed the air appreciatively. 'Thank God he doesn't smell of farmyards at the moment. Unless I'm losing my touch I'd say that was definitely Caroline Herrera aftershave and not eau du silage.'

Feigning amusement, Rod acknowledged the rest of the group and made his way to the bar making sure that when he returned he sat next to anyone other than Francesca. An hour and a half later he looked at his watch, announced that he ought to be leaving and produced the envelope of photos from his pocket. 'Would you mind giving these to your father?' he said, passing half of them across to Francesca.

'Of course, dahling. I take it you do know he's in Manchester until the end of the week, so I hope these aren't important.'

'Yes I did and no they're not,' Rod replied. 'They're only extra copies of the cottages and barns at Whycham le Cley. He said he'd like to see them.'

Also curious to see the photos, particularly as Francesca was still pondering Rod's reply and not in any hurry to pick them up, Jeremy reached out and spread them over the table. 'Manchester, Franny. Good Lord! What's your pater doing in Manchester? I wouldn't have thought that was quite Henry's scene.'

'That's where you're wrong, Jeremy dear,'

Francesca drawled, lazily. 'Daddy's making quite a killing up there at the moment. Did you know there are places where you can pick up a three-bedroom house for less than twenty thousand pounds?'

'Bloody hell! You've got to be joking.'

Francesca shook her head and drained her spritzer. 'No. I'm not. In fact, only last night when Daddy rang, he was convinced that if he played his cards right he'd be picking up a row of terraced houses for half a million. I might not know much about this property lark but you ask Roddy. He'll tell you it's true.'

Rod cleared his throat when all eyes turned in his direction. 'Henry was saying there's quite a slump in the Manchester property market at the moment, which means it could also be a good time to speculate.'

Shifting uneasily in his seat while those around him did some verbal speculation of their own, Rod was happy to withdraw from this topic of conversation. For some considerable time both he and his father had chosen to extricate themselves completely from the Henry Davenport way of doing business. While it was common knowledge there was plenty of money to be made in both property management and development, everything at Marchant Associates was very much above board and within the law. Henry, on the other hand, always managed to find a way of bending it a little.

Gathering together the photos and bending them a little, Jeremy gave a low whistle. 'Jesus! If all these properties are part of the Whycham Estate, Rodders old chap, then you my friend are sitting on a little goldmine. You'd have to pay a darned sight more than twenty thousand for one of these terraced cottages. As for the barns . . . '

Deeply embarrassed and longing to get away, Rod interrupted, 'Don't be fooled by what you see on the photos. Structurally, those cottages and barns aren't too bad. Inside it's quite another story. They need a hell of a lot of work.'

'Even so,' came a voice by his side. 'Once the cottages have been tarted up and those barns subjected to one of those pretty amazing makeover/conversion thingies you see on TV, you'll be worth an absolute fortune — that's if you're not already. What will you do, rent them out as holiday homes or sell them to commuters? Only last week I had lunch with a couple of chaps who've decided to commute from Norwich to London.'

'I'm not sure,' Rod said, preparing to put the rest of the photos back in his pocket.

Anxious not to miss out on anything concerning the monetary aspect of Rod's inheritance, Francesca stretched out her hand. 'What have you got there then, more cottages?'

'I don't think you'd be interested in these, Francesca. It's only the village May Day celebrations.'

'Definitely not,' Francesca sneered. 'Seeing a group of country yokels dancing round a maypole is hardly riveting stuff, is it?'

'Actually, it was a very enjoyable occasion. The children each made floral displays, for which there was a competition. Then, they all lined up on either side of the maypole waiting for the May Queen to arrive before performing a dance in her honour.'

Reminded of a beauty queen pageant he'd seen recently on terrestrial TV, Jeremy pricked up his ears. 'May Queen, eh? I don't suppose that little dairy maid of yours was part of the proceedings to perform a dance in your honour?'

'If you mean Catherine,' Rod bristled, 'no, she wasn't. The May Queen has to attend the village school.'

'Not only that,' Francesca broke in. 'Aren't May Queens supposed to be fair-haired and blue-eyed? As Cathy's got ginger hair, she's hardly got the right credentials.'

About to say it's Catherine not Cathy and that her hair was the colour of burnished copper not ginger, Rod grew even more angry when Jeremy chortled, 'I don't know about that, Franny. From what I saw of the little poppet, I thought her credentials were pretty spot on. I expect Rodders does too.'

Somewhat put out and anxious to change the subject, Francesca snatched the May Day photos from Rod's grasp. 'Oh, all right. I suppose you'd better show us then. Just who was the May Queen?'

Counting to ten beneath his breath, Rod flicked through the photos, all the while asking himself how could he have spent so much time in the presence of these people seated here tonight. Was it himself who had changed or them? Or was it simply the fact that he'd been spending so much time amongst decent, ordinary village folk that Jeremy and Francesca now appeared like some horrible caricatures of the friends he'd once known? Regarding an assortment of discarded bottles and empty glasses on the table, he tried to make excuses for them. Perhaps they'd all had far too much to drink. All that is except himself, who like Catherine and her aunt had decided two glasses of wine were more than enough.

'This was our May Queen,' Rod said,

through tight lips, passing Francesca the relevant photograph.

'There, you see!' she announced, triumphant. 'What did I say? A fair-haired, blue-eyed May Queen. Perfect! Not like that peculiar little creature holding the stick with the flowers on. Why is it that kids with ginger hair and freckles always look so ugly?'

Trying to conceal his exasperation, Rod retrieved the photo. 'That's Daisy Barnes, my gardener's youngest granddaughter. Far from being ugly, she's an absolute delight and one of the most enchanting children I've ever met.' Placing special emphasis on the word *children* (he hated it when adults called them kids), Rod decided against trying to explain the significance of the *flowers on sticks*. What was the point? Anyone could see they weren't at all interested.

Refusing to give in to their requests to go on to a night club, Rod was adamant. Not only was he going back to his flat but also he was going alone! No amount of pleading on Francesca's part would make him change his mind.

'It's not fair. I've scarcely seen anything of you for weeks,' she simpered. 'Whenever I ring you're always busy. Either that or never at home.'

'That's hardly surprising when I'm trying

239

to be in two places at once. Believe me, Francesca, it's not easy having to divide my time between Marchant Associates and Whycham le Cley.'

Happy to dismiss any further mention of such a dreary place, Francesca turned her thoughts elsewhere. In this instance, Rod's Docklands flat. Hard as she'd tried, she'd never succeeded in spending a night there. Sidling up to him, she placed a hand on his arm and cooed, 'Poor Roddy. How tiresome of me not to have realized before. Of course you don't want to go clubbing. Come to think of it, neither do I. Why don't we just say goodnight to the others and go back to your flat? As for what you were saying earlier, about dividing your time between Norfolk and the office, just think what fun we could have with me giving you *my* undivided attention.'

Always careful to avoid such a prospect, Rod remembered only too well how he'd been tricked into taking Francesca to Norfolk. On the other hand, if Francesca hadn't pestered him into going to the hall before Easter (as originally planned) or been driving like an idiot, he might never have come across Catherine, ankle-deep in the ford. Filled with a warm glow as he relived that never-to-be-forgotten moment, Francesca mistook Rod's subsequent thoughtful smile as a 'yes'.

'Good. That's settled, then. Shall we go?'

'Go?' Rod, asked, shaking his arm free from Francesca's grasp. 'Go where?'

'Your flat, dahling.'

Realizing that Jeremy and the others were already making their way to the door, Rod knew he had to act quickly. 'I'm sorry, Francesca. I think somewhere along the line we've got our wires crossed. I know we've known each other for ages — what with you and my sister being in the same class together at school and even our fathers being in a similar line of business — but I thought I explained months ago there can never be anything other than friendship between us.'

'Yes, you did. And, as you described most correctly, it was months ago. Months and months ago, just before Henrietta left for Nepal, when she asked you to keep a brotherly eye on me.'

'Precisely. A brotherly eye,' Rod repeated. 'Which I did — '

'Most admirably,' Francesca said, stumbling against a table and clutching at his jacket sleeve. 'Can't you see, sweetie. I no longer need a brother, I need something else. I need a lover.'

A lover! Alarm bells rang in Rod's head at that moment. Unlike the harmonious bells of

St Andrew's welcoming him to Sunday service, these bells were of a more strident and discordant nature, filling him with a sense of dread. From where he was standing, it soon became painfully clear that Francesca had had far too much to drink. As for the original plan of going on to a nightclub . . . Unless she was putting on an act for his benefit, she was utterly incapable of making her way home on her own.

'Believe me, I'm truly sorry, Francesca,' Rod whispered as an aside, spying Jeremy and the others heading into the street. 'As for what you were suggesting . . . '

'Why can't I come back to your flat?' Francesca pleaded, her voice becoming louder as they all gathered on the pavement.

'Quite simply, old girl, because poor old Rodders here looks all in,' Jeremy announced, coming unwittingly to Rod's aid. 'In fact, in the last few minutes I'd say he's turned positively peaky. It must be all this travelling between two homes that's doing it. Either that or the glazed expression on his face is a result of him staying up half the night counting all his money.'

'Is it that obvious?' Rod said, forcing a smile, glad to have escaped from one very embarrassing situation. There was, unfortunately, still the delicate problem of Francesca, who appeared to be finding it even harder to stand upright. Again, Jeremy came to the rescue. Hailing an approaching taxi, he nodded to the others to go ahead on foot, held out a supporting arm and relieved Rod of his very unwelcome burden.

'Don't worry, old chap, I've been doing quite a bit of this in recent weeks. As you've probably gathered, Franny here had more than the odd sherbet or two before we arrived tonight. If it's all right with you I'll take this taxi and make sure she gets home safely before joining the others at the club. As for you, why not take yourself back home for a bit of shuteye. You look as if you could do with it.'

Completely oblivious to Francesca's tear-filled eyes as he bundled her carefully into the taxi, Jeremy gave the cabby her address, before leaving Rod standing on the pavement. Raising an arm in a gesture of farewell to the departing couple, it was several moments before Rod realized he was alone.

'My God! What an absolute nightmare,' he muttered, turning in the opposite direction.

Undecided whether or not to take a tube or a taxi, he opted for a combination of both, highly relieved when he eventually stepped off the Docklands light railway at Canary Wharf. Even there he half expected Francesca to appear from the shadows. Only when he was safely installed in the calm and tranquility of his flat did he allow himself to relax.

Shucking off his jacket and making his way to the bathroom, he doused his face with cold water, almost as if trying to rinse away the disturbing vision of Francesca getting into the taxi. Not only the disturbing vision, he reminded his reflection in the mirror; what alarmed him more was her almost public announcement that she wanted him for a lover. Rod shuddered at the very prospect. At that precise moment he couldn't think of anything worse.

'What you need is a drink, and a stiff one at that,' he told himself, dabbing at his face with a towel. Ten minutes later, with the lights dimmed and a favourite CD playing in the background, he turned away from the calming view across the Thames, and reached for a bottle of whisky and a heavy-based, cut-crystal tumbler.

'Steady on, old chap,' an inner voice rebuked. 'We don't want you dancing on the table at tomorrow's board meeting.'

Knowing there was absolutely no danger of that, Rod was reminded of the portfolio left on his bedside table. Hurrying to retrieve it, he caught sight of the original photo of Catherine and Daisy at the impromptu May

Day celebrations held in the grounds of Whycham Hall. As predicted there hadn't been that much time to arrange a full-scale May Day festival. Nevertheless, with Catherine's help the children had been taught how to dance round the maypole (without getting in too much of a tangle), the May Queen chosen (without too many tears of disappointment), the decorated floral pole judged fairly (he'd resisted the temptation to award Daisy first prize) and Mrs Bailey and her stalwart team of helpers (Mrs Barnes, Basford and Martindale) coming up trumps with an excellent tea for everybody.

How I miss you all, Rod thought, picking up the photo. Life seemed so very much simpler at Whycham le Cley, unless of course you were given the job of judging the competition for the best-decorated floral pole. Replacing the photograph, Rod picked up the portfolio and headed back to the open-plan living-room. Laughing quietly to himself, he remembered the morning he'd arrived back at Whycham Hall to find Daisy (accompanied by her grandad and Catherine) gazing longingly up at the wisteria.

'Please, mister, can I have some purple stuff for my stick?' Daisy had entreated. 'Grandad says we're not to pick the *hysteria* cos there's only three bits out. But I only want one and that still leaves a bit for you and Catherine.'

'Grown-ups won't be needing floral poles, Daisy,' Catherine had announced, meeting Rod's bewildered gaze, before going on to enlighten him. 'The children all make a floral decoration using a margarine tub, a small bamboo cane and — '

'An' Catherine's goin' to help me make mine,' Daisy said matter-of-factly, 'Cos Mum says she's far too busy. The twins are bein' little buggers at the moment.'

Trying hard not to laugh, Rod had sucked in his cheeks and bent down to lift Daisy high into his arms. 'Let's see, shall we? As you're only going to need one piece of wisteria and there's masses more to come into flower . . . Which one would you like, Daisy, or do you think we ought to ask Catherine to decide, especially as she's going to be helping?'

Daisy beamed from ear to ear; not only had she come up with the brilliant idea of asking Catherine to help her, Mister was going to let her have a piece of that purple stuff with the funny name, after all. 'See, Grandad,' she called back when both she and Catherine chose the same cluster of blossom, 'I told you Mister wouldn't mind. He's my friend.'

'Mr Marchant to you, young lady,' Mr Barnes corrected, trying to hide his embarrassment.

'And what about you? Do you mind?' Rod had asked Catherine when they'd headed off for lunch together. 'I know how strongly you feel about picking things from the garden.'

Kissing his cheek, Catherine had reached for his hand. 'In the circumstances I don't mind at all. As you say, there's still masses more to come. Promise me one thing, however. On no account are you to give Daisy first prize.'

'Why ever not?'

'Because she's at an unfair advantage. No one else will have anything quite so striking as *hysteria* for a centrepiece.'

In the end, it had been Polly Kazer, from Kazer's Farm who was chosen as the winner. Later, when they were having their picnic tea on the lawn, and Daisy was picking off hundreds and thousands from one of Aunt Em's iced buns, Catherine said softly, 'Daisy, I hope you weren't too disappointed that you didn't win.'

'Nope,' came the simple reply. 'Cos Mister's goin' to give me a running-up prize.'

About to say don't you mean the runner's-up prize, Catherine saw Rod hold a finger to his lips. 'Shh, Daisy. It's supposed to be our secret.'

Pausing with a blob of pink icing stuck to her finger, Daisy's face filled with alarm. Oh, dear! Mister was right; it was supposed to be a secret. At the same time, she also remembered the person who'd helped make the very pretty floral pole resting on the grass at her side. Shouldn't Catherine also share the running-up prize? The same *running-up* prize which resulted in Rod, Catherine and Daisy heading off in the Range Rover for another picnic when the wisteria was well and truly in bloom and all thoughts were turning to the next event at Whycham le Cley — the fête on August Bank Holiday Monday.

More than happy to have his attention diverted by Whycham wonders as opposed to Francesca's fatuous desires concerning their relationship, Rod opened up the folder containing the latest stock market figures. All extremely satisfying but hardly as warm and inviting as the figure he longed to hold in his arms.

17

'Mr Velvet's waiting for you in reception,' Janice called, popping her head round the office door at the library. 'I told him you'd be down in five minutes.'

Catherine looked up, unable to believe her ears. 'Rod? I thought he was still in London. What's he doing here?'

'Despite him being your very own Superman, and the fact that he wasn't wearing his pants over his trousers, I can only assume he left early to avoid the Friday afternoon snarl-up. You know what it's like at the start of Bank Holiday weekend.'

Thrilled at the prospect of seeing Rod earlier than anticipated, Catherine studied the piles of books on the table in front of her. They all needed to be sorted and catalogued. At the same time, there was still another week before the autumn term began. If she explained the situation to Janice and made a special point of coming in early next Tuesday morning . . .

'Don't even say it,' Janice began.

'What?'

'Catherine Wickham, stop being so bloody

conscientious. You've been here every day this week as it is. Leave what you're doing this minute and go and spend the afternoon with that gorgeous man of yours. As for coming in early next Tuesday morning . . . '

'How did you know that's what I was going to say?'

'Because I'm a genius. Added to which I not only love books and work with books, I've also been working with you long enough to read you like one.'

'You really don't mind me leaving now?'

'No, but it will cost you. I shall be expecting double helpings at that pig roast you're holding on Monday.'

'You're actually coming!' Catherine's face flushed with renewed delight. For weeks she'd been trying to persuade Janice and Dave to join in the Bank Holiday celebrations at Whycham le Cley. As usual (with most public holidays), Dave's parents were expecting their son and his wife for the entire weekend. This time Janice had decreed it would be different. Besides, as she'd told her husband only last night, when he'd produced and opened a nice little number from Chile, if Dave promised to explain the slight change of plan to his mother, she'd search out the other little number (decorated with ecru lace and pale pink rose buds) that he'd bought for her birthday. Her ploy had obviously worked.

'I think you deserve more than double helpings,' Catherine said, switching off her computer. 'Rod still can't thank you enough for introducing him to Romy Felden. Needless to say he's thrilled to bits she's agreed to open the fête.'

'And I'm thrilled to bits I'm going to be ogling Stephen Walker. But don't tell Dave, or he might subject me to an extra day with the SAPs instead.'

'SAPs?' Catherine puzzled.

'That's Sweet Aged Parents when they're being charming and Selfish Awkward Parents when they're not.'

Catherine looked up, a glimpse of sadness in her eyes. With fate being so cruel, her parents had never reached either stage.

'Catherine? Are you OK? You look sort of upset.'

'No, I'm fine, Janice. I was thinking about Mum and Dad and wishing they could have met Rod.'

'Speaking of meeting, have you met Rod's parents yet?'

'No, apparently they're arriving on Sunday evening. Luckily, I shan't be around as I'm helping with some of the costumes for the children's fancy dress parade and also decorating the village institute.'

'Why luckily?'

'Because I'm dreading meeting Mr and Mrs Marchant. I . . . er . . . don't actually know if Rod's told them about me yet.'

'As in telling them that he intends to marry you?'

'I'm not sure that he does. He still hasn't asked me, officially.'

'Rubbish!' Janice snorted. 'He's talked about it often enough, hasn't he? Anyway, how do you quantify officially?'

Giving a sigh, Catherine looked down to her engagement finger. 'I suppose a ring would be nice. Nothing too flashy, of course. Just something to prove that this isn't all a dream. Then again, as we haven't really known each other all that long, perhaps it is better to wait until we're both really sure.'

'Sweet Jesus! What am I going to do with you? You're sure and Rod's sure. And before you ask, I only have to see the way he looks at you or hear him mention your name whenever he rings, to know that he's head over heels in love with you. I'm only surprised the pair of you haven't yet — '

'Haven't what?'

'Well . . . you haven't, have you? I'd be able to tell if you had.'

Sparing Catherine's blushes, Janice refrained

from further comment, not altogether surprised when her friend replied, 'No, we haven't
. . . yet. Rod did suggest I go and stay at his
flat a couple of weeks ago but I declined. I
suppose I was worried that some of his old
friends might turn up unexpectedly.'

'Like that awful Francesca and Jeremy you
mentioned a while back.'

'Mmm, and with so much going on at
Whycham Hall at the moment there never
seems to be time for anything else.'

About to declare she certainly wouldn't
define making love as *anything else*, Janice
looked at the clock on the wall. 'Blimey!
Speaking of time, hadn't you better be going?
I told Rod you'd only be five minutes.
Knowing him he'll probably take you out to
lunch. Would you mind if I had that tuna and
mayo sandwich?'

Tossing the packet of sandwiches on to
Janice's desk, Catherine called back, 'Bye.
Have fun with the SAPs and I'll see you on
Monday.'

★   ★   ★

Rod raised his glass in Catherine's direction.
'Good. Now that we've decided what we're
having to eat, you'd better remind me. What's
the plan of attack for Monday?'

Reaching into her handbag for a copy of the timetable, Catherine reeled off the proposed order of events for Bank Holiday Monday. Beginning with the opening of the fête and judging of the children's fancy dress parade by Romy Felden, the day would draw to a close with a tug of war on the village green — with the unfortunate losers no doubt ending up in the village pond. A unanimous decision had also been taken for a brief interlude to allow for people to change (or dry out in the case of the tug-of-war team), have tea, put the children to bed and collect babysitters, before heading off to the barn dance in the institute.

'In between times,' Catherine continued, 'there'll be all the produce displays, assorted events organized for the children, the pig roast and of course Aunt Em and Mrs Basford doing their wonderful cream teas.'

'Don't forget my pre-barn-dance supper at the hall,' Rod reminded.

'As if I could. Particularly as you've asked me to do all the table decorations and place settings.'

Rod reached for Catherine's hand. 'You don't mind, do you? I know you've already got a hundred and one other things to do that day. I still think how nice it would be for families and friends to get together before the barn dance. You know . . . break the ice and that sort of thing.'

'Of course I don't mind. In fact I think it's a lovely idea, as long as it's only the ice that gets broken. It's going to be pretty cramped round the dining table with all the people you and Damian have invited. Even Mr and Mrs Erskine never had that many guests in the dining-room.'

Rod smiled indulgently. 'I had to think of some way of having you close by my side at some point during the day. From what you've been saying, we're going to be like ships that pass in the night.'

'Speaking of ships, your idea of a *Pirates of the Caribbean* theme for the barn dance went down extremely well with everyone who's bought tickets. With your looks, they're all expecting you to turn up as Johnny Depp's Captain Jack Sparrow.'

'Jack Sparrow. You've got to be joking! I was thinking of dressing up as a simple buccaneer.'

'Rod, darling. Nothing you do can ever be simple,' Catherine added shyly.

Rod swallowed hard, touched by the gentle way she'd called him darling. How different it sounded from Francesca's contrived 'Roddy dahling'. Preferring to concentrate more on his lunch, thus dismissing any further thoughts of Francesca to the back of his mind (at least she wouldn't be coming to Monday's fête), he saw Catherine scribble down an addition to her already long list of notes. 'Don't tell me you've forgotten something?'

'Not exactly. It's merely some last-minute bits and pieces from the craft shop for Daisy's flower costume. I'd planned to get them in my lunch hour but — '

'I came along and scuppered your plans.'

'That's a very appropriate turn of phrase. You see, you're already getting into Jack Sparrow mode. Now all you need is the eyeliner and the earrings.'

'Eyeliner and earrings? Heaven forbid!'

Leaving Catherine outside the craft shop, Rod made his way once more to Tyrrel and Robinson the estate agents. So far the information gleaned from their property management side of the business had been extremely helpful, especially in relation to holiday cottages. He'd also made some very useful contacts with a local firm who specialized in barn conversions.

Her errands completed, Catherine was surprised to see Rod emerge with yet another bulky envelope under his arm. Was he now having second thoughts about keeping the Whycham Estate in its entirety? Perhaps even to the extent of selling some of the outlying barns in need of extensive renovation? Telling herself she had no right to pry into his affairs, it was none of her business (as long as the village itself remained untouched), Catherine patted the carrier bag she was holding. 'At least I shan't be letting Daisy and her brothers down. This time I managed to find everything I wanted.'

'Daisy *and* her brothers? I thought it was only the girls who were interested in dressing up. Don't tell me the twins are going to be flowers?'

'No, while you were in London there was a slight change of plan to include the boys. The girls are going to be flowers and the boys insects.'

'I would imagine pests would be far more appropriate with regard to Brett and Carl,' Rod said, reminded of Daisy's somewhat forthright description of her younger brothers. 'I suppose I don't need to guess what Daisy is going to be.'

Catherine demurred, thinking back to the afternoon when Daisy and her grandad had come knocking at the door of Aunt Em's cottage. At the time she and Aunt Em had been working on a simple menu for Rod's pre-barn-dance supper. Once again it seemed Daisy's mum was far too busy to cope with the forthcoming project (and according to

Aunt Em utterly useless at sewing) so could Catherine please help instead? Especially as Daisy knew exactly what she wanted to be.

Following Rod's gaze to the crisp white organdie and yellow crêpe paper, visible from the corner of the carrier bag, Catherine merely nodded and smiled. 'Which reminds me, just in case you see Daisy before Monday, you are not to ask her about her costume. She says she wants it to be a surprise for Mister.'

'A surprise, with a name like Daisy,' Rod chuckled.

Once back at Whycham Hall, Catherine and Rod found Aunt Em dashing round like a thing possessed; her arms filled with freshly laundered linen and a wonderful aroma of home baking wafting from the kitchen. Surprised, because her niece and Master Roderick had arrived far earlier than expected, she also began to panic. She hadn't given any thought to an evening meal.

Leaving Rod to go and check the fax machine in his office, Catherine placed a reassuring arm about her aunt's shoulder. 'Don't worry, Aunt Em. Rod and I had a very substantial lunch. We'll only be wanting something light this evening. Wait a minute! Why don't I make us a fish pie, using Janice's recipe? And if Mr Barnes gives me a lettuce from the greenhouse and I persuade Rod to let me have a bottle of white wine from the cellar.'

Convinced there were umpteen last-minute details requiring Catherine's attention before Monday, Emmy shrugged her shoulders. 'Fish pie would certainly be very nice, but won't you be needed elsewhere?'

'If you mean Rod, as usual he's brought masses of paperwork home with him from London. He also collected a huge folder of information from Tyrrell and Robinson's.'

Emmy's face filled with renewed alarm. This time not from the burden of household chores but more from the rumours circulating about the village. 'Catherine . . . I know you and Master Roderick are very close and what you talk about when you're alone together is none of my business, but I don't suppose he's mentioned anything specific about his future plans for the estate, has he?'

Future plans? As far as Catherine knew, Rod wanted everything kept just as it was. OK, so he had been showing a great deal of interest in the empty barns and cottages on the periphery, and taking detailed photos of every occupied dwelling they'd come across within a fifteen-mile radius. At the same time, he was only too aware that renovating the vacant properties with a view to selling on to townies was an absolute anathema, at least as far as she was concerned.

'Aunt Em,' Catherine said, intrigued. 'You're looking worried. Is there a problem?'

'It depends what you mean by problem. For the moment it appears it's only rumours.'

'What's that supposed to mean?'

First checking on the trays of buns and scones in the oven, Emmy then looked towards the door into the hallway. Making sure it was securely closed she went and sat at the kitchen table.

'Oh, my dear I hardly dare tell you. According to Barry Martindale and even Mr Barnes, there's been all sorts of people traipsing through the village for the past couple of weeks.'

'That's not so unusual, is it? It is holiday time and we usually get a few holidaymakers or day-trippers at this time of year. We're even hoping some of them will come to the fête.'

'They're not day-trippers,' Emmy insisted. 'Since when have you seen day-trippers walking round taking measurements and consulting architects' drawings? Before you ask how do I know they were architects' drawings, Mr Barnes and Barry were in the Whycham Arms having a drink when a group of them turned up. Spread their plans all over the table, apparently. That's until their lunch arrived and they hid everything away from view.'

'I see,' Catherine said, without expression. Only she didn't really. Doubtless she'd like to think Rod and herself were so close that he'd take her into his confidence if he was planning anything out of the ordinary for Whycham le Cley. Then again, as she'd remarked to Janice only a few hours ago, although Rod had frequently referred to her as the love of his life, he still hadn't proposed.

Deciding to be completely philosophical, at least for the moment (especially with a fish pie to prepare and Daisy's and the twins' costumes to finish), Catherine's immediate concern was to reassure her aunt.

'As far as rumours go,' she said, holding up a pair of oven gloves, 'I'm convinced that's all they are. As for these scones and fruit buns, however, I'd say they're more than ready to come out of the oven.'

With a gasp, Emmy leapt up from her chair and made a grab for the oven gloves, all thoughts of strangers traipsing through the village forgotten. Passing her aunt a cooling tray, Catherine smiled diplomatically. 'If it will make you feel any better, once Rod's sorted through his faxes and emails, I'll see if I can have a quiet word with him. At the end of the day I'm sure we'll find it's all conjecture. Far better to clear the air now, don't you think? We certainly don't want anything to spoil Bank Holiday Monday.'

★ ★ ★

Down in the cellar, Catherine followed Rod along the quarry-tiled floors past seemingly endless racks of vintage wines and champagne.

'Goodness! Janice's Dave would be in his element down here,' Catherine said, marvelling at row after row of bottles.

'Really? Then perhaps I should give him a guided tour on Monday.'

'What a good idea. Particularly if you can arrange it while Janice is ogling Stephen Walker.'

Rod chewed his lip, reflectively. 'Hmm, and with me out of the way as well, will you also be doing a bit of ogling?'

'I think I'll be doing more than just a bit,' Catherine teased.

'And only moments ago there was me thinking you were being honest and true when you said you loved me,' Rod replied, pretending to be hurt. 'Now it seems you've not only got eyes for another man, you've also brought me down here under false pretences.

All you're really after is a bottle of my finest white for your fish pie.'

'It doesn't have to be your finest,' Catherine said, linking her arm in his. 'Only according to Janice, the better the wine the better the flavour for the sauce.'

Halting by a specific wine rack, Rod turned and drew out a bottle of 1986 Pouilly-Fumé Silex. 'Definitely not!' Catherine cried. 'That's far too good. I'm only making a fish pie.'

'Nothing's too good for you,' Rod said, slipping the bottle carefully back in place.

Catherine tilted her head to one side. 'Really. That's very kind of you to say so. But am I good for you?'

Pulling her into his arms, Rod stroked her hair and murmured softly in her ear. 'Oh, yes. Absolutely. If only there was a nice comfortable bed down here, instead of all this wine. I don't suppose you know where there's a spare mattress, do you? At least this is one place where we could really be alone.'

'Cheek!' Catherine said, digging him playfully in the ribs. 'All this time I've been saving myself for you and that promised weekend of unadulterated luxury. Now all you're offering is a mattress on the floor in a musty old wine cellar.'

Rod's eyes glinted wickedly as he rubbed

his side. Turning, he kissed the tip of her nose. 'That's because you're worth it and I know you don't mind spiders.'

'Hmph! Thank you very much.'

Emitting a long, drawn-out groan, Rod drew her back into his arms. 'Oh, my love. Believe me, at this very moment I can think of nothing I'd like more than to whisk you away to somewhere truly romantic.'

Catherine fixed him with a wan smile, wishing if only that that were possible. 'You certainly pick your moments, Mr Marchant. With umpteen people descending on Whycham le Cley this weekend, we can hardly go and confront Damian and Aunt Em with the news that we're heading off to Venice or — '

'Would you like to go to Venice?'

'Yes, very much. Isn't that where Edwina's little frog came from?'

'Then that's where we'll go for our honeymoon.'

About to remind him they still weren't officially engaged so hardly in the position to make plans for a wedding, let alone honeymoon, Catherine advised, 'For the moment can I suggest you concentrate more on the weekend ahead. Far from cruising down the Grand Canal, if you're not in the winning tug-of-war team on Monday after-noon, you'll be waist deep in the village pond!'

Determined to go for a workout and a jog round the estate before supper, Rod reached for a 2002 Sauvignon Blanc and walked hand in hand with Catherine back to the kitchen.

'Well,' said Aunt Em, watching Rod head off in the direction of the tennis courts. 'Have you managed to discover anything?'

'No. Not yet,' Catherine replied. 'To be honest I didn't think it was the right moment. I thought it would be better to wait until tomorrow or Sunday when he's more relaxed.'

18

Early on the morning of the fête, Catherine and Rod parted company, each to their allocated duties. Catherine going in search of wild flowers for the table decorations and Rod heading off to join Mr Barnes, who at this very moment was carrying assorted chairs and trestle tables into a giant marquee. Rod's parents, meanwhile, had already set off for a leisurely walk into Whycham le Cley. There, Rod's mother (Mr Erskine's niece) was hoping to reacquaint herself with familiar haunts from her youth, and his father (at Rod's request) was to make a special point of looking at the almshouses.

Alone with her thoughts, Catherine wandered through the spinney and into the fields beyond. Already the sun was shining in a virtually cloudless, azure blue sky and swallows were flying high on the wing. Following yesterday's talk with Rod, what could be more perfect? This morning she'd been able to reassure her aunt that his plans for the village were to be in everyone's interests, though, in truth, she hadn't seen them for herself. Rod had simply laughed and tapped the side of his nose when she'd enquired further.

An hour and a half later, and deeply content, Catherine made her way back to the hall, her arms filled with a profusion of wild flowers. 'And how's my little woodland nymph?' a voice called from the summerhouse.

'Rod! You quite startled me. I thought you were with Mr Barnes.'

'I was. When I caught sight of you emerging from the spinney I nipped back here in the hope of snatching a few precious moments in your company. I also managed to persuade your aunt to make us a flask of coffee.'

'You did what? Poor Aunt Em, as if she hasn't got enough to do.'

'She didn't appear to mind. In fact she was positively glowing. Maybe it was just my imagination but she didn't seem her usual self on Friday.'

'I expect she was feeling overawed by all the preparations for today,' Catherine lied, knowing full well this wasn't the case at all. Aunt Em had been desperately worried by rumours and speculation running rife throughout the village.

'Are we going to have this coffee or not?' Rod asked, leading her by the elbow into the summerhouse.

'As long as it is only coffee. I need to get these flowers in water as soon as possible.'

'What a pity. To think I left my mobile with Mr Barnes so nobody could get hold of me.'

Catherine lowered her flowers carefully on to a large wicker table. 'At least you can get hold of me.' Comforted to feel Rod's arms curl protectively about her shoulders, Catherine heard him whisper huskily, 'If only you hadn't put those flowers on that table, perhaps we could have . . . '

'Rod Marchant! First mattresses in the cellar and now tables in the summerhouse. Shame on you! Are you still trying to wriggle out of taking me somewhere luxurious?'

'Considering the state of those cottages on the far side of Great Whycham, this is luxurious,' Rod said, releasing her from his embrace and pouring out two mugs of coffee. 'Henry still reckons I should pull them down and replace them with a modern block of one-up, one down — '

'You'd never get planning permission,' Catherine interrupted.

'Who needs planning permission when you know people like Henry? Come along and drink this coffee before it gets cold. I'm no flower expert but those poppies look as if they could be wilting already.'

'That's because their stalks need singeing

with a flame to stop the sap oozing out.'

'Ouch! That sounds painful.'

*   *   *

Waving him goodbye, Catherine walked back to a deserted Whycham Hall, feeling decidedly less content than before. Rod had only been joking, hadn't he? He'd never entertain anything as grotesque as a modern block of brick-built terraces in place of those lovely cottages. Reminding herself that he was almost always disapproving of Henry Davenport's ideas, Catherine took comfort from Rod's recent announcement. His parents had liked her immensely and also thought her 'charming'.

'And they were charming too,' Catherine acknowledged, telling herself how silly she was to have been terrified at the prospect of meeting them. Rod's father was simply an older version of his son and Davina Marchant had been delightful, and as far removed from Francesca as was humanly possible.

Highly relieved that Francesca would not be putting in an appearance today, Catherine wasn't quite so fortunate when trying to dismiss Francesca's father to the back of her mind. Moments later, separating the scarlet poppies from the rest of the wild flowers, she reached for a box of matches. It wasn't only the bitter poppy sap she needed to stem but also any unpleasant influence oozing this way from Henry and Francesca Davenport.

Having completed three dining-table decorations (kept specifically low at Rod's request — he wanted people to see and speak to one another across the table), Catherine was in the process of filling large vases for the porch and deep bay windows in the hallway, when a young lad knocked at the kitchen door.

''Scuse me, miss, Mr Barnes sent me to look for Mr Marchant. Seems someone keeps trying to get him on his mobile.'

Remembering that Rod had deliberately left his phone in the marquee, Catherine explained that he'd gone to collect the tannoy system. 'I expect he'll be back soon. If it's urgent, I'm sure Mr Marchant will deal with it immediately.'

'Actually, I . . . um . . . think it is,' the young lad said, shuffling his feet in embarrassment. 'When Mr Barnes got fed up listening to the same bit of music — he says he can't stand Vivaldi — he asked me if I . . . er . . . knew how to switch the phone off.'

Slightly surprised, even taking into account Mr Barnes's aversion to mobile phones and PlayStations (Daisy's older brother bore witness to that), Catherine added brightly,

'That's probably just as well. Mr Barnes has more than enough to do today without constant interruptions. Thank you for coming to explain. I'll certainly pass on your message.'

When he made no attempt to leave, Catherine guessed there was still something the young lad hadn't divulged. 'Erm . . . Mr Barnes said I ought to tell you I also read a text message sent to Mr Marchant. I wouldn't usually but with that mobile ringing and ringing, I thought someone might have been hurt or something.'

'And had they?'

'I'm not sure, miss. I wrote the message down just in case . . . '

Reaching out for the folded scrap of paper, Catherine read: '*R. Insist U keep plans secret. Need 2 speak 2U. Urgent!*' 'Did you happen to note who the message was from?' she said, trying hard to conceal the anxiety rising in her breast.

'Yes, it was signed, 'Henry'.'

Henry! Catherine couldn't believe her ears. Why would Henry send Rod a message marked urgent, today of all days?

Listening to the young lad murmur his apologies as he walked away, Catherine gave a shudder. Less than an hour ago she'd been walking arm in arm with Rod, feeling the warmth of the sun upon her face; now all she could feel was the distinct chill of being on her own with a deadly secret to conceal. Despite all Rod's protestations to the contrary, he was planning something secretive with Francesca's father after all. Choking back tears, she finished the rest of the flowers, thankful that at least Aunt Em wasn't here to see her niece in such distress. Like Janice at the library, Emmy Bailey could also read her niece like a book.

It was thinking of Janice that prompted Catherine to look at the clock. Cautiously carrying the precious Majolica vases into the hall, she knew it wouldn't be long before Janice and Dave were due to arrive. At the same time she needed to go and help Daisy and her brothers into their costumes. As for herself, did it really matter what she looked like?

'Yes, of course it does,' an inner voice appeared to protest. 'You've been working and planning for weeks to get this show on the road. Even if you and Rod don't see eye to eye concerning what he plans to do with his inheritance, that doesn't mean he'll no longer love you.'

'But can I still love him?' Catherine asked herself, washing away the remaining traces of poppy juice from her fingers. If only it were that easy to wash away all traces of doubt and fear she felt at that moment.

* * *

'Ooh, Catherine, you do look pretty,' Daisy called, when Catherine appeared in Grandma Barnes's kitchen. 'You look like one of those fairies in the flower book.'

Dressed in green tights and matching leotard, Daisy jumped up and down with excitement. Where was Grandma's fairy book? She wanted to find the picture of the Queen of the Meadow Fairy. The fairy with the very pale yellowy-green dress and golden, fluffy hair.

Asking Grandma if she could show Catherine the special book she'd had when she was a little girl, Daisy clasped it to her chest before sitting herself down on Catherine's lap. 'Of course, Grandma's really old now,' she said. 'Once upon a time she was little like me and this book was a present from Father Christmas.'

Catherine smiled, grateful for anything to divert her attention from that wretched text message. Oh, for the innocence of childhood. Concentrating hard on each and every picture, Daisy studied the pages of the Cicely Mary Barker *Flower Fairies Treasury*. Turning each page slowly and carefully, she announced, 'Grandma says I have to be very careful cos books aren't toys. An' we don't let Brett and Carl have this book, do we, Grandma?'

'Certainly not,' Mrs Barnes replied, with a knowing look in Catherine's direction.

'By the way, where are the twins?' Catherine asked. Time was already pretty tight. If she had to dress Daisy and then the boys .. On the other hand, Rod could manage quite well without her. By now he ought to be making his way to meet Romy Felden and Stephen Walker. And, providing she planned the rest of her day accordingly, it might be possible to avoid too much contact with him until this evening. As for what would happen then, that was anybody's guess. She wasn't going to worry about it now. She had far more important things to do.

'See. There she is,' Daisy said, pointing to the Queen of the Meadow Fairy. 'She's one of my favrits. An' did you know she has little frog servants to wait on her.'

How very appropriate, Catherine thought, feeling tears prick her eyelids, the memory of the treasured Murano glass frog still fresh in her mind. Would she have to return it if she and Rod went their separate ways? How could she possibly face him if he were to change the whole fabric of the village?

It was fabric of a different kind that commanded Catherine's attention. Daisy slid off her lap, closed the book and handed it back to Grandma. Now she was ready for her sunflower costume.

Standing patiently while Catherine straightened the leafgreen tights and leotard, Daisy looked up in earnest. 'Do you think Mister will be surprised?' she said, her eyes widening in delight. Catherine was reaching into the biggest carrier bag she'd ever seen for a beautiful circle of yellow petals, framed at the centre with soft, furry, brown edges.

'I'm sure he will, Daisy,' Catherine found herself replying, easing the rest of the costume over Daisy's head, before tying it under her chin and securing it in place with hair clips. 'So will everybody else.' Other than Daisy's immediate family, everyone had assumed she would want to be a daisy. It was that never-to-be-forgotten picnic (her *running-up prize*), when Rod had taken them all off in the Range Rover, that had prompted her to choose otherwise.

Fascinated by Mrs Bannister's newly laundered sunflower curtains (used that day as their picnic cloth), Daisy had declared sunflowers to be her most favourite bloom. Asked why, she'd declared in the most delightful way that they made her feel happy, just like she did when the sun shone through her bedroom window early in the morning. 'An' the brown bits in the middle are like bumble bees' tummies,' she'd added as an afterthought, reminded of all the bees in the garden at Whycham Hall. 'An' bees make honey and I like honey.'

'Don't forget they also provide food for the birds in winter,' Catherine had explained, describing what happened once the sunflower's brown, furry face had turned to seed.

Knowing that Catherine couldn't give her a brown furry face (cos she wouldn't be able to breathe), Daisy stood stock-still while Catherine set to with some brown face paint. Presently, and with two green, crêpe paper leaves fixed strategically in place at her elbows, Daisy was ready to blossom. Now, where were those brothers of hers?

As expected Brett and Carl weren't quite as cooperative when getting them in to their costumes. Eventually, and with Grandma lending a hand and Daisy threatening to tell their mum if they misbehaved (meaning no candyfloss and no ice creams), two little boys soon became two little bees. Or should that be two little Bs? Catherine thought, struggling to arrange each set of organdy wings. Grateful for Mrs Barnes's contribution (it must have taken her ages to sew that gold and brown ribbon on to two black polo-necked sweaters), Catherine prepared to add the finishing touches. Pipe-cleaner antennae, stitched firmly on to child-size balaclavas, again courtesy of Grandma.

'I only hope they're not going to be too hot with those on,' Catherine said, regarding her two charges.

'I shouldn't worry too much,' Mrs Barnes replied. 'I knitted them nice and loose and they're acrylic not wool. Once the judging's taken place, I doubt whether they'll keep them on for long, anyway.'

'Right, then. Daisy, boys, are you ready to go?' Highly relieved when three eager faces nodded in unison (mercifully they hadn't decided they suddenly needed the loo), Catherine produced two tiny plastic pots of honey from her bag. 'Can you believe I managed to find sunflower honey?' she said, as they walked down the garden path and headed across the lawns.

★ ★ ★

'Catherine! We won! We won!' Daisy squealed excitedly. 'Did you see us? The lady said we was the bestest.'

'Yes, Daisy, I saw you, and I'm delighted. Well done.'

'An' Mister was so surprised, cos he thought I was goin' to be a daisy.'

At the mention of Rod's name, Catherine looked across to where a sea of tiny, human blossom was milling round Rod and the author Romy Felden. Rod was speaking to a pansy and Romy to a daffodil. As for Stephen Walker, Romy's actor husband, he was nowhere to be seen, unless . . .

'Oh, heavens!' Catherine whispered, under her breath. It looked very much as if Stephen was being attacked by a pair of bees. Brett and Carl were literally buzzing between his legs, balaclavas askew and antennae dangling. Grateful they'd stayed still long enough for the judging, she saw Rod dashing off to rescue Stephen, before he got well and truly *stung* in a rather delicate part of his anatomy.

With a questioning look in her direction, Rod motioned to the candyfloss stall. 'It's OK,' Catherine called. 'They were promised candyfloss if they were good. Will you please get some for Daisy as well?'

'That's being good. Blimey, I'd hate to see those two little Bs when they're being bad.'

'Janice! Dave! You made it. Oh, I'm so pleased to see you both.'

Hugging her friend warmly, Janice realized she was suddenly having to compete with the tannoy system. 'Wouldn't have missed this for

278

the world,' she shouted. 'And an invitation to supper followed by a barn dance. Great! However, having seen those amazing kiddies' costumes, I hope you're not expecting similar standards from Dave and myself.'

'It's not the costumes that are important. It's having fun and keeping the spirit of the village alive.'

'As long as the spirit comes in bottles and *you're* not dead on your feet at the end of it. What time did you get up this morning?'

'It's all in a good cause, don't forget. Any profits made today are going to ROKPA, the Nepalese charity Rod's sister is working for at the moment.'

Pushing an envelope containing a very generous cheque in Catherine's direction, Janice began, 'While I remember, there's our contribution. Dave and I thought it would be easier to do it this way. Of course, we'll still do our bit on the stalls.'

'I don't know what to say.'

'Then say nothing,' Janice replied, no longer vying with the tannoy. 'Just remember I'm your other good cause for the day. I'm relying on you to take care of Dave for a few minutes while I go and ogle Stephen Walker.'

'No problem. I'll even give you more than a few minutes. Rod's offered to take Dave on a a tour of the wine cellars and Daisy wants her photograph taken with Romy. If you don't mind waiting a bit while I see to that and then hand the sunflower and her brothers back to the queen bee, namely Hayley, their mother.'

Janice nodded appreciatively when Catherine reappeared and promptly whisked Dave away and introduced him to Rod. Watching the two men depart, presumably in the direction of the cellars, she patted Catherine on the shoulder. 'Wow! Now that's what I call service. I hope Rod realizes what a little treasure he has in you. I know you've been working your socks off getting ready for today, and unless I'm very much mistaken, everything seems to be running like clockwork.'

'So far so good,' Catherine replied. 'And the next few hours should pretty much take care of themselves. It's usually the senior members of the village who deal with the flower and produce show. The only flowers I had to worry about were the two-legged variety. Which reminds me, I'd better go and rescue Romy from that bunch of tulips. I expect she could do with a break by now, especially after posing with the children for all those photographs.'

As usual, Janice read Catherine's mind. 'And if you take Romy off for a leisurely cup of coffee, I can . . . '

'Precisely.' Catherine nodded. 'You can drool over Stephen Walker, only please remember that he's a happily married man and we need Romy's continued support for our future Wordswork events.'

'And I'm a happily married woman,' Janice said, with a wicked gleam in her eye. 'In my book that means look but do not touch.'

'Definitely no touching!' Catherine teased, walking away.

Pleased to have a few quiet moments away from the gathering throng, Catherine took Romy into the conservatory for a cup of coffee and a well-deserved break. It was there Rod came to look for her, having first reunited Dave with his wife.

Explaining that Stephen was outside in the drive, Rod reacquainted Romy with her presentation bouquet of flowers and a selection of Whycham Hall's finest wine. 'I can't thank you both enough for coming,' he said, walking with Catherine and Romy to the waiting car. 'I'm only sorry you couldn't stay on for tonight's supper and dance.'

'So are we,' Romy replied. 'As you know, Stephen's guesting on a chat show this evening. Believe me, we'd far rather stay here with you than head off down the motorway in all that traffic. Give me Norfolk any day. So much more restful than London.'

'Hardly restful at the moment,' Stephen broke in, fixing Rod and Catherine with a knowing smile. 'I really admire what you've achieved today, particularly as it's in such a good cause, but you two will be absolutely exhausted by the end of the day.'

'Exhausted but content, hopefully,' Rod murmured, linking his arm in Catherine's as they waved Stephen and Romy good-bye and walked back to the open doorway.

Standing together in the shade of the Gothic-style porch, Rod drew Catherine into his arms. Kissing her mouth, her face and her hair, he whispered longingly, 'Mmm. You smell utterly delightful. A wonderful blend of flowers, fresh air and perfume. I know everyone's enjoying themselves and the day's going swimmingly but when are we going to have some time together on our own?'

Momentarily forgetting her earlier doubts and fears, Catherine was almost tempted to suggest they sneak away to the top of the house and her attic bedroom. For the most part Whycham Hall was out of bounds to anyone other than invited guests and not many of those knew the exact location of what Rod still referred to as her turret. Even so, Catherine thought better of it. For a start it was too risky; it was also extremely impolite. They were, after all, supposed to be hosting today's event. Leastways, Rod was supposed to be hosting it, she was merely helping out in an advisory capacity.

Lost in thought for a moment, when Rod broke away to answer the telephone in the hallway, Catherine could almost imagine Janice's reaction to her self-proclaimed job description. *'Advisory capacity! Of course you're not here as his bloody adviser, you're here because this is where you belong, as his wife, his lover, mother of his children and mistress of Whycham Hall.'*

'Yes, this is Whycham Hall and it's Rod Marchant speaking,' Rod said, casting a furtive glance in Catherine's direction. 'And yes, I will accept the charges.'

Wanting to remain by his side partly out of curiosity as to the identity of the mystery caller, Catherine was also deeply hurt that Rod was deliberately keeping something from her. Usually, when he received a phone call, be it business related or from a friend, he never made any attempt at adopting the somewhat mumbled and hushed tone he was using at present.

With a resigned sigh, Catherine stepped outside into the sunlight. Sitting herself down on the serpentine steps, she was glad to have her attention drawn to a pair of magnificent stone urns filled with Mr Barnes's current pride and joy — huge plumes of brilliant blue *Agapanthus Africanus*. Mr Barnes had been hoping and praying for them to be at their best in readiness for today's celebrations. Unlike his poor lilies, Catherine recalled, sadly. Three weeks ago, Mr Barnes's display of prize-winning flowers had been stripped bare by the much hated and dreaded lily bug.

Surprised to hear Rod's raised voice echo through the confines of the porch — 'No, Henry, definitely not. This was supposed to be a secret, remember . . . ' — Catherine edged slowly backwards on the steps, regretting her action almost immediately when she heard Rod proclaim, 'Lord knows I feel bad enough as it is, keeping this from Catherine and her aunt. If I tell them now . . . What? Of course I can't come to London. I also have absolutely no idea what we can do now. You're the one who drew up the plans. You sort it out but whatever you do don't involve Francesca!'

Recognizing the smell of Catherine's perfume, Rod turned to find her eyeing him suspiciously. Fully expecting her to ask what was going on, she merely informed him that she was going to look for Janice and Dave. It was time for the pig roast.

Despite last Friday's request at the library, Janice refrained from a second helping of freshly roasted pork, offering it to her husband instead. All that interested her now were the arrangements for the rest of the day. Wiping her mouth with her serviette, she turned to Catherine and enquired, 'So if Dave and I nip home for a while and come back in time for supper, that will still be OK?'

'Absolutely.'

'And what do we come back as? I mean, do we come back in our pirate gear or . . . '

'That's entirely up to you,' Catherine said. 'Either way it doesn't matter. If you come in your usual clothes you can always change into your pirate outfits up in my room. All I'm asking is that you make sure you do come back.'

'You try and stop us. By the way, what are you and Rod going as? Orlando Bloom and Keira Knightley?'

'No. Rod's planning on doing a Johnny Depp and I'm going to be a cabin boy. It's Damian who's opted for the Orlando Bloom character.'

'Damian? Isn't he the vicar?'

'Yes, and an exceptionally good-looking one at that. I'm surprised you haven't been drooling over him as well.'

'That's because I haven't had the chance. In which case lead me to him, immediately.'

'What are we going to do about your wife?' Catherine said to Dave, as Janice made a beeline for Damian, who was organizing the egg and spoon race for the children.

'Nothing,' Dave called back, a broad grin illuminating his face. 'She's perfect just the way she is.'

'Yes. She is,' Catherine whispered to herself. 'I'm also glad she's got broad shoulders. I've a horrid feeling I might be needing them to cry on before the evening's out.'

19

Watching the remaining stragglers make their way to the village green for the tug of war, Catherine made her excuses to Rod. With the last-minute table preparations to deal with, including the place settings, wouldn't it be better if she remained at the hall with Aunt Em? Seemingly reluctant not to have her there, to cheer him on, Rod concluded it was perhaps the better option. The look on Catherine's face as he'd hung up the phone still filled him with a combination of despair and foreboding. If only . . .

'Master Roderick's just rung,' Emmy said, popping her head round the dining-room door. 'He said to tell you his team won — unlike you, he won't be coming home covered in duckweed.'

'If that's supposed to be funny, Aunt Em, I'm not amused.'

'Catherine? What is it? You two haven't fallen out, have you? Not today of all days. With the supper and dance still ahead of us . . . '

'No. Not fallen out,' Catherine said, fixing her aunt with a sardonic smile. 'But I wouldn't mind betting there'll be a great deal of fallout before too long.'

Leaving the pile of place cards on a corner of the table, Catherine took her aunt by the hand and led her back to the kitchen. With assorted guests milling about and Rod's parents offering to help virtually every five minutes, it seemed the only place where Catherine could safely reveal to her aunt what she'd overheard.

Aunt Em shook her head in disbelief. All colour drained from her face. 'That's dreadful, absolutely dreadful. No wonder you looked so strained when you came back after saying goodbye to your friends. There was me putting it down to tiredness, when all the time it was . . . Of course, you know who I blame for this. That wretched creature, Francesca! I bet she's put Master Roderick up to it.'

Not entirely sure what Aunt Em meant by 'it', Catherine was more concerned about Henry and those secret plans. What exactly did they involve? How much of the village would be affected by them? More importantly, how soon were they planning to carry them out? Pressing her fingers against her temples, Catherine recalled Rod's angry retort: '*No, Henry. I cannot come to London.*' From the urgency in Rod's voice, she could only assume their plans were imminent.

Hmm, Rod's not the only one who can make secret plans, she thought to herself. Five minutes later, with Aunt Em in charge of keeping Charles and Davina Marchant occupied (opening the wine and folding table napkins), Catherine let herself in to Rod's study. Unlike all the spy films featured on TV, she had absolutely no intention of hacking into his computer — she wouldn't have known how to. She was, however, hoping to locate his briefcase.

'Damn!' she hissed, discovering it was nowhere to be seen. That meant it could only be in his bedroom. Shaking her head in Aunt Em's direction as she passed the dining-room, and pointing a finger in the direction of the stairs, Catherine breathed a huge sigh of relief. Davina and Charles were still busily engaged. At the same time, just as a precaution, she paused by the landing window searching for any sign of Rod making his way up the drive. Knowing it wouldn't take him that long to help Damian and Mr Barnes pack away the rope and markers used for the tug of war, Catherine continued with her own war: the tug of her heart strings and the conflict of interests raging in her head.

Moments later, slipping quietly into Rod's

bedroom, Catherine spied the Whycham crest above the familiar tester bed. If only she'd been born a boy and lived a couple of hundred years ago. Fiercely protective of the family name, Catherine tried to suppress the recurring vision from her mind as she hunted for Rod's black leather briefcase. A vision which included, Rod, Henry and Francesca on one side, surrounded by bulldozers and construction traffic, while on the other was Catherine, Aunt Em and the residents of Whycham le Cley. OK, so in years gone by they might not have possessed the same advantages of modern armour as their opponents, but pitch-forks and scythes could be just as lethal. Look what happened to the French at Agincourt.

'*Agincourt!*' Catherine's other self broke into her reverie. '*Good grief! This is neither the time nor place to think of Agincourt. Find that damned briefcase!*'

'At last!' Catherine gasped, hauling the briefcase from beneath the bed, even more relieved to discover that it wasn't locked. What she did discover, however, were simply masses of papers, photographs and a sapphire-blue ring box. With no time to think of the significance of the tiny jewellery box, Catherine pulled out what she considered to be the most relevant pages. Oh! If only she'd thought of this sooner. If only she had more time. Already she'd discerned the sound of Rod's car coming up the drive, which left her with only two options. That of throwing the papers back in the briefcase any old how, a sure sign that someone had been riffling through Rod's private correspondence, or else putting all the pages back as neatly as she'd found them and wait for Rod to discover her in his bedroom . . .

'Catherine! What are you doing here? I thought you were downstairs with . . . '

'And I thought you might want to spend some time alone with me — before supper.'

'Whew!' Rod gasped and ran a hand through his hair. For weeks he'd been waiting for this moment. Now that it had arrived . . . it wasn't that he didn't want to. It was more that he was simply overwhelmed at finding Catherine semi-naked on his bed!

'Oh, my love. You do pick your moments,' he murmured, sitting down beside her, his fingers trailing down her cheeks and throat until they reached the gentle curve of her breasts. 'There was me thinking I'd upset you by not explaining about the phone call and all the time you were planning this.'

When Rod began unbuttoning his shirt, Catherine closed her eyes, trying to shut out the memory of that fateful phone call and the secrets hidden beneath the bed. If only she could put back the clock to yesterday morning when they'd walked home from St Andrew's together, making plans for their future. If only she didn't feel so guilty for being here like this. Alone in her bed at night she'd often wondered what that first time would be like . . . giving herself utterly and completely to him. Certainly, she'd never ever dreamt it would be like this. Yes, his bedroom was far more luxurious than the cellar or the summerhouse, but giving herself to him purely as a result of her scheming, because she had something to hide — the very thought of it made her feel cheap. On the other hand, she considered, conscious of Rod getting up from the bed and moving about the room, in her heart of hearts she knew she still loved him desperately. The haunting memory of making love this once would be something she could . . .

Feeling a solitary tear prick her eyelids, Catherine heard Rod whisper huskily, 'Catherine, darling. Much as I'd love to go downstairs and tell everyone to go away so I could be alone with you, I don't really think that would be a good idea, do you? They've been so looking forward to this evening — and it is after all only one evening. After tonight we shall have more than just an evening together.'

Rod smiled lovingly as Catherine opened her eyes to look at him. A tiny frown furrowed her brow. 'And it's not only evenings,' he continued, stroking a finger across her forehead, 'There'll be nights too — and mornings. Lots of lovely mornings. In fact, when I saw you emerging from the spinney, carrying all those flowers in your arms, I got to thinking what it would be like waking to find you in my arms. Hmm. What a delicious thought. So . . . what do you say? Shall we stay or shall we go? I'll leave it entirely up to you.'

'I-I think perhaps we should go,' Catherine said softly, reaching out for her dress.

★   ★   ★

'Rod's having a shower. He won't be long,' Catherine announced to Rod's parents and Aunt Em. Turning to Charles Marchant she resumed, 'He also said to ask you if you wouldn't mind pouring out some champagne for the guests.'

Charles nodded approvingly, watching Catherine follow her aunt in the direction of the kitchen. 'Mmm,' he said, turning to look at his wife. 'Does that mean we're going to be celebrating something this evening?'

'I sincerely hope so,' Davina replied. 'I think she's absolutely charming. They're so right for each other, don't you think?'

Charles reached for a bottle of Moët. 'Absolutely! I'll certainly drink to that.'

Listening to the chattering voices as friends and neighbours gathered in the drawing-room and spilled out onto the terrace, Emmy and Catherine worked together in silence. To anyone looking in the kitchen at that moment, they would have seen aunt and niece busily employed in decorating silver platters of whole poached salmon, flown down at Rod's request from Scotland. With two bowls containing thinly sliced cucumber in front of them (one raw and one plunged briefly in hot and then cold water), aunt and niece created a delicate pattern resembling fish scales. That task completed, there only remained the slices of stuffed olive to make the eyes, and a mixture of chopped mint and parsley to be added to the home-grown potatoes, once they'd finished cooking on the Aga.

Unlike the bright eyes now gracing the salmon, Emmy and Catherine's eyes were listless and sad. Emmy still couldn't believe it. Unless Catherine was very much mistaken, Rod was not only going to erect some modern, brick-built monstrosities but also planning to demolish the almshouses! 'Over my dead body!' Emmy had declared angrily. 'Those almshouses were bequeathed to the villagers of Whycham le Cley in the reign of Queen Victoria!'

Greeted by this outburst, Catherine had given a laconic smile. It was the only time Queen Victoria's name had been mentioned in positive vein. Usually, it was with that other affair. That of Catherine's rightful inheritance. Once again calling to mind the saga of unpaid death duties and what might have been had she been born a boy, Catherine remembered the cabin boy's costume she planned to wear this evening. Should she change into it now or later? The majority of guests present had decided to come in their costumes, anxious not to delay the start of the dance. Already, aided and abetted by the odd glass (or two) of champagne, shouts of 'Ahoy there!' and 'What ho, m' hearties. Splice the main brace' echoed through the house.

'At least some of them appear to be having a good time,' Catherine said, wistfully.

'And you must too, Catherine. I know you still love him.'

'Love him, hate him. Aunt Em, what am I going to do? Rod says he wants me to sit next to him during supper. As well as that horrid photo of the almshouses, with the word DEMOLISH written all over it in black felt tip, I-I also saw a ring box.'

'A ring box! Do you think . . . ?'

Catherine stifled a sob. 'Oh, I don't know what to think.'

Mindful of the late Edwina Erskine's collection of jewellery (she'd been given the task of handing it over to Mr Hayes to take to the bank for safe-keeping), Emmy asked, 'This ring box, what was it like?'

'Like any ring box, I suppose. Small. Square.'

'What about colour?'

Catherine faced her aunt in utter bewilderment. At the time she hadn't been interested in the ring box. She'd only been interested in architects' drawings and photos.

'Was it green or was it burgundy?' Emmy prompted.

About to snap, 'What the hell did it matter whether or not the box was green or bugundy in colour? If Rod was planning to give her the ring tonight, she'd probably throw it back at him,' Catherine decided otherwise. Aunt Em was already distressed. As if it wasn't bad enough that Rod had insisted his housekeeper join them for supper (people wouldn't need her to serve them, Rod had reminded — it was a sit-down buffet and people were perfectly capable of helping themselves), she didn't need her niece yelling at her just because of some stupid ring box. 'No . . . I'm sure it wasn't,' Catherine said at length. I think it was blue. Why do you ask?'

'Then it couldn't have been a ring belonging to Edwina. All her jewellery came in green or burgundy leather boxes, engraved with the family initials.'

Catherine shrugged her shoulders. Unlike the walnut-shaped box containing the precious glass frog, she couldn't recollect any lettering once she'd slid the briefcase back in its exact same position. She'd been far too preoccupied, stepping out of her dress and climbing on to Rod's bed. Even now the very thought of Rod finding her in her bra and panties brought a rush of colour to her cheeks. Consigned to sitting by his side during the meal she should, for the most part, be able to avoid eye contact. 'The place settings! I never finished them,' she called to her aunt, hastening away to the dining-room only to discover Rod had beaten her to it.

'Just making sure I have you where I want you, at least for supper,' he said, fixing her with a playful smile. 'I'm sure we can think of something more interesting later.'

Blushing, Catherine followed him round

the table, noting as she did so Rod was keeping to their original seating arrangement. Catherine and himself at one end, Charles and Davina Marchant at the other, Damian somewhere in between on the left and Janice and Dave on the right.

'I see you haven't changed yet, either,' he said. 'I thought I'd save my Johnny Depp bit for after supper. Keep it as a surprise. From the sound of that laughter outside I reckon they'll be staggering across the fields to the institute. In fact,' he joked, reaching for her hand as they made their way to summon the guests to eat, 'if most of them hadn't come on foot anyway, I'd be insisting they all left their car keys on the table in the hall.'

Once back in the dining-room and with everyone about to stand, while Damian said grace, Rod heard a screech of tyres on the gravel outside, followed by a loud slamming of a car door and hurried footsteps clamouring down the hallway and into the dining-room. Knowing that all the expected guests were present and correct, Rod's face registered unmitigated surprise and subsequent delight. 'Henry! How on earth? I thought you were stranded at Heathrow.'

'Henrietta!' Davina Marchant clasped her husband's arm. Like some of the assembled guests, had she too perhaps had more than her share of champagne? Was she seeing things or was it really her daughter, framed in the open doorway?

'Hello, folks!' Henrietta said, beaming. 'Sorry if I'm a bit late.'

'A bit late!' Rod called, leaving the table to embrace his sister. 'You were supposed to arrive yesterday. First your plane was held up at Qatar, then your luggage went missing. By lunchtime you told me your coach had broken down on the outskirts of Heathrow and . . . '

'Ahem,' came a voice from the far end of the dining-room. 'Excuse me, Roderick,' Charles Marchant began, 'would you mind if we left your sister's seemingly unfortunate travel arrangements until later What your mother and I want to know is why Henrietta is here in Whycham le Cley, when only this morning you told me you'd spoken to her in Kathmandu?'

Answering on her brother's behalf, Henrietta called out, 'Sorry, Dad. I told Rod not to let on. I've come to collect the cheque.'

'The cheque on behalf of ROKPA,' Rod explained. 'I thought it would be a nice surprise if Henrietta came and collected it in person. Of course, when I sent her the air fare, I had hoped she'd arrive before everything kicked off but as usual she's late.'

'Not too late to join us for supper,' Damian broke in, looking in Mrs Bailey's direction. 'I'm sure we can squeeze in another place at this magnificent table.'

Suddenly aware of the murmured voices and shuffling in the room as people began moving their chairs, Rod took control of the situation. 'Mrs Bailey, would you mind setting another place and . . . '

'Um, I think you'd better make that two,' Henrietta hissed in Rod's ear. 'You haven't asked me yet how I managed to get here.'

'Well, no, come to think of it, I haven't. How did . . . ?' Alarm bells rang in Rod's head at that moment when he heard his sister's apologetic, 'I'm sorry, Rod. I know you specifically asked me not to involve her but other than taking a taxi, which would have cost an absolute fortune, it was the only way. You do realize the train service to Whycham le Cley on a Bank Holiday is non-existent. In fact it's probably on a par with Kathmandu.'

At that moment Rod wasn't interested in listening about non-existent train services. As he made his way along the hallway to the front door, he was more interested in the identity of Henrietta's chauffeur, or should that be chauffeuse? Though delighted to see his sister after such a long absence, he was less than delighted to see her friend.

'Roddy dahling,' Francesca cooed. 'Is it safe to come in now? Henry thought it best if I gave you five minutes to say your hellos and also give your ma and pa chance to recover from the shock.'

Recover from the shock was right, Rod thought to himself; he'd need more than five minutes to recover from the shock of finding Francesca in such close proximity. And it was close proximity, he discovered to his cost ten minutes later, once Henrietta and Francesca had chance to freshen up and the two extra places laid at the table. It was Francesca, not Catherine, who was sitting by his side.

Still registering the horrified expression on Catherine's face as Francesca sashayed into the room, Rod recalled how Mrs Bailey and her niece had volunteered to have their supper in the kitchen, thus avoiding any need to rearrange the dining-room.

'Absolutely not!' Rod had said angrily, as aunt, niece and employer stood in the kitchen embroiled in a verbal battle of wills.

Eventually, it was Rod who won. Regrettably, there was nothing he could do about moving Francesca and whether or not he was imagining it, it was almost as if Catherine was happy not to be sitting anywhere near him. On the contrary, it was Damian who appeared to be the happiest all through supper. With Catherine on his right and Henrietta on his left, Damian could have been forgiven for thinking his two supper companions were as manna from heaven.

20

Almost relieved when supper came to an end, Rod watched in bemused silence as the Revd Damian 'Orlando Bloom' Cooper led a happy band of pirates across the fields in the direction of the village institute.

'He's very nice,' Henrietta said, coming up behind him. 'Not at all like a country vicar.'

'I know,' Rod acknowledged. 'Like me he's also a bit of a new boy. After five months he's still trying to find the path in more ways than one. Some of the parishioners have accepted him with no trouble at all. As for the rest . . . '

'I expect they'll all come round eventually.'

Henrietta eyed her brother suspiciously. 'Speaking of finding your way around. From what you've been saying in your phone calls, you haven't been doing too badly. I found Catherine extremely easy to talk to. Damian too come to that. The three of us hardly stopped talking all through supper.'

'So I noticed.'

'What's that supposed to mean?'

'Nothing in particular.'

'Oh, yes, it does,' Henrietta said, digging him in the ribs. 'You were jealous of Damian talking to Catherine.'

Rod shrugged his shoulders, making no comment, slightly irritated when his sister continued, wide eyed, 'Rod Marchant, I do believe you're in love. I know you told me you were fond of Catherine, but it's really serious, isn't it? At long last you have found a soul mate. Oh, I'm so happy for you. Gosh! Can I be a bridesmaid?'

'Hold on a minute, Henry. It's not official — yet.'

'Are you admitting you haven't actually got down on one knee and all that sort of thing? Shame on you, brother. Why ever not?'

'Hard as it might seem, because I wanted my parents *and* my sister to be here in order that we could all celebrate together? I had hoped that yesterday — '

'When I was due to arrive?' Henrietta volunteered.

'Mmm. You could say that. And today I was going to announce it over the tannoy system at the fête.'

'Oh, bum! I'm sorry. No wonder you let rip at me on the phone this morning. What will you do now? Ask Catherine to marry you tonight, at the dance?'

'I'm not sure. Catherine's been a bit strange this evening. My original intention was to find out what was wrong, during supper. She was supposed to be sitting next to me, only — '

'Francesca arrived and scuppered your plans.'

Rod forced a weak smile. Hadn't he used a similar expression when he'd taken Catherine to lunch last Friday? Although he was three years older than his sister, people often remarked how alike they were. 'Well and truly scuppered,' he agreed. 'And as Francesca's obviously intending to come to the dance . . . '

'Crikey! Speaking of the dance. Hadn't we both better go and get changed? We don't want to be late, do we? By the way, what are you wearing? Needless to say, I've come totally unprepared, unlike Francesca. I can only assume the moment I rang and asked for a lift, and also explained about this evening, she must have ransacked her entire wardrobe for something suitable.'

Walking upstairs together, brother and sister parted on the landing. There Henrietta planned to go in search of her mother, who'd offered to look in one of the old cabin trunks stored at the other end of the attic, while Rod still refused to give anything away about his own costume. All he would say was that neither of them had much time in which to change. 'Make sure you pass that message on to Francesca,' he advised, turning the handle of his bedroom door. 'If she's not down by quarter past, tell her we'll go without her. To save time, I've ordered a taxi from Whycham Halt.'

Ready in record time (he'd had the presence of mind to lay out his costume before supper), Rod surveyed his reflection in the mirror. OK, so his hair was nowhere near as long as Johnny Depp's but with his dark eyes and tanned complexion . . . Not only that, Catherine's contribution of assorted necklaces, courtesy of Norwich charity shops, and even a solitary hooped earring (clip not pierced) also helped to add a certain *je ne sais quoi*. It was thinking of Catherine that prompted Rod to think of something else. Looking at his watch, and deciding that there was still time, he set off to find Francesca.

Catherine, meanwhile, dressed as a simple cabin boy, closed her turret door and descended the stairs. Checking in the pocket of her black, cropped trousers, she hesitated outside Rod's bedroom door and knocked gently.

'He's not there,' came a voice. 'I saw him going into Francesca's room five minutes ago.' Walking past her and heading downstairs, Henrietta remarked with a smile, 'If he's not out in another five minutes I suggest you go and drag him out, Catherine. To think

Rod had the cheek to tell me not to be late.'

Trying to make light of Henrietta's remark, Catherine toyed with the idea of waiting in the hall with Rod's sister and parents or else hovering here on the landing. After several minutes she made her way slowly towards the blue room, somewhat saddened to hear the sound of Francesca's horsey laugh coming from within. Eventually, plucking up courage, she tapped gently on the bedroom door and waited.

'Oh, hello, Cathy. What's the problem? Come to check up on us, have you?'

'No. I've merely come to tell you the taxi's been waiting for the past five minutes and everyone else is ready to go.'

Holding the door ajar, Francesca drawled, 'Roddy dahling, come along. Looks like we're being summoned downstairs by the little librarian. From the look on her face you could say we're not in her very good books!'

Catherine bit her lip, listening to Francesca's derisive laughter as she set off to join Henrietta and the others waiting by the open front door. Unconcerned about the look on her own face (she no longer cared what Francesca thought of her), it was Rod's face that prompted attention. At first glance he'd looked almost embarrassed at being discovered sitting on Francesca's bed. And what was that around his eyes? Makeup!

'What do you think?' Rod asked, as they walked downstairs side by side. 'Do I look the part?'

'Y-yes. Very much so. How did you . . . ?'

'You mean the eyes. I asked Francesca to do it for me.'

Overhearing the tail end of the conversation, Francesca turned to meet Catherine's gaze, catching her arm on the floral display in the porch as she did so. 'I take it you're admiring my handiwork, Cathy. He looks rather gorgeous, doesn't he? Then he always does. Speaking of handiwork, Roddy, I've been meaning to ask ever since I arrived. Why on earth have you got jugs of weeds everywhere? If it's not bad enough here in the porch, you've got them on the windowsills in the hall and even on the dining table.'

Thinking he was springing to Catherine's defence, Rod said without thinking, 'They were Catherine's idea. She prefers wild flowers to cut flowers. She likes simple things.'

'I suppose that figures, if the locals are anything to go by.'

Highly relieved that Henrietta and his parents were already making their way down the steps, closely followed by Francesca, Rod made a desperate grab for Catherine's hand.

'I'm so sorry,' he whispered. 'Ignore her. Please don't let it spoil the evening.'

Listening to Francesca complaining as she climbed up into the people carrier — *Didn't they have proper taxis in this godforsaken place, and why were there old curtains draped across the passenger seats?* — Catherine fixed Rod with a look that said. 'Spoil the evening. Isn't it spoiled already?'

★ ★ ★

Returning home at midnight, Catherine made her excuses and hurried upstairs to the attic, leaving Rod, his parents, Henrietta and Francesca to make their own way into the drawing-room for a late-night coffee and brandy. This was one time Rod could fend for himself! Telling herself this wasn't quite true (coming back home in the same taxi, Henrietta had already volunteered for coffee duty), Catherine also wished that she'd remained downstairs with them. She really liked Rod's sister and would have loved to stay and chat. It wasn't only Damian who'd been interested in hearing all about ROKPA's work in Nepal. Catherine herself had been fascinated, particularly in the soup kitchen they ran during the winter months, the women's workshop which supported and trained women to sew and weave, and last but by no means least the children's home, where Henrietta worked.

Finishing her brandy, Francesca yawned and gazed longingly across the drawing-room. 'I don't know about the rest of you but I'm going to bed. What about you, Roddy? Do you want me to help you take off your makeup? I've some wonderful eye makeup remover. Frightfully expensive, dahling, and — '

'I don't think that will be necessary, Francesca. I'm sure good old soap and water will do just as well. Apart from that, there's something I need to discuss with my father. Sleep well and we'll see you in the morning.'

Watching her go, four pairs of eyes waited until they saw the drawing-room door open and close. Hearing her footsteps on the stairs it was Henrietta who spoke first. 'Rod, what can I say? I'm *so* sorry, *so* very sorry. When you begged me not to involve Francesca in our surprise plan for Mum and Dad I had no idea why. I knew Fran could always be a little bit sniffy but tonight she was an absolute bloody cow!'

'Henrietta!'

'I'm sorry, Mum, but she was. Just think yourself lucky I didn't use the F word because she certainly deserves it! She was an absolute bitch to Catherine. As for the '*I've* some *wonderful eye makeup remover, frightfully expensive, dahling . . . '*, I wouldn't mind betting that what she pays for one single bottle of eye makeup remover would feed a hundred and sixty people at the soup kitchen between December and March.'

'What!' Charles Marchant raised his eyebrows in disbelief.

'It's true, Father,' Rod began, 'Henrietta sent me ROKPA's brochure ages ago. That's why I wanted today to be such a huge success, in addition to some other ideas I have in the pipeline. I was hoping to go through all that with you tomorrow.'

'Why not now? There's no time like the present.' Reaching forward, Charles Marchant drained the remains of the cafetière into his cup. 'Henrietta,' he said, with a winning smile, 'I don't suppose you'd care to make your dear old dad another pot of coffee? I'm sure Rod wouldn't mind another cup.'

'Charles! It's gone midnight. I thought you were supposed to be cutting down on coffee. Besides, Rod's had an exhausting day and what about Catherine? Won't she be waiting for him? Having been subjected to an evening of Francesca I would have thought the poor girl would be in dire need of some TLC.'

It took Rod several moments to register the significance of his mother's statement. He

311

might be nearly thirty years old but he certainly wasn't in the habit of discussing his sleeping arrangements with anyone, least of all his mother. 'Erm, Catherine sleeps in the attic.'

'The attic? Good God!' Charles Marchant looked horror struck. 'Last night, when you were talking of Catherine's turret, I assumed it was your idea of a joke.'

'I think I'd better go and put the kettle on for another pot of coffee,' Henrietta said, making a dash for the kitchen.

'And I think I'd better go and get those plans I mentioned earlier.'

Waiting until both of their offspring were out of earshot, Charles and Davina turned to face each other. 'Phew! What do you make of that, old thing?'

'Less of the old thing, if you don't mind,' Davina replied. 'As for what do I make of my daughter swearing like a trooper and my son with a girlfriend sleeping in an attic . . . '

Charles rubbed his chin thoughtfully. 'You don't think it's got anything to do with Whycham le Cley air, do you?'

'I honestly don't know. What I do know, however, is that our own Whycham heir is deeply in love with Catherine and at some time today — before Francesca arrived — something went horribly wrong. Before we leave tomorrow I intend to find out what it is and hopefully put it right.'

Practically colliding with his mother when he re-emerged from his bedroom, carrying several folders and a small ring box, Rod sniffed the air appreciatively. 'Good old Henry. A fresh pot of coffee.'

'You're getting as bad as your father,' Davina teased, kissing her son goodnight. 'Oh! I thought you were taking those downstairs.'

'I am,' Rod said, following his mother's gaze to the bulky folders. 'I just need to pop something in to Francesca. I know she's awake, because the light's shining below the door.'

'I expect she's struggling to untie that ridiculous yellow bandana she had tied round her head, and also take off all that war paint she plasters on her face. Still, I suppose she does have that wonderful makeup remover. *Frightfully expensive, dahling.*'

'Mother! And to think you were having a go at Henrietta!'

★ ★ ★

Ready for bed, Francesca loosened her long blonde hair, examined her face in the mirror and frowned. Was that a wrinkle? Probably not. It could only be a shadow or a trick of the light. At twenty-seven, she supposed she was looking pretty good for her age. After all, she not only had the financial benefits of being able to buy the most expensive products for her skin, but also the other perks to go with it. Wealthy parents, a luxury home, fast car and every imaginable item of clothing in her wardrobes. 'Unlike Cathy,' she whispered. 'And now I have this. Hmm. I wonder . . . '

Opening the sapphire-blue ring box, Francesca took out an eye-catching, square-cut aquamarine and slipped it on her engagement finger. Then, tying the sash on her pale-blue silk kimono, she crept slowly to her bedroom door, opened it and, making sure no one else was on the landing, tip-toed towards the attic stairs.

Unable to sleep, with myriad thoughts racing through her head, Catherine tried to concentrate on reading her new library book. Having decided that if she couldn't get beyond the first twenty pages (or first chapter, whichever came first) she would give up completely and start counting sheep, she'd just turned to page thirteen when she heard a noise. A noise that sounded suspiciously like footsteps creeping along the landing outside her bedroom door.

Thinking it could only be Rod, she braced herself for a verbal onslaught. The one she'd been practising all evening while she'd been dancing, when really she should have been concentrating on her footwork instead. No wonder she'd returned home with swollen toes and bruised ankles. 'Right, Rod Marchant,' she hissed under her breath. 'This is where I tell you what I think of you and your plans to demolish half the village!'

Bracing herself as she made her way across the floor (she needed that element of surprise as she flung open the door to confront him), Catherine grabbed hold of the latch and pulled.

'Francesca! What on earth . . . ?'

'Cathy, sweetie. You are still up. Good. Can I come in?'

Standing with her mouth gaping open and the door ajar, Catherine watched in stunned silence as Francesca padded barefoot into the room.

'I left my mules downstairs,' Francesca explained, sitting down uninvited on Catherine's bed. 'I thought they might make a noise on the stairs and I didn't want to disturb anyone.'

'But it's all right to disturb me?'

'Oh, very funny, Cathy. You do have a very unusual sense of humour. That's one of the things I like about you, as well as your expertise in getting this house back into shape. Though I wasn't there to see it, I understand you worked tirelessly at yesterday's fête. Perhaps I didn't quite see eye to eye with you over your choice of flowers, but no matter. I've decided to remedy that myself tomorrow.'

Glancing towards the open door, Catherine was in two minds whether or not to shut it. Hardly worth it, she thought to herself, Francesca would be leaving in a couple of minutes or so, once she's finished her drunken ramblings.

'Is that what you've come to talk about, Francesca? My lack of flower arranging skills? Because if you have, I'd very much appreciate it if it could wait until morning. In case you hadn't noticed it's almost one o'clock. You might not need any beauty sleep but as for us lesser mortals.'

At the mention of lesser mortals, Francesca's gaze alighted on the cabin boy's costume, hanging on the bedroom door. 'Yes, well,' she drawled. 'I suppose I'd better get on with explaining why I'm here, especially as you'll need to get up early and pack.'

'Pack. Why? Where am I supposed to be going?'

'Leaving here, of course. Hasn't Roddy

told you? Hasn't he shown you what he's planning to do here?'

Catherine felt her mouth go quite dry. She couldn't admit to seeing Rod's plans because she wasn't supposed to know anything about them. If they were only recently filed away in Rod's briefcase, and Francesca had only arrived this evening, how did she know about the plans? In an attempt at remaining nonchalant, Catherine enquired, 'And you've seen Rod's plans, have you?'

'Yes. To begin with he mentioned some of them during supper, and also when I was doing his makeup. Then, after you'd gone to bed he came back to see me. He also gave me this.' Wriggling her left hand so the aquamarine caught the light radiating from the bedside lamp, Francesca continued. 'To be honest I would have preferred a diamond this size. No doubt that will come later. Roddy said he bought this ring because it matched my eyes. Don't you think that's sweet?'

'Yes, very.'

Still standing and feeling decidedly shaky, Catherine suppressed the urge to sit down. First, she must get this wretched woman out of her room. 'Congratulations, Francesca. I'm sure you and Rod will be very happy. You can also tell him I'll pack up my things and leave as quickly as I can tomorrow. As you can see

317

I don't have a great deal here.'

'Hmm. Actually, I had noticed. Far be it for me to say anything.'

Holding on tight to the Suffolk latch, her knuckles showing white, Catherine suppressed a deep sigh of relief; her unwelcome guest was at last taking the hint and also making ready to leave.

'About Roddy,' Francesca said, her fingers brushing against the costume hanging on the door. 'Isn't it strange how I call him Roddy, whereas you call him Rod? Funny, really, because after tonight — or should that be tomorrow — I won't have to call him either of those names.'

Knowing that she shouldn't have, because she was practically asleep on her feet, Catherine fell almost immediately into Francesca's trap like a fly into a spider's web. In a daze she heard herself ask, 'What will you be calling him, then?'

'Isn't that obvious, sweetie? I shall call him *mine*.'

Doing her utmost to hold back the tears that threatened to spill over, Catherine prepared to close the door. Before she did so, however, and to her abject horror, Francesca reached out to touch her face. 'Hmm. I suppose in a way you are quite pretty. And even though Roddy made a rather dishy

Johnny Depp lookalike, you're certainly no Keira Knightley. Take my advice, Cathy, dear, forget about Roddy and stick to your own kind. Earlier in the evening when we were talking about flowers, wasn't it you who said you like simple things? Don't get me wrong, I'm not suggesting you marry the village idiot, but there must be someone simple enough in the village to make you happy.'

With tears coursing down her cheeks, Catherine slammed the door shut. As for packing in the morning, why wait for morning? Why not do it now? Trying to be as quiet as she could, she gathered together her few belongings and waited for the dawn.

21

'Has anyone seen Catherine?' Rod called, going down for breakfast.'

Davina and Charles both shook their heads. 'No, sorry. We haven't seen anything of Henrietta either. Even Mrs Bailey appears to have done a disappearing act this morning.'

'Oh, well, perhaps Catherine and Henry have gone for an early morning walk together. As for Mrs B. that's most unusual. She's normally here at the crack of sparrow.'

'Catherine hasn't had to go into work, then?' Davina said, passing Rod a cup of coffee.

'Not today. Janice told her to have a well-deserved rest.'

Charles Marchant peered over the top of the morning paper. 'Speaking of sparrows, Francesca's certainly sounding chirpy today.'

Rod paused with his cup to his lips. Francesca sounding chirpy at this time of the morning. It was unheard of for her to be up so early. 'Must be the Whycham air,' he said, draining his cup.

Reminded of last night's conversation between herself and her husband, Davina gave Charles a knowing wink and then approached her son. 'Roderick, I was wondering . . . Could we have a quiet chat together? In the garden, perhaps?'

Knowing that whenever his mother called him Roderick, there was always something afoot, Rod replied, 'Of course. When do you want to go?'

'I was hoping we could go now.'

About to say couldn't it wait until later, Rod registered the concern in his mother's voice.

'Ok. Just let me fetch a sweater. Do you need anything, Mother?'

'You could fetch my pashmina. I think you'll find it on the chair in the bedroom.'

Running up the stairs two at a time, Rod soon found himself in what had once been Edwina Erskine's bedroom. The one he hoped would soon be occupied by Catherine, if only for the storing of her clothes and personal effects. For the most part he was hoping they would share the giant tester bed in Uncle Cedric's old room. Edwina's bed wasn't nearly as roomy. Though perhaps a great deal more cosy, he thought with a satisfied smile.

Leading his mother by the arm, Rod took her through the conservatory and into the back garden. 'I think this way's probably best,' he said. 'From what Father says, Francesca's picking flowers in the front garden at the moment. Not wishing to appear rude, I'd prefer to avoid seeing her until after I've spoken with Catherine.'

'As long as it's only seeing her you intend to avoid, and not speaking of her.'

Rod's brow creased into a frown. 'Pardon?'

'It's Francesca I need to speak to you about. And also . . . Catherine.'

Seated in the summerhouse, Rod listened to his mother recount the tale of what had prompted her, when unable to sleep and waiting for her husband to come to bed, to seek out Catherine's whereabouts and pay her a late-night visit. Like her daughter, Henrietta, she too had been outraged at Francesca's behaviour earlier in the evening. Unlike her daughter, she was of the generation that tried to keep their thoughts to themselves. As for the obscenities that literally tumbled from everyone's mouths these days, be it on radio, television or even at the theatre, Davina was horrified. Reconsidering her daughter's description of Francesca, however, even Davina was forced to admit that she agreed with her wholeheartedly. It was for this reason she'd felt duty bound to apologize to Catherine on the family's behalf and perhaps even discover the reason for the current rift in Rod and Catherine's relationship. Fully expecting to hear a tale of some silly tiff that had got blown out of all proportion, it wasn't Catherine's voice Davina had heard as she'd made her way stealthily up the attic staircase but Francesca's.

'Rod, I need you to be perfectly honest with me,' Davina urged. 'Have you proposed to Francesca?'

'Proposed to Francesca? Mother, is this a joke? Why on earth would I want to propose to Francesca? I don't even like her, let alone love her!'

'Fair enough. So can I ask, have you given her a ring?'

'Yes. I gave her a ring. I gave it to her only yesterday evening, in fact. As you know she was the last person I expected to see but I'd bought that ring ages ago and it had been rattling round in my briefcase for weeks. As I explained to her last night, it was meant as a token of farewell.'

Davina's eyes registered incredulity. 'Some farewell token. If it's that very striking aquamarine she was sporting on her engagement finger this morning.'

'What! It wasn't meant as an engagement ring! The chap in the jewellers said it was a dress ring.'

'And you made that perfectly clear?'

'Of course I did!'

'Hmm. Not wishing to sound as if I've suddenly gone completely ga-ga,' Davina said, pulling her pashmina about her shoulders, 'how did you make it clear?'

'When Francesca was doing my makeup, I started to explain about what I planned to do with the estate. At the same time I also tried to break it gently to her that Catherine and I were getting engaged with a view to marrying as soon as possible.'

'What was Francesca's reaction to that?'

'Extremely dismissive at first. She said she couldn't concentrate on listening to me and do my eye makeup at the same time. Which was why, after her shocking behaviour all through supper and at the dance, I decided to put it to her once and for all, before I took the architect's drawings to show to Father. Call me a coward if you like, but I hoped the ring might soften the blow. She also doesn't know yet about her father's affair and that her parents are about to split up.'

'Oh, Roderick,' Davina sighed. 'I regret to tell you that far from softening the blow, you only made matters worse, my dear. A moment ago you mentioned Francesca's shocking behaviour at the dance; believe me, that was nothing compared to her behaviour in Catherine's bedroom in the wee small hours of this morning. Francesca not only told Catherine about the ring, implying that the two of you were engaged, she also told Catherine to pack her bags and go because you're planning to sell half of the estate.'

Rod sat in stony silence, all colour draining from his face, his eyes deeply troubled and his jaw set hard. 'She did what! No, I can't believe it. As Henrietta says, we've always known Francesca can be a bit waspish but that . . . that's utterly despicable. Where is Catherine? I must go and explain. Oh, my God! I think I'm beginning to understand now. Yesterday, when Catherine caught me on the phone to Henrietta, she must have thought I was speaking to Henry Davenport. I've been joking for weeks that Henry's been trying to persuade me to demolish some of the cottages and barns on the estate.'

Davina regarded her son gravely. 'In hindsight perhaps that's not something you should have joked about with Catherine. From what you say, she's extremely keen to preserve the village and its way of life.'

'Not only Catherine but also her aunt. According to Mrs Bailey, Catherine is the rightful owner of Whycham Hall. She's a direct descendant of . . . '

Davina stifled a cry and reached for her

handkerchief. 'This is becoming even more tragic by the minute. First Francesca and the ring, then Catherine thinking you plan to demolish part of the estate.'

'I'm not demolishing it! I'm planning to repair and renovate. I've even applied for planning permission to build several starter homes in the hope of bringing young families back into the village, once that small industrial unit is completed on the far side of Great Whycham.'

Placing a reassuring hand on her son's elbow, Davina whispered softly, 'Roderick, you must find Catherine and explain. And from what you've just said, the sooner the better. Once you've clarified this dreadful catalogue of misunderstandings, I'm sure she'll understand.'

'If only it were that easy,' Rod replied, feeling an icy shiver trickle down his spine. Now he knew why he hadn't seen Catherine this morning. Even without checking her room, he knew he'd find it empty.

'Maybe Catherine's aunt will be able to tell you where's she's gone.'

Rod shook his head. 'I doubt it, Mother. Knowing how close Catherine is to her aunt, it wouldn't surprise me if Mrs Bailey has also packed her bags.'

Making their way back to the hall in

silence, Rod and Davina got as far as the conservatory when they heard the most amazing commotion. Walking round to the main entrance, they discovered Mr Barnes shouting and gesticulating angrily. Equally loud was Francesca, her high-pitched screams echoing across the drive.

'You stupid little man! How was I supposed to know?' Francesca was yelling at him. 'If you didn't want people to pick them you should have put up a sign. Anyway, who are you to dictate to me what I can and cannot pick? Have you any idea who I am?'

'No an' I don't bloody care!' Mr Barnes retorted. 'All I know is that the likes of you don't belong round here. You shouldn't even be let loose in the garden with a pair of nail scissors, let alone secateurs. Look what you've done to my Agapanthus!'

'Roddy, thank God!' Francesca cried, when Davina and Rod came into view. 'Did you hear what that odious little man said to me? Will you tell him who I am?'

Rod shook his head. 'As far as I'm concerned there's nothing to tell. Mr Barnes has said it for me, most eloquently.'

'Why? Because I picked his wretched flowers?' Francesca demanded, clutching an armful of what had once been majestic *Agapanthus africanus*. 'Anyone will tell you

327

they're a darned sight prettier than those jugs of weeds.'

The same *weeds*, Rod noticed, thrown into an open bin bag at Francesca's feet.

Stepping forward to retrieve the pair of secateurs from her right hand and the Agapanthus clutched against her left side, Rod said quietly, 'It wasn't the flowers I was referring to, Francesca, it was Mr Barnes's other comment. Come to think of it, I couldn't have put it better myself. Regrettably, dahling, Mr Barnes is quite correct. You do not belong around here. Now, if you wouldn't mind packing your bags and leaving.'

EPILOGUE

TWO YEARS LATER

'Come along, sleepy head, wake up. I'm taking you somewhere special, remember?'

Catherine stirred, feeling Rod's lips brush gently across her forehead. From the early morning sunlight filtering through the curtains, she knew she couldn't have overslept. As for going somewhere special, no, she hadn't remembered.

Watching her stir sleepily and rub at her eyes, Rod was filled with a deep longing for his wife. This morning, however, that would have to wait. What he was planning had to take place before the sun was too high. The last thing he wanted for his heavily pregnant wife was for her to be sitting out in the heat of the midday sun.

'Where are we going?' Catherine asked, vaguely recollecting being told weeks ago that Rod was planning something special for the end of July. At the time she hadn't given it too much thought. It wasn't their wedding anniversary, that wasn't until October, and it certainly wasn't her birthday. At the same time, there had been several occasions, recently, when Rod had disappeared and returned with a self-satisfied smile upon his face. Questioned about it, he'd merely said he'd been checking on progress of the starter homes now under construction, or else some new crops he was experimenting with.

Catherine eased herself up against her pillows, her gaze taking in the bedside clock. It was only 6.30 in the morning. Not the time they usually got up on a Sunday. More often than not in recent weeks they'd had breakfast on a tray, with Rod insisting that she stayed put until he appeared with orange juice, coffee and croissants. This morning it was tea he was handing to her, not coffee, and there was no sign of a breakfast tray anywhere.

'We're going out for breakfast,' he said, as if reading her mind.

'Out for . . . We never go out for breakfast. Why are we? And what shall I wear? You haven't forgotten that I'm the size of a house and nothing fits me at the moment.'

'Questions, questions,' Rod teased, sitting down beside her on the bed. 'As for where we're going, that's a surprise; as for what to wear, that's easy: wear what you're the most comfortable in. Trousers and a loose top and something sensible on your feet.'

'That means there's got to be walking

involved,' Catherine said, eyeing him suspiciously. 'You're not taking me fishing, are you? Do I have to catch my own breakfast?'

'No. And stop fishing for ideas. It will get you nowhere, Mrs Marchant. All will be revealed almost as soon as you're up and dressed.'

'You're right about that,' Catherine said, when Rod helped her from the bed and slipped her bathrobe over her shoulders.

Standing behind her, knowing that his wife was once again referring to her size, Rod clasped his hands protectively across her swollen stomach. 'Will you stop thinking you're the size of a house? You're not. You look absolutely delightful. Only last Sunday at St Andrew's everyone was saying how pregnancy suits you. And I'm inclined to agree with them.'

Marginally comforted, Catherine turned to face him. 'By that I hope you're not expecting me to be in a permanent state of pregnancy.'

'No, not permanent. I am hoping perhaps to persuade you to try it at least once more — maybe twice?'

'Hmm. I'll reserve judgement on that if you don't mind. I think I'd rather wait and see what happens in two weeks' time when baby Marchant puts in an appearance.'

Picking up on Catherine's frisson of fear,

Rod adopted a less light-hearted tone. 'I will be there with you, you know. I'd even give birth myself, if I could.'

'I know,' Catherine said, hugging him warmly. 'And I appreciate the thought. Unfortunately, there's only one problem.'

'What's that?'

'It's a bit late to swap places now. And I suppose if I don't get a move on, we're also going to be late for breakfast. How many people are going to be there, by the way?'

'None. It's just the two of us.'

Even more confused than before, Catherine padded towards the bathroom.

Half an hour later, dressed in a white T-shirt, pale-sage linen drawstring trousers and matching overshirt, she made herself comfortable in the Range Rover. 'Right, are we ready to roll?' Rod began, switching on the ignition. 'And before you say anything, I wasn't referring to your size.'

'Hmph,' Catherine said, fixing him with a mock glare and sticking our her tongue. 'If it hadn't taken me so long to get comfortable I'd open this car door and roll back to bed. I still can't believe it's so early in the morning.'

'Don't worry, I'm sure you'll think it's well worth it. At least I hope you do. And you'll be able to have a lovely, long rest this afternoon. Aunt Em will insist on it.'

Catherine smiled to herself as they headed off down the drive. As if it wasn't strange enough hearing Rod refer to their house-keeper as Aunt Em, it had been even stranger for Emmy Bailey to address Rod purely by his Christian name. 'I can't possibly call Master Roderick, Rod,' she'd declared emphatically, immediately following her niece's wedding.

'You'll have to,' Catherine had replied. 'He certainly won't entertain you calling him Master Roderick. He's family now, don't forget.'

In the end, with a little cajoling, Emmy had succumbed. Still adamant about 'Rod' she'd at least agreed to drop the 'Master' prefix. These days the name Roderick seemed to flow relatively easily from her tongue.

'Penny for them,' Rod said, slowing down for the level crossing at Whycham Halt.

'Oh, I was just thinking about Aunt Em coming to terms with your Christian name.'

'Mmm. It is a bit of a mouthful, I'm afraid. Are we still agreed on something shorter for baby Marchant? As I recall, it took me ages to learn how to spell my name when I first went to school. All those different letters.'

'Me too. I had a similar problem.'

'What? Of course. Your name's even longer than mine. Although, I suppose once you'd learnt how to master the first 'e' the second one at the end was a great deal easier.'

Puzzled by Rod's observation, Catherine heard him continue, 'In case you're wondering, I lost count of the amount of times I actually wrote your name following that awful misunderstanding with Francesca after the night of the dance.'

Waiting for the approaching train to come to a halt, Rod reached out for Catherine's hand. These days there was never a problem whenever Francesca's name was mentioned. Having flounced out of Whycham Hall, both in anger and indignation, it had been some months before Francesca had made contact again with either Rod or Henrietta, by which time Catherine and Rod were man and wife (ably assisted by their bridesmaids: Henrietta and a very proud Daisy). Joined together in matrimony by the Revd Cooper, the wedding had been a truly memorable occasion.

Thank God for Damian, Rod thought to himself, reliving the nightmare of his mother's revelation as to why there was no sign of Catherine or her aunt on the morning after the dance. It was only when his sister had reappeared that he'd discovered aunt and niece's whereabouts. Henrietta, having arranged the previous evening to join Damian for breakfast as he was keen to learn more about ROKPA, had been both surprised and concerned to find Catherine and Mrs Bailey already there.

Surprised because she'd assumed Catherine would be at Whycham Hall with Rod celebrating their engagement, and concerned because from the state of Catherine's red-rimmed eyes it was obvious that she'd been crying. Equally perturbed to hear that Mrs Bailey was enlisting Damian's help in transporting some of Catherine's belongings to her flat in Norwich, Henrietta became even more anxious when she overheard Mrs Bailey ask Damian if he was still looking for a housekeeper. What on earth was happening? What on earth had gone so horribly wrong? As for the look on Mrs Bailey's face whenever Rod's name was mentioned, from the way she was busy wielding that huge earthenware teapot, it was probably just as well that Rod was out of harm's way.

Meeting Damian's gaze, Henrietta had followed him from the kitchen into the hallway. There, sharing their combined anxieties, Damian had mentioned only briefly Mrs Bailey's disquiet for the future of Whycham le Cley. On hearing of Rod's supposed intentions to demolish the almshouses, Henrietta had sprung immediately to her brother's defence. She knew only too well that wasn't the case at all. Nothing could have been further from the truth. At the same time she also knew from the banging and crashing in the kitchen, where Mrs Bailey was in the process of preparing breakfast, there wasn't that much time before Damian's ancient Volvo was pressed into action as a removal van.

'Just keep Catherine and her aunt here for as long as you can, while I go and fetch Rod,' Henrietta had urged.

'But if you want me to stay here and you're on foot, won't it take you ages to walk?'

'No, because I'm not on foot. I borrowed Catherine's bike. She doesn't know that, of course, so better not tell her. Don't tell her where I'm going, either.'

'I'll do my best,' Damian had added, blinking in the early morning sunlight. Last night he'd been extremely taken by Rod Marchant's younger sister. This morning, looking up to find her breezing into his kitchen, she'd been like a breath of spring.

'Bless you,' Henrietta said, hurriedly plonking a kiss on his cheek. 'I knew you were the sort of fellow a girl could rely on in an emergency. Back soon. Bye.'

Ten minutes later it had been Rod who'd looked out of his study window to see Henrietta hurtling up the drive on Catherine's bike. 'Rod! For God's sake leave what you're doing and come with me. Catherine's going back to Norwich and her aunt's taken over Damian's kitchen.' Spying the pile of papers cascading to the floor from Rod's desk, Henrietta had called, out of breath, 'And bring all those photos and things you were showing Dad.'

Totally numbed and confused, still registering the cause for Catherine's disappearance and Francesca's subsequent departure, Rod had merely nodded, picked up the bulky folder and his car keys and followed his sister to the door. 'Not the Range Rover, the Morgan,' Henrietta said, tugging at his sleeve. 'It will be quicker.'

Hearing the commotion coming from the hallway, Davina Marchant had confronted both her son and daughter. 'Henrietta? Roderick?'

'Not now, Mum,' Henrietta had called back. 'No time to explain. Just tell Dad to put some champagne on ice. I think we could be needing it.'

*　*　*

Watching the Norwich train move away and the crossing gates swing open, it was Rod's turn to think of champagne. In particular the bottle packed away in the picnic box with the

337

rest of the items he'd selected for this morning's breakfast. He only hoped he hadn't forgotten anything. 'Not long now,' he said, spying Catherine rub at her bump.

'I hope not. I've a horrid feeling the next two weeks are going to feel like an eternity.'

Rod grinned, 'Actually, I meant not long until breakfast. Goodness! You're not having a contraction, are you?'

Catherine shook her head. 'No, but I am getting hungry.'

Watching her husband turn from the main road and into a country lane that she didn't recognize, she became even more suspicious when he pulled over into a passing place and produced one of his mother's silk scarves. What was he doing with Davina's silk scarf, when she distinctly remembered him saying that he hadn't been able to find it?

'I know what you're thinking,' Rod said, folding the scarf across his lap. 'Rest assured I'm merely borrowing it. I need to blindfold you.'

'What! In my condition? Isn't it a bit late for all that bondage stuff,' Catherine joked, reminded of Janice and Dave.

Jumping down from the driver's seat, Rod ran round to the passenger door, carefully released Catherine's seat belt over her precious bundle and loosely tied the scarf across her eyes.

'I'm afraid I'm going to have to leave you here for a bit, while I unload all this stuff from the boot and set it up. In the meantime, I suppose you could have forty winks if you like.'

'As long as it is only forty winks and you promise not to forget about me.'

'My darling. I could never forget about you,' Rod said, kissing her lingeringly. 'Now, if you'll allow me to get on.'

Grateful to have a few extra moments to catch up on some sleep (with the baby's head engaged, sleep was becoming extremely difficult), Catherine closed her eyes beneath the blindfold. Ten minutes later, waking to the sound of birds singing in the hedgerow and the gentle hum of bees, buzzing in the fields beyond the open window, she reached up to adjust the silk scarf. Unless she was very much mistaken, the knot was already working loose. Knowing that she'd promised Rod she wouldn't take a crafty peek at their whereabouts in his absence, she decided to leave well alone.

Presently, hearing approaching footsteps and recognizing Rod's jaunty whistle, she turned in his direction. 'Right, breakfast's all ready for you, ma'am. If you'd care to follow me.'

Catherine giggled. 'That's not exactly

going to be easy, is it? First you're going to have to heave me down from the car and I'm still wearing this blindfold.'

'And you're going to have to wear it for a little while longer,' Rod said, reaching out his arms to help her down on to terra firma. 'It's OK, I won't let you stumble, but the ground is a bit uneven. Thank goodness we haven't had any rain for a while and that you took my advice and wore sensible footwear.'

Reminded of her less than elegant sandals, Catherine clasped hold of Rod's hand and let him lead the way. He was certainly correct about the uneven terrain beneath her feet. 'Where on earth are you taking me?' she queried. 'At the moment it feels like the middle of a ploughed field.'

Making sure she remained perfectly still, Rod untied Catherine's blindfold and instructed her to open her eyes. 'Hmm, well, it was a ploughed field at the beginning of the year. Now as you can see it's full of — '

'Sunflowers!' Catherine cried, her face radiant. 'Row after row of sunflowers. Oh, Rod, they're beautiful, utterly beautiful! I had no idea. When — ?'

'When did I plant them, or when did I first get the idea?' Rod finished for her.

'Both, I suppose.'

'Initially, after seeing Daisy dressed up as a

sunflower. Then, last year, I remembered you buying some from that farm shop when we drove out to Deeping St Nicholas. As a result I got to thinking exactly like you and Daisy. Sunflowers are wonderful things for cheering people up on even the darkest days.'

'So you intend to sell them?'

Rod shook his head. 'Not really. I prefer to leave that to the chap at Vine House Farm. It's not my intention to set myself up in competition. Shall we just say this is a sort of early wedding anniversary celebration?'

'How lovely! And are those really Mrs Bannister's sunflower curtains?' Catherine said, spying a table laid for breakfast.

'Mmm, I must say your aunt made a superb job of turning one of those into a tablecloth and picnic cushions.'

Catherine frowned, admiring her aunt's handiwork. 'But I thought Henrietta had taken those curtains back with her to Kathmandu.'

'Only some of them. And they went with Mrs Bannister's blessing. I can't wait to see her face when she sees the photos Henrietta sent from the orphanage.'

'I expect Damian will be pretty thrilled too,' Catherine added, reminded of the latest photos of her sister-in-law standing with a group of happy, smiling children against a backdrop of sunflower curtains. 'Only the other day he was asking me when Henrietta was due home again on leave. Rod, do you think Damian and Henrietta will — ?'

'If they do I'm sure we'll be the first to know. In the meantime can I suggest you take a seat while I pour you a glass of buck's fizz.'

Listening to Rod explain how he'd driven to Deeping St Nicholas to ask for advice on when and how to plant sunflowers, Catherine heard how the field had been prepared for planting and seeds eventually drilled at the end of April. 'That explains all your mysterious disappearances,' she said, reaching for her glass. 'And is it my imagination or are they sunflower seeds on those breakfast rolls next to the sunflower honey and sunflower-decorated napkins?'

'Very observant of you, Mrs Marchant. I suppose you could say the only thing missing is that other little sunflower, namely Daisy. Though no doubt she would have loved to have joined us. In the circumstances, however, I thought it would be nice if it was just the two of us. Happy Anniversary, darling.'

'Even if it is two months early,' Catherine said with a lazy smile.

'Hmm, especially as it's two months early.

You do realize we shall be three on our anniversary.'

'And I shall have to decorate the church for Harvest Festival,' Catherine enlightened him, 'but now I no longer have to worry about it. These sunflowers plus some of those lovely rose hips and hawthorn, over there in the hedgerow, would be absolutely ideal for the windows at St Andrew's.'

★ ★ ★

Sitting in her regular pew in St Andrew's, Emmy Bailey felt a lump rise in her throat as she waited for her niece and her husband to arrive. Could it really be only two years ago since she'd stood here waiting for Catherine to walk down the aisle to become not only Mrs Roderick Marchant but also mistress of Whycham Hall? Given away by Dave (with Janice watching anxiously from a nearby pew), Catherine had looked positively radiant in the exquisite antique lace dress, worn by Edwina Erskine herself at her own wedding. Like today, Catherine had decorated the windows to resemble a Norfolk hedgerow in full autumnal glory and Emmy (in brand new coat and hat) had excelled herself with her own display of flowers by the lectern.

Reaching for her handkerchief, Emmy was

glad of the sudden murmur of voices echoing through the church; at least it drowned out the sound of her blowing her nose. It also meant that Catherine and Rod had arrived, only this time it wasn't just her niece and her husband making their way to the Whycham family pew, it was also the youngest member of the family. Edwina Emily Marchant was making her first public appearance. As usual, escorted by Barry Martindale, Rod and Catherine made their way forward, Catherine carrying assorted baby paraphernalia and Rod cradling his precious daughter in his arms. Coming to a halt by Emmy's side, Rod was heard to say, 'Come along, Aunt Em. This Sunday we're not going to take no for an answer.'

Momentarily wishing the ground would open up and swallow her, Emmy was on the point of remonstrating with them, when she heard Catherine announce softly, 'Rod and I are doing the readings, Aunt Em, which means we need someone to hold the baby. Besides, you, too, are a Whycham don't forget. It is, after all, where you belong.'